I0831755

S W E V E N

Andrew Matarazzo

SWEVEN

TABLE OF CONTENTS

1 3 2 2 14
2 6
10 19
5 3 4
7 2 4
17
6 8 13 3
10 7 10 7 11 10
2 12
1 14
10
19
7 10 4 3 7 14 10

10 7 11
10
14|
19 2 3 5 10 5
17
6 8 3 7

10 7 11 10 2 12
1 14
13

1.

I stared into the cloud of dust trailing behind our Humvee as we sped down an empty road towards the forsaken city. In the distance, the towering border wall glared back at me, reminding me that I'd left its safety of my own will and may never see it again.

I leaned against the transport basket on the back of the Humvee, eyeing the two soldiers as they shared a cigarette. They had introduced themselves earlier when I climbed aboard. She went by Eve and he, Jax.

"So, Willa, what you reentering for?" Jax asked, exhaling a small puff.

"I'm going to find my brother," I said.

"Figured it was something like that. Almost everyone who goes back is looking for someone that never showed up," said Eve.

Behind that wall I'd endured a month of training, and I was now a certified volunteer in the government's FORESIGHT program. The crash course had covered survival tactics, combat, and a handful of protocols, all of which I'd aced with flying colors.

FORESIGHT recruited individuals to collect data and report observations as they ventured back into the contamination zone for their own pursuits. Mine was a singular goal: to find my brother, Malik. I learned he'd reentered just a week before my arrival at the border. Likely in search of me at our home in Seabird, unaware that I had set out on my own for salvation months earlier.

Our town of Seabird was known as "the least desirable beach town in the nation." It was a small seaport just outside a major city: quaint, lower-middle-class neighborhoods against an industrial backdrop. We'd moved there when my father got an opportunity to work as an import-export specialist, coordinating shipments to and from the bustling harbor. My mom helped him log inventory. Although Seabird was on the water, the congested marine traffic and industrial pollution had turned the beaches into trash pits. No one wanted to visit those beaches. Not even marine life.

Luckily, I was more of a city girl at heart. Much to my parents' distaste, I would frequent the inner city with my friends, a creative bunch of musicians and artists. We'd go to exhibitions and concerts, sometimes indulging in vices before and after, but overall, I was never the wayward kid they thought I was. I simply wanted more for myself than a town like Seabird could offer. I wanted to be around interesting people, make mistakes, and explore. I wanted a fuller life and it made me restless.

My parents had aspirations of their own. They envisioned a future where we'd achieve enough success to support them in their golden years. I, for one, killed that dream early on, so my brother Malik was their shining hope. He was the studious one, proudly dedicating himself to his studies and harboring ambitions of attending an Ivy League school. We were polar opposites, but he meant everything to me. He was the one person who truly understood the depths of my soul. While my parents and I frequently got into fights, Malik always remained on the sidelines. More often than not, he'd have one-on-one conversations with me, offering advice and perspective, and I cherished that about him. He exuded kindness and recognized how our parents had a talent for applying pressure on both of us.

When Malik earned a scholarship to attend an out-of-state university, he left home to begin the journey of his biochemistry career. Consequently, things between my parents and me got worse. That year, all their attention turned to me, and the more they tried to control me, the less I wanted to listen.

Just before a visit to see Malik at his campus, a particularly bad argument made me stay behind. I couldn't bear a six-hour car ride with them only for them to berate me, all while using my brother's life as the benchmark for what I needed to strive for.

It was three days later, the day they were due to return home, when everything unraveled. First came the screams from outside my house, and as I watched from my bedroom window, I saw groups of rabid-looking creatures attacking my neighbors. Gunshots were going off in the distance. Cars were fleeing their driveways. I called 911 and when I got a busy tone, I knew something was terribly off. I tried my brother and my parents, but the lines went down. I closed all the windows, locked the doors, and hoped that my parents would get back at any minute. I caught a brief news bulletin reporting that *"reanimated human corpses are spreading a virus through biting."* Then, the power went out.

I watched the mayhem from my rooftop, gobsmacked by the surrealism of a world turned upside down. Soldiers in war vehicles showed up hours later, eliminating a lot of the creatures and helping control the chaos the best they could.

Then, Seabird became a ghost town. The soldiers had evacuated as many survivors as possible, but I chose to stay behind. I barricaded myself inside my house for two weeks, peeking through the blinds to watch for any changes. I still had hopes that my parents or my brother would come back. However, after the second week went by, I had nothing left in my house to allow me to survive a third. So, I left.

Even though I had just arrived at the border camp, I was adamant about leaving as soon as possible ... and then the FORESIGHT program offered me a deal I couldn't refuse. Along with two soldiers to escort me to a drop-off point anywhere I requested within five miles of the border wall, I was given some survival gear, ammo, and my pistol with an extended magazine. Other than my silver septum ring, my dad's handgun was the only thing I truly owned from the old world.

Inside my military-grade backpack was a solar-powered tablet for me to note any useful information I gained on my journey. It would be logged and reported back to the program instantly, ensuring that even if I didn't return, any valuable insights gathered would still make it.

"I'm heading deep out there next week, after training," said Eve. "Joined the EMBER program."

"Haven't heard of it," I replied, just as we were passing a line of abandoned cars on the road. I was trying to sound easygoing, but my palms were damp and my heart was racing. I was still wrestling with the fact that I'd willingly volunteered to go back into this hellscape.

"Those things out there feed on the dead and it makes more of them," Eve said. "They even feed on each other. After they lose that initial life-spurt, another one will bite into it and reanimate it. It's a never-ending cycle.

"So, they've just launched a program for squads—EMBER Squads—to go out there and burn as many bodies as we can to keep their numbers down. No hosts, no reproducing," she concluded proudly.

I nodded, the mountain of bodies lying on the lobby floor of the Don Lux Hotel flashing through my mind. That day, it had seemed that those would be my final moments. I remembered looking into Tye's eyes and feeling a strange sense of comfort in knowing he would be with me for my last breath. Even though I had known him so briefly, our spirits recognized each other in a way unlike anything I had felt with anyone other than my own brother. My biggest regret in leaving the camp was not getting the chance to say goodbye to him. While my other friends had been cleared for release after a few weeks, there had been no updates on Tye, despite our relentless inquiries... In a strange way, that lack of closure would never leave me. Even the uncertainty surrounding my parents' whereabouts hadn't troubled me as much, as their status was at least categorized as *alive,* but Tye's was frozen on *pending.*

My eyes shifted to the street ahead, taking in what was to come. We were still in the middle of nowhere, but I knew the nearest city was within a few miles. When deciding my drop-off point, I'd tried to choose a location I knew was in the general direction of where I used to live.

"You nervous?" asked Eve.

Was it that obvious? There was no doubt in my heart about going back to find my brother, but now that I was truly reentering, unfamiliar anxieties were creeping in. This world felt different. It had a different energy.

"No," I said, covering.

"Well, we haven't seen any Teeth anywhere near the border yet, so don't feel too uneasy," said Jax, ignoring my denial.

Eve laughed. "You remember the first time you saw one? Bet you had Hershey squirts in those tighty-whities, huh?"

"You're sick, you know that?" Jax retorted, flicking away the butt of the cigarette.

She laughed harder. "When I first—"

The shriek of rubber on asphalt rang in my ears. Our Humvee skidded to a halt. The two soldiers immediately stood up with their weapons in offensive positions. I followed their lead a beat later, peeking over the rooftop of the truck to see what the problem was.

A little blonde girl in tattered clothing was in the middle of the road, shaking and waving at our truck.

"Please, help me!" she screamed, running towards the Humvee.

Eve and Jax pulled masks over their faces.

"She could be infected," said Eve, adopting her on-duty demeanor once again.

"Help me!" the girl repeated, shrilly, standing on her tiptoes and tapping the driver's window.

The two soldiers jumped down from the transport basket to flank the Humvee, scanning our surroundings. On both sides of the road were dense, far-reaching woods. The driver stepped down from the truck to deal with the little girl as Jax and Eve secured the area. My hand was gripped tight around my pistol. My intuition rarely failed me, and at that moment, I had a strong feeling something was coming.

As if to answer my suspicions, a stampede of Morts exploded from the woods in a frenzy. I fell back as they crashed against the Humvee. Gunshots fired from all directions. I jumped onto the rooftop, firing at the ones climbing up. The driver wailed as a Mort tore into him and dragged him off into the woods. The little girl was devoured so quickly that she never made a sound.

Eve managed to fight her way to the driver's seat, kicking away a Mort that I shot a moment later. She slammed on the gas but realized the keys had fallen from the ignition port. That millisecond of bad luck cost her. A Mort shattered the driver-side window, climbing inside and sinking its teeth into her thigh. She screamed, shot it point blank in the face, then retreated to the backseat as more monsters surrounded the vehicle.

My magazine clicked after several more shots and I realized what I was leaning against—the turret gun, mounted on the roof of the Humvee. My training would be put to use already, it seemed. I holstered my handgun and jumped onto the mount, firing in a circle around the truck. The bullets hit each creature with an explosive spray of guts.

In a matter of minutes, a bloodbath of lifeless bodies lay strewn across the road. One of them was Jax, a large bite taken out of his neck. I grabbed my bag and reloaded my pistol in anticipation of another attack.

"Eve?" I called down from the turret hatch.

"It's bad," she replied, sounding pained.

I jumped down into the interior. She was holding her leg. It lay at a revolting angle, the muscles completely torn apart. Blood spilled onto the seat between us.

"I'm done for. No coming back from a bite like this," she said, her face tensed in agony. "Yo, please don't let me turn... I can't go out like that."

My forehead grew hot. I knew what she was asking me to do.

"Should I use my radio? I can call for help," I said, trying to swallow my alarm.

"Hah, you think they're sending anyone out here to help a goner? No chance. Please, I hate to ask it of you... You're young, I know, but I can't do it myself. That's some tough shit."

Tears were pooling in her eyes now. She handed me her gun. I couldn't even make eye contact. I locked up. I'd been here before.

"Kid, *please*," she said, the desperation rising in her voice.

I felt a rush of panic.

"I'm sorry," I said, opening the door and stepping out.

"Hey, where are you—"

"I'm *sorry!*" I called back.

I ran down the street, away from the Humvee, zigzagging between a myriad of abandoned cars. I heard Eve yelling frantically after me for half a mile.

I knew leaving someone like that was brutal, but I couldn't bring myself to do it. Killing undead came easy to me. I could see in their deep, black eyes that they were soulless. The light was out, replaced by a rageful void. But an innocent, living, breathing person, no matter how close to death they were, that was a place I couldn't go ... again.

As I walked, I kept my eyes peeled, keeping the dumped cars between me and the surrounding woods. If anything ran at me, I'd at least have a barrier between us.

The sense of security was brief. Up ahead, the wooded area ended and the wide road gave way to vast wheat fields as far as I could see. Although, at least in open land nothing could sneak up on me.

I ducked into an abandoned car at the end of the forever-frozen traffic jam and took the tablet from my backpack. Part of my training had included drilling in the idea that any time we had an encounter with the infected, we were to immediately log it on our tablets. I had used it in simulations, but this was the first time I would be logging real information.

I tapped the voice note feature and took a moment to gather my thoughts.

"Our Humvee was ambushed by a horde of infected ... Observation ... I noticed this particular group looked different than the last time I saw any ... They appear to have changed a bit ... More humanoid than human ...

More decayed and thin, but no sign of lost strength... Could possibly be the virus developing over time."

I clicked the green arrow and my report was sent instantly. I slid the tablet back into my pack and resumed my trek, passing more cropland.

After no more than a minute, I heard the tablet beep from inside my pack. I veered to the side of the road and reached in to grab the device, but then realized the sound was actually coming from my compact radio.

I pressed down on the side button. "... Hello?"

"*Willa?*" came a male voice.

"Yep?"

"We tried contacting your escort unit. No one answered," the man said in an articulate English accent. *"I received your voice note about the attack. What is your status?"*

Each member of the FORESIGHT program was given a 'point person' who would be their direct contact. This guy must have been mine.

"I made it, but the others didn't. I'm continuing on without them," I said, letting him know that aside from research, I had my own reason to be there.

"Very well. Stay safe," he said, and the transmission went dead.

In training, they'd told us the radio was for limited use and only for mandatory communications. The briefness of the convo was expected.

I followed the road for miles through farmland. My heart ached with every cattle field and ranch I passed. The area looked very much like where Imani lived... where I first met her.

After I left home, I tried to walk to my friends' places nearby, praying I'd find someone familiar. All I found were Jumbees. Firing my first bullet into a walking, bleeding thing solidified that none of this was a passing moment of delusion. It was very real, and it was the new world.

As the realization set in that I wouldn't find anyone I knew, I decided to leave Seabird in search of any form of help at all. After another lonely and strenuous week on my own, I came upon a ranch outside the city. That's where I found Imani. She caught me snooping around what I thought to be an abandoned property. Pointing a shotgun barrel in my face, she asked me who I was and what I was doing.

Turned out, our stories were very similar. She lived there with her parents, who had gone to the store the night before and never come back. When the chaos broke out, she too stayed inside, hoping they'd return.

And just like that, Imani had fallen into my story like a comet from space. We spent the next four days together inside her ranch house, talking all day and night about our lives up until that point, debating over theories on what had happened, and holding each other up when things got emotional. She was one of those rare people I felt I had known before, in another life. It was no coincidence that the first human interaction I had after being separated from my family was with a kindred spirit like Imani. The universe had my back.

Her features were kind. Her gap-toothed smile shined so bright against her dark skin. She was soft, but strong, like me. We quickly realized how well we balanced each other out. She was very smart on random but useful topics, and where I was impulsive, she was thoughtful.

Coming to terms with the fact that her rations were depleting and her parents would most likely never return, she joined me in hopes of a better option.

I walked aimlessly for an hour before finally starting to see the shift from the rural part of town to the urban areas. I hadn't planned on my drop-off being cut short, so figuring out where I was was the immediate challenge. Navigational skills were never my forte; my mother had never missed a chance to criticize my lack of a driver's permit or any interest in getting one. Most of my friends were older than me and drove me around, and other than concert venues, I didn't usually go anywhere further than where my bike could get me.

The last blowout I had with my parents was sparked after a tatted-up musician friend of mine dropped me off at home, two hours past my curfew. It would be one of a hundred arguments I'd end up regretting forever. I wished I could take it all back.

As I guardedly approached the city limit, the golden light of the setting sun made my readied pistol glisten. The concrete jungle ahead would serve as a hiding place for all sorts of dangers. Morts weren't the only threat out there. I'd learned the hard way that other wanderers could be just as dangerous. Desperation and survival bred hostility. I needed to find shelter before night fell.

Like in most cities I'd passed through since the outbreak, the storefronts of once-thriving businesses were all shattered and ransacked. The glass crunched beneath my combat boots as I made my way to a large square building down the block. The front read *Augustine County Public Library.* Seeing one of the windows near the front door had been busted out, I approached with caution. The library was in good shape compared to some of the surrounding facades. I guess books weren't a top-priority resource during an apocalypse.

The sun had set enough to warrant the use of my flashlight. Once inside, I unclipped it from my backpack and shined it down the aisles of books. Walking slowly, I combed through the place until I felt sure I was alone. I struck gold when I came across a reading corner in the back, complete with multicolored bean bags. I'd sleep on those over a hard floor any day.

I lay in my makeshift nest, eating a ration bar and planning the following day. First priority was figuring out where I was. This place was definitely not the drop-off point I had picked so strategically. If only the tablet they'd given me could do more than annotate and take photos. The computers along the back wall were useless without power. Maybe this library had a printed map somewhere.

A sound from behind one of the aisles had me cocked and loaded in a blink. I stood up slowly, aiming into the dark. I didn't dare reach for my flashlight. Morts were inhumanly fast.

From around the corner emerged a wolf, of all things. Its fur was so black it was almost invisible in the lack of light. It snarled, baring its wet teeth in warning. With the human population diminished, wild animals were finally bouncing back, it seemed.

I aimed to kill. My finger touched the trigger, but I lowered my gun a millisecond later when a beam of light cut through the darkness. Another flashlight?

"Hound! Come here, boy!" came a young voice.

In the new light, I could see it wasn't in fact a wolf, but a very large dog. Its growling stopped when the scrawny boy grabbed it by its leather collar. He shined his light on me and I lowered my weapon.

"Oh!" he said in surprise. "Sorry about that. Didn't think anyone would be in here."

2.

The boy's name was Archer. We spent a portion of the night talking in whispers with his black German Shepherd, Hound, planting himself nearby to keep watch. I was hesitant to reveal too much until I realized he wasn't a threat, just a lost boy. Archer was fourteen years old, he said, and had been wandering on his own for a while by that point. His sun-kissed face and overgrown buzz cut made his boyish looks endearing. He was looking for shelter, so I sacrificed a few of my bean bags and let him stay the night.

The next morning, I expected him to be on his way, but he joined me in foraging through the library to see if there was anything of value. Hound was sniffing around as we followed close behind. Every few minutes, the dog would turn and throw me an untrusting glare, as if to make sure I knew he was *Archer's* ally, not mine.

While we rifled through some drawers behind the library's checkout desk, I started to wonder if Archer might have some insight into our whereabouts. "Are you from around here?"

"Not at all. I'm from what people call the 'wrong side of the tracks,'" he said, a slight twang revealing itself in his accent.

"Trust me, where I'm from probably isn't much better," I said.

"Where are you from? Is it a trailer park too?" he asked, light-hearted.

"Not quite, but it's a small town called Seabird. I left when they started taking over... Then I found out my brother went looking for me. I'm heading back there to find him. It's the first place he'll look."

"How far is it from here?" he asked.

"That's the thing. I'm not exactly sure, but I know it's nowhere near here. I need to find a map or something to figure out exactly where I am," I explained.

I pocketed a pair of keys I found in a drawer, hoping they'd lead to something useful.

"Are you a soldier?" he asked, pausing in his search to eye my gear.

"No," I said with a laugh. "The gear was given to me by this government program I'm part of. I've been taking data for them in the contamination zone. This is only my second day back in."

"*Back in?* You made it to the other side?!" he exclaimed. "I heard people talking about 'safe' cities. Wasn't sure if it was true or not."

"Let's check upstairs," I said, turning from the desk and leading the way. "It's true. They managed to stabilize some states. There's checkpoints between the contaminated states and the contained ones. It took me months to make it to the one at the border, but I got there. They have tests, vaccines, even housing for refugees. I never made it beyond the halfway camp, though. Couldn't leave my brother behind."

"That's the best news I've heard in forever... I had to leave my mama. I told her I was gonna make it to one of the safe zones. To find help for her."

I stopped halfway up the stairs. "She's alive?" I asked, wondering why he'd chosen to go alone.

Archer's face dropped. Hound whined as if he was in sync with his owner. "She was bit... I'm gonna go back for her, once I find a cure," he said.

"How long ago was she bit? I know the vaccines can stop someone from turning if they're given it early enough," I said.

"Well, she... It was like, two weeks ago. I don't remember," he said, avoiding my eyes.

I decided not to pry, seeing the subject was difficult for him. It wasn't my place to tell him there was no known cure for anyone who turned. I tried to hide the concern seeping through my expression.

Hound went ahead of me on the way up and began to growl at something. I raised my pistol, instinctually putting a hand out to keep Archer back. I climbed to the top slowly, then peeked around the corner.

Hound was barking at a dead body on the floor. It looked only a few days old. I approached it warily, Archer hanging back in the stairwell.

I nudged the body with my foot. It didn't move. I flipped it over and saw no sign of bites. This was clearly someone who had made the library their home before us. I could tell from how skinny they were that they had been malnourished when they passed.

"You're good, Archer," I called to him.

He approached warily. His lack of reaction to the body indicated he had seen one before. Hound stuck close to his side. "What do you think happened?" he asked.

"Probably dehydration or lack of food. If he was infected, the body wouldn't still be here," I pointed out.

We left the body and moved vigilantly around the study area, past long work tables and more rows of books.

Towards the back of the space was a hallway with two doors, one a restroom and the other a staff room. Both were locked. I fumbled with the keys I'd found, but while I was trying to force one into a keyhole, I realized it was labeled *Ford.* Most likely belonging to an older car. The second key wasn't a fit either.

"Shoot, these are car keys... Probably parked out on the street somewhere. Too bad I don't drive," I said, more to myself.

"I can," said Archer.

My jaw nearly dropped. "You can *drive?*" I repeated, unsure I'd heard correctly.

"Well, kinda. I used to drive to the store and back to help my mama out. It was only down the road, though."

"I see. Well, as sweet as that is, I'd need to get a lot further than just down the road."

Hound barked and we both jumped as a forceful slam shook the door in front of us. I knew all too well what was trapped behind it. I was suddenly grateful the keys hadn't worked after all.

"A Mort," I said, taking Archer by the arm and backing away.

"A what?" he asked.

"A Mort. It's what my friends and I call them."

He mouthed the word to himself, and we turned and ran back downstairs.

"Do you have a gun?" I asked him, stopping to lean against the checkout counter.

"No. Just this," he said, pulling an aerosol can of body spray from the leather satchel that hung across his body. "And a lighter."

I gaped at it. "Homemade flamethrower?" I asked, letting out an incredulous laugh. I had seen my friends try something similar one summer and it had not ended well for my buddy's eyebrows.

"Yeah. I'm a decent shot, though. Used to go hunting with my pops when he was around, but when things started going crazy, our neighbors raided our shed and took all the hunting gear. I already killed a 'Mort' using this. Plus, I got Hound."

The jet-black dog wagged his tail at the mention of his name. Archer rubbed his head.

Their bond reminded me of Imani and her horse.

Asha was the only animal on the ranch that was solely hers. She had saved up for the Chestnut by helping her dad with crop work. When Imani left her home behind to join me, we traveled for three days on horseback. The steed covered ten times the distance we could have ever done on foot. The perk was welcomed, along with Imani being a much better navigator than I was. She'd learned the lay of the land while assisting her father on cross-country product deliveries.

We took shelter in abandoned office buildings and large homes along the way, but as more time passed, the harder it became to avoid the undead. Imani was devastated when one encounter resulted in the death of her beloved horse. It was our first major setback.

I pulled my canteen out of my bag and took a swig. I offered some to Archer.

"Thanks," he said, taking it and pouring a splash into his mouth. "I was trying to find some food yesterday before it got dark. There's a small convenience store off the main road, but there were looters camped inside."

"How many?" I asked. A pit stop there could be a good opportunity to find a roadmap.

"Three, I think."

"Let's go check it out. We'll get you something to eat and I can find a map," I proposed.

"But what if things get bad? I don't even have a gun."

"I do," I said.

We ducked in and out from behind permanently parked cars. I could tell this area was once a shopping hub. Almost every shop window had mannequins on display. Their vacant stares made me feel like we were being watched.

Hound was sniffing the ground in a frenzy, only stopping every few minutes to look up and turn his ears to assess any potential danger. Archer had just told me we weren't far from the bodega when Hound growled. I immediately pulled the boy by his shirt behind a stack of newspaper boxes. Hound cowered under a mailbox just ahead of us.

A cluster of four twitching Morts turned the corner.

Three looked thin and demonic, like the Morts who'd attacked my Humvee. The other was the typical decayed-looking human I was used to encountering. All of them had the signature hauntingly black eyes.

As the first Mort limped by the mailbox, it froze, apparently sensing flesh nearby. Hound kept stone-still, waiting for the horde to pass. Archer watched through a narrow gap between the boxes, his hand reaching into his bag for the lighter and aerosol can. The second Mort drooled grotesquely over the mailbox. It was virtually on top of Hound, but the dog made no sound.

After a couple of agonizingly tense minutes, the undead finally limped off.

"Are you gonna shoot them?" Archer asked me in a shaky whisper.

"Never use ammo unless mandatory. No need for confrontation," I said. "Let's cut through this store."

Behind us was a stretch of empty retail space. Where a trendy storefront once stood, the window panes were now destroyed. On the far side, I could see a second entrance leading out to the adjacent street.

Ducking low, we stepped through the shattered door. Hound trotted inside a beat later.

Inside was an abandoned remodeling project. Scaffolding, paint buckets, and power tools littered the ground. It was difficult to walk freely. We crossed from one end of the store to the other on tiptoes, like we were in some booby-trapped ruin.

"I thought Hound was done for," Archer said, petting the dog's head. Hound whimpered.

"I think sight's their weakest sense. Noise and blood attract them most. You did good, pup," I said to the animal.

"My sister used to call him that," said Archer.

"Sister? Where is she?"

"Don't actually know. She's kinda like my pops, always off somewhere doing who knows what," he said, with little emotion.

"Older?" I asked as we stepped over a pile of scrap metal.

"Yeah, by ten years. My mama got really sick with MS so we were both taking care of her once my pops stopped coming around," he said flatly. "My sister was always... difficult, but I think my mama getting sick was too much for her. She started staying over at her boyfriend's place more and more. He made my pops look like a catch. Eventually it was just my ma and me."

"That's a lot to handle. I fought a lot with my parents, but it can't compare to what you were dealing with."

"Well, with everything happening now, I'd trade it in for any of my old problems," he said.

I laughed weakly. "Fair."

We reached the other side of the store. Unlike its counterpart, this entrance was still intact. I pressed my forehead to the glass and peered outside. The street was empty. I opened the door gently and stepped onto the sidewalk, looking up and down the street to confirm we were alone.

I beckoned. "Come on."

"See that billboard?" Archer asked, pointing up at a building across the street.

The advertisement depicted a brooding blonde woman, delicately holding a colorful fragrance bottle. The image seemed utterly out of place against the barren backdrop.

"What about it?" I asked.

"I could see that from the bodega. We're really close," he said. "Hound, remember those meat sticks you wanted? Take us back to them."

The dog perked up and started sniffing wildly again. We tailed behind him, staying vigilant, but quickening our pace to keep up.

Five blocks later, a small convenience store appeared in an empty lot on a corner along the main road.

"That it?" I asked, ducking behind a van.

Archer knelt beside me. "Yeah," he said excitedly. "I see their sleeping bags inside, but I don't think they're home."

"You and Hound keep watch. I'll go in and grab as much as I can," I said, gripping my gun.

"Alright. Be careful," he called after me.

As I drew closer, I spotted the three sleeping bags and a handful of empty water bottles between the aisles. Whoever was staying there had either stepped out or didn't make it through the night.

I opened the door. The twinkling welcome bell sent a jolt through me. A few mice scurried under some dusty boxes. Calming myself, I walked over to the clerk's counter. Strewn wrappers from gas station snacks crinkled under my footsteps.

On the counter was a collection of brochures and pamphlets, organized in holders. I immediately spotted a roadmap. My biggest hope, fulfilled. A weight lifted off my shoulders.

Moving on to my second need, I shoved the map in the side pocket of my pack and grabbed a plastic bag from behind the register.

Hurrying up and down the half-empty aisles, I threw as much food into the bag as I could. Everything left for the taking was the kind of junk food parents would only let their kids have on special occasions. It'd be welcome calories, but by no means nutritious. Still, anything to beat the bland ration bars I was given by the program.

I bagged three bottles of water from inside a darkened fridge, then headed straight for the door. I contemplated whether the sleeping bags were fair game, but decided not to be too brutal in case the occupants returned to their camp.

A warning bark from outside made me look up. I lunged for the door. The second I stepped outside, a sharp point pressed into my side. I dropped the bag. Two greasy-haired guys blocked my path. One held the knife at my waist, the other a small gun to my chest.

"And what the fuck do you think you're doing?" demanded the taller one with the gun.

"Shopping," I said simply.

"And how do you plan on paying for that stuff? We claimed this spot," said the other, his knife pressing slightly harder into my side.

I clocked his poor grip around the blade. "I'm gonna let you walk away, alive," I said.

The two guys burst out in scornful laughter, like I was nothing to them, but their cackling was cut short. An aggressive, canine growl from behind them made them turn in alarm. Archer and Hound revealed themselves.

I took full advantage of their distraction, shooting the gunman in the foot, then pushing the other guy's arm with such force that the knife clattered to the floor.

Wailing in pain, the gunman shot off a round in my direction as I backed away to put distance between us. Hound lurched forward, locking his teeth around the guy's wrist. Blood dripped and he screamed louder. His accomplice made to run off, no doubt terrified of suffering the same fate.

Archer jumped aside and let him pass, but a beat later, a crazed Mort appeared out of nowhere, grabbing the fleeing man by the neck and burying its teeth into the meat of his shoulder. Two other Morts, possibly the ones from earlier, ran towards the rest of us.

"Get inside!" I shouted to Archer.

He sprinted for the door, Hound at his side. I snatched up the bag of goods and the injured guy's handgun, locking the door behind me a mere second before a Mort ravaged him. Red liquid spread by the gallon over the sidewalk outside.

I handed the bag and weapon to Archer, then jumped behind the counter.

"What are you doing? Let's go!" he said, urging me towards the back door.

"One second," I said, rummaging under the register.

As expected, I spotted a box of bullets at the back of the cabinet. Store clerks usually kept small handguns behind the counter for protection against theft, and it was probably where my assailant had found his. I pocketed them and we sprinted for the rear exit.

Racing down the street with no clear direction in mind, we tried to get as far away from the bloodbath as possible, until Hound gave another warning bark and we stopped dead in our tracks. An emaciated Mort had appeared in the middle of the street.

BAM! The monster dropped instantly.

I turned to see a wide-eyed Archer holding his new pistol, smoke rising from the barrel. Despite his evident shock, I was impressed.

We jogged a bit further until we spotted a fire escape and climbed the steps all the way to the rooftop of an abandoned office building. We stopped to sit on a large radiator unit, catching our breath. Hound was panting. Archer reached into his bag for his water and poured a little onto the dog's tongue.

"Good shot back there," I praised him.

"Thanks. I told you I was decent." He held up the handgun. "This mine now?"

I smiled. "Guess so. You earned it."

He turned it over in his hands. "Says here it's a Ruger LC9."

I unhooked my backpack and took out the map, spreading it across the concrete. Archer popped open a bag of chips and handed me a couple.

"Thanks," I said through a mouthful. "So, this is the road I was on when I left the border base. Looks like we're ... *here.*"

My finger landed on a city called Talson. From there, I moved it almost all the way down to the edge of the map ... to Seabird. "Shit. My hometown's way further than I thought," I said, more to myself.

"Let me see," Archer said, peeking over my shoulder.

"See that half-moon cutout on the coast? That's the port my town's built on. We're all the way over here."

"Wouldn't be so bad if you had a boat, or could drive straight there," he said jokingly. I shot him a look. He shrugged. "Hey, I told you, I know the basics of driving. Even though it was just to the store and back, I was pretty decent at it. Might be some roadblocks, but with no other drivers on the road I could probably get us there in one piece."

"Aren't you heading to the border checkpoint? You realize Seabird's hundreds of miles in the opposite direction, right?" I countered.

He looked pensive. "After you find your brother, are you heading back to a safe zone?"

"That's the plan."

"I'll help you find him if you take me with you to the border," he said abruptly.

"But... we're not far from the border *now*. You should find a car and make it there yourself, not go in the opposite direction," I said.

Archer huffed. "Look, this last week on my own's been tougher than anything I've ever gone through. I've been mostly staying put, barely making any progress, because I'm scared out here alone. But seeing the way you get around, you know what you're doing. I promise I'll pull my weight if you let me stay with you," he pleaded.

Hound sat up, his big amber eyes on me, as if they were teaming up to convince me. I contemplated Archer's pitch. I was hesitant to take someone else on. The trauma of losing people close to me was fresh in my mind. Turning him down wasn't out of the question, but then, remembering my own experience of traveling alone after I lost Imani, I started to reconsider. This world was dark, and the only light that peeked through had come from the friends I had made along the way.

Although he was four years younger than me, he had shown that he was beyond his years, and today had proven that I could use someone having my back. Hound was also a surprisingly valuable asset to the team.

"You realize this is gonna push you unlike anything you've gone through before, right?" I said seriously. "Your week alone, and what you saw today, was nothing compared to what we'll run into traveling that deep into the contamination zone."

He shrugged. "I have nothing to lose. I have no family left other than my ma. I don't want to die out here alone. Anything that will increase my chances of reaching the border to get her some help, I'll take it. We made a good team today... and Hound likes you," he added with a smile.

The German Shepherd wagged his tail. Then, as if to hide his moment of friendliness, he resumed his serious demeanor.

I took up my canteen and raised it to Archer. He smiled and picked up the water bottle next to him, then tapped it against mine.

"Welcome aboard. Don't let me down, kid," I said with a wink.

We shared some snacks as the sun dipped beneath the horizon. Before long, Archer fell asleep nestled against an already slumbering Hound.

As I peered over the edge of the rooftop at the phantom city below, a series of glowing lights in the distance caught my attention. It took me a few minutes to realize that they were fires, dotted all along the horizon.

I remembered Eve telling me about the EMBER Squad, whose job was to dispose of as many bodies as they could find in hopes of lowering the spread rate. For a second, the thought of colleagues out there was comforting, until I realized how many pyres I could count... That was a lot of dead people.

A faint beep chimed from my bag, interrupting my morbid thoughts. I took out the radio. "Hello?" I said, keeping my voice low to not wake Archer. Hound's ears twitched, but he didn't stir.

"*Willa?*" came the familiar voice.

"So, you already know my name, but what do I call you?" I asked, sitting on the edge of the roof and letting my feet dangle.

"You can call me Thirteen."

"Okay... Well, listen, Thirteen, I've had a pretty crazy day. I just sat down for the first time since waking up," I said, as if I was speaking to one of my parents. "I'll enter my observations for the day in a bit."

"I was just calling to simply check if, well, you were still alive," he said matter-of-factly.

"How sweet of you. Yes, I'm still alive. And I picked up a teammate along the way. It's only been forty-eight hours and I've run into more undead than I hoped to this early on."

"While I have you, can you share today's experience?"

The last thing I felt like doing right then was launching into a full-on discussion, but the information was part of my deal with the program. "Like

I noted yesterday, the main thing that's catching my eye is some of them changing in appearance. Before coming back in, I didn't see any that looked so deformed." A slight chill ran up my spine at the visual recall.

"When a body is bitten, alive or dead, the virus spreads until they turn," Thirteen said. *"Once they become a full Host, they have a spurt of rage that can last up to an hour before they go limp. If the body is fed on again, it will reanimate. This cycle can continue, and from the little data we've studied, it seems the more a Host body is reanimated, the more its appearance changes. It makes sense that you'd see more of the Phase Two specimens now that more time has passed. We're still conducting studies to find out if there's a limit to how many times a body can reanimate."*

I found myself pretty impressed by his knowledge. "Phase Two, got it... Thirteen, I know you're keeping your identity under wraps, but what exactly is your background? I figured you were just some volunteer processing the notes I take out here."

"I'm an epidemiologist, among other things. I'm on one of the government teams investigating every aspect of this outbreak. Think of me like a disease detective. That's why your role in the FORESIGHT program is essential to our studies."

I had joined the program solely for the perks it provided, but hearing the role I played within the context of potentially helping the world rid us of this virus made me feel like I was actually doing something valuable.

Another beep cut in, along with a blinking light on the radio labeled *Overuse.* I rolled my eyes. "Guess that means you gotta go?"

"I'll continue to check in. Note any further data from today. Take care."

The radio fell silent.

After entering a few notes into my tablet about Morts' poor eyesight, I slid my backpack under my head and tried my best to get some sleep. I wished I had taken the sleeping bags from the bodega.

My final thoughts were of Tye and his friends. My friends.

3.

Like Greek columns, thick beams of light trace the ground frenetically. I can hear the beat of chopper blades. The behemoth metal birds are looking for something. One spotlight catches a young man, freezing him in place. He's panting. He's been running for miles. The light's so bright that I can't quite see his face. But when I do, I see it's Tye.

My eyes flew open at the sound of screaming engines as three fighter jets zoomed overhead. I winced from the sonic boom. The sky above was shrouded in haze from all the pyre smoke, veiling the dim sun.

I watched the military planes disappear into the distance as I redid one of my hair ties that had come loose overnight. I must've been tossing and turning.

"Good morning," said Archer, trying to offer a Twinkie to Hound, who refused.

I knew the difference between regular dreams and those with deeper meaning. This dream had been in high definition. I could see actual dust particles in the beams of light. I could feel the breeze from the helicopters on my skin. Though it was vivid, I was still unsure how to interpret it.

I recognized one thing, though. Tye had fear in his eyes. It hurt me to see him like that, even if it was just in slumber. Still, seeing his face so lucidly assured me he was still alive somewhere.

"Quite the wakeup call," I said, still recalibrating. "But good to know there's some military presence."

"What's with all this smoke?" Archer asked, looking at the sky. "Did we sleep through a battle?"

I sat next to him and spread out the map. "They're burning the dead. To make sure the Morts can't keep feeding on the bodies and reanimating them."

His face paled as he stared out at the distant plumes.

"Might mean less Morts, but the ones already out there will be extra hungry," I added, almost to myself.

He decided to evade the grim topic. "So, what's our plan for heading towards your hometown?" he asked, eyeing the map.

I traced my finger across three cities towards the ocean. "It looks like if we can make it to State Route 2, we can take that all the way up the coast to Seabird. We'll have to make stops, but it'll be easy to follow straight there."

Archer could clearly tell by the way I was delivering the plan that he would be the driver afterall. We'd have to make do with his limited experience.

"And where are we getting a working car?" he asked.

I dangled the set of keys we found at the library in front of his eyes. "With these, hopefully. There's a good chance whoever left them behind had to leave their car too. We'll head back to the library and try every Ford we can find."

We were more familiar with the city center by then, so finding the library again was no issue, but the number of cars parked around it was. Wandering outside for too long wasn't safe. We had to be quick about it.

It would have been ten times easier to find the car if we had smart keys, but the set we had was old-school. We'd have to manually test every Ford we found.

Archer spotted the first one, a silver sedan parked by a meter across the street. A thin layer of ash blanketed the exterior. The keys jingled as I pushed it into the door. Immediately I could feel it wasn't a match.

"No go," I said, and we were off to the next one right away.

I was aware that just because the keys were found inside the library, it didn't necessarily mean the car was nearby, but it was our only lead. My eyes darted to the grill of every vehicle we passed.

The Ford logo on a green SUV caught my attention. It was closer to the building's entrance, and like the keys, it looked older. I had high hopes.

Hound sat on guard as I made a second attempt. I tried both keys and neither worked. I knew this was going to be a challenge, but my patience was already being tested. I didn't want to be out in the open.

"There's another one up there," said Archer, keeping his voice down.

Parked at the top of the slanted street was a black hatchback. We jogged up to it, guns drawn in case anything came at us. Archer tried the keys this time as I kept watch.

DOOT! DOOT! DOOT! DOOT!

The car alarm blared. Hound barked and Archer's face went white, but he quickly snapped out of his shock and grabbed a potted plant from a table outside the coffee shop behind us. He slammed it into the driver-side window, shattering it and reaching inside to put the car in neutral. He jumped away from the car as it began to roll downhill.

"Let's get out of here!" he said, grabbing me by the arm, and we ran down an alley to the back of the library building.

The alarm sound faded more and more until we heard the hatchback slamming into a storefront with a final *crash*. It fell silent.

"Sorry about that," said Archer, catching his breath.

"I'd kill you, but that was fast thinking. Good job," I praised.

He looked up and pointed behind me. "Willa ... "

I turned quickly with my gun drawn, but it wasn't a Mort. Parked in the loading bay was a large white transit van. Above the grill was the recognizable blue-and-silver Ford emblem.

I grabbed the keys and marched up to the car like I was about to confront it. I shoved the key in the lock with ease. I glanced back at Archer, who looked on edge with anticipation, then turned it, praying the alarm wouldn't go off.

It clicked! We'd found the matching vehicle. I opened the driver-side door with a sigh of relief. Archer climbed behind the wheel as I slid over to the passenger side. Hound leapt into the spacious rear compartment, which was filled with boxes of books.

"Pop the back doors," I said, jumping into the cargo hold. With limited gas, I wanted to lighten the load, so I pushed everything out of the car. Books clattered to the ground in a pile.

Back in the passenger seat, I asked, "Do you know how to back this thing out of here?"

"It feels a lot different than my mom's small car," he said, nervously fidgeting with the seat.

"Well, take it easy, but we can't stick around here long. Morts will be swarming us any second now after all that noise," I said, strapping myself in.

After several key turns and some sounds of struggle from the engine, he was finally able to switch the van into reverse. It beeped as we backed up slowly, then lurched with a creak over the pile of books.

"*Shh!* Are you kidding me..." he muttered, checking all the mirrors for any creatures being summoned by the sound of it all.

Once he'd straightened out the hefty vehicle, we drove forward onto the main street, peeling away just as a throng of Morts turned the corner.

After several uncomfortable minutes of stop-start driving, I was able to guide Archer onto the main highway towards the coast. We drove slowly. The open, multilane road was much easier for him than the sporadic city streets. I kept track of our route on the map and we were well on our way.

Hound climbed over me to stick his head out of the half-open window, and Archer and I laughed. I realized it was actually nice to have company. Half the battle of survival was mental stamina, and I knew all too well that loneliness was just as dangerous as any other obstacle.

"Thanks for letting me tag along," said Archer, probably having similar thoughts.

I smiled. "Glad I did."

"When you first left home, were you traveling alone?" he asked.

He kept his eyes on the road, so he didn't see my smile fade. "Mostly. I met friends along the way... Not all of them made it."

"Sorry, I didn't mean to bring that up," he said, turning a little red.

"It's okay. I'm always thinking about it, even when no one asks."

Hound jumped back into the cargo hold, lying down for a nap.

"It's been just me, Hound, and my mama for so long, it's kinda nice to have a new friend," Archer said.

I patted him on the shoulder. "You'll learn quick, the friends you make out here are friends for life. No one understands what this is like unless you've lived it—"

All of a sudden, he'd started to cry. The car slowed gradually until we came to a full stop. He put the gear in park.

"What's wrong?" I asked, feeling terrible that I'd said the wrong thing.

"It's not you. Just thinking about my ma now," he said, covering his face.

I needed to choose my words carefully. I knew his mom had been bitten, and from everything I'd gathered about the turning process, there was no chance Archer was making it back in time to save her.

"How was she doing when you left her?" I asked. "Did she have any symptoms?"

He looked up at me, his eyes pink and lip quivering. "She turned already," he whispered.

He looked agonized. I finally understood why he was so distraught. He already knew saving her was impossible.

"Archer... I'm so sorry," I said.

Hound stirred behind us. He whimpered and licked Archer's arm.

"Is there any cure? Did you hear anything when you were at the border?" Archer asked, sniffling.

"Not yet, but I'm sure there's teams all over working to get one as fast as possible," I said, trying to sound hopeful.

He put the car back in drive, and we continued down the highway.

"After she was bit, it took four days before she turned into one of them. Only two to completely forget who I was. I locked her in her room and told her I'd be back for her…" He looked pensive. "I want to find her a cure. I just can't accept that there's no hope for her."

"Don't lose that hope," I said. "It's all we got."

We passed a few more cities as we approached State Route 2. The topic of Archer's mother waned and I tried to keep things light by asking him what music he was into. When I realized his idea of a band was a country music group, we laughed at how wildly different our tastes were.

A tiny *ping* cut through our banter. The gas light had lit up. It had only had a half tank when we left.

"Oh, frick, I didn't think about gas," said Archer. "What do I do?"

We'd been driving for a couple hours, but the warning still felt abrupt.

"It's okay, we'll take the next exit and find some. One of my friends taught me how to get gas out of other cars. We'll need some sort of tube, though," I said. "Get off here."

Archer drifted across three lanes onto the exit ramp. He slowed the car as we rolled into a gloomy city. The smokey sky made it hard to tell what time of day it was.

We drove around town, looking for any type of auto shop or hardware store. We pulled over when we came across a series of strip malls along the road.

"Don't get distracted. We're not any safer in this city than the last one," I cautioned as I climbed out.

He nodded, then raised his small pistol and jumped down from the parked van. Hound followed.

We walked by the windows of many rundown businesses—a Chinese restaurant, a nail salon, a pizza joint—before one heavily tinted storefront caught my eye.

“What’s this place?” I wondered, stepping back to look at the sign. It was impossible to see inside through the darkened glass.

“Aquarium store,” said Archer, disinterested, but then a beat later, his face lit up. “Wait, they’d definitely have tubing!”

He tried the door and it pushed open. It was our only viable shot.

All along the walls were rows of grimy fish tanks. The nauseating smell of dead aquatic life made my nostrils sting. Even Hound was scrunching up his snout.

“Still think we should take a look?” I asked, lifting my shirt over my nose. I clicked on my flashlight.

Archer’s eyes were watering. “Let’s make it quick.”

We bypassed the murky aquariums and were heading for the accessory aisles when Archer picked up a small goldfish bowl and looked at it fondly.

“When I was little, I kept begging for a dog. Drove my parents nuts. Finally, my mama got me a goldfish instead and told me if I could keep it alive for a year, they’d get me a dog. I don’t think she realized goldfish can live up to fifteen years. Did you know that?”

“I did not.”

“They do! Anyhow, I kept it alive, and one day my pops brought home a puppy. Told me he was for hunting. But since my pops was never home, Hound spent way more time with me and basically became mine.”

We turned down another row of supplies. So far, nothing looked to be of use.

“No denying he loves you,” I said, looking down at the canine wagging his tail.

“We’re best friends. He’s probably the only good thing my pops did for me.”

We scanned the back wall and my flashlight landed on a row of filtration system boxes. One showed a hose-like contraption, labeled *Clean and Refill Aquarium Maintenance System.* I took it down from the shelf. “This is perfect,” I said, taking out the long, clear tube from the packaging and winding it into a coil. “We need something to hold the gas.”

Archer went to the other end of the store and came back a moment later with a plastic bucket. He dumped out a pile of river rocks. "This work?"

"Great. That'll do."

We hurried back outside, cautious to recheck our surroundings. Luckily, we were still alone.

I recalled Otto's siphoning technique. One end of the tube would go into a parked car, I'd suck the air through the other end, and then I could pull the gas from inside the tank through the hose. If the car had any gas left, it'd pour into our bucket. I'd have to do the reverse to get the gas into our van.

Conveniently, there were several cars still in the strip mall's parking lot. I knelt beside the nearest one and put the routine into practice. Archer and Hound kept watch as I worked. Only a few minutes later, amber liquid was streaming into the bucket.

The fumes were pungent, but it was the smell of success. Having a car to get around in drastically increased our chances of survival. Seabird didn't feel so out of reach now.

The tube coughed as the car's tank ran empty. I hurried to the next car a few spaces down, lugging the bucket with me.

After three cars, the bucket was full. We'd most likely need more than a bucket's worth to get very far, but we'd already tempted fate by roaming the parking lot for this long.

I completed one final siphon into our tank and poured the remaining gulp of gas into the gas hole, trying my best not to spill any of the precious liquid. With the gas cap clicked back in place, we jumped back into the safety of our van.

We both let out a long sigh of relief, realizing that despite not running into any trouble, it was always unnerving being outside and exposed. The van at least felt sturdy, and with only one small back window in the cargo hold, it was a mini fortress on wheels.

"Sun's going down. I think we should just sleep in the van tonight," I proposed.

Archer eyed the metal flooring in the back. "Guess it's not much different than a concrete floor."

I grabbed my canteen from my backpack and took a swig. Archer mirrored me, going through the plastic bag and grabbing a water bottle and a small pack of cookies. He opened it and handed me one, then poured a little water into the cup holder of the center console for Hound. He slurped it hastily, but after a few seconds, looked back up at his owner and whined.

"He okay?" I asked.

"Yeah, I think he's just really hungry. Hasn't eaten since before we met you," he said, petting the mewling dog.

I offered the rest of my cookie to Hound, but he turned his head away.

"Hound hates human food. He only likes meat. He used to hunt for himself in the woods around our trailer," said Archer, a little defensively, like he was worried the dog would seem spoiled.

I felt a twinge of stress, realizing it wasn't just Archer I was going to be liable for on this journey. "So, what does that mean? We need to get him meat . . . ?" I asked, trying not to sound impatient.

"Well, he can get it on his own, so maybe now we have gas, we can find him a wooded area?"

I unfolded the map, and was relieved to see a green patch bordering the city limit: the outer rim of what was labeled *Mariposa National Park.* It wouldn't be too much of a detour. "You're in luck," I said, more to Hound. "We can drive a few miles to this area and park over there. It's technically on the way."

"Deal," said Archer.

The engine spluttered to life. We drove towards the park, slowly but surely.

Archer parked alongside a curb and opened the trunk to let Hound out. The dog was bouncing with excitement at the sight of the dense maple trees ahead. I, on the other hand, was not. These woods would provide cover for all sorts of dangers, and the sun was going down quickly. My hand was tight around my gun, trigger finger ready.

"He's usually pretty quick about it," said Archer. "We can walk slow, and he'll go ahead and come back when he finds something."

The Shepherd was already sniffing the ground furiously.

"Alright, but let's make sure we don't go too far and can't find our way back to the car," I said, scanning ahead for any movement.

We walked guardedly behind Hound, who darted further into the trees.

"You think animals can turn if they get bit?" Archer asked me after a few minutes.

"Don't think so. Haven't seen any animal Morts, and a lot were showing up dead all over at the beginning of the outbreak. Maybe the one silver lining. Can you imagine an army of undead squirrels?" I asked, quirking an eyebrow.

He laughed.

We hiked for another twenty minutes. Hound would briefly disappear while following a specific scent, then return to check on us. Pre-devastation, these woods would have been teeming with wildlife, but not even a bird chirped in the canopy.

I put my hand out to stop Archer's step. Ahead of us was a large tent between two trees in a small clearing. I heard him click off the safety lock of his gun.

We tiptoed towards the camp. Hound was still off somewhere.

Seeing the tent up close, I could tell it was military grade. A small firepit was just outside the open entrance. No one was inside, but embers still smoked in the campfire's ashes. Someone had been there recently.

I turned quickly, hearing a creak of a branch, but saw nothing.

"Don't … move," said Archer, staring at my chest.

I dared to glance down. Over my heart was a tiny, glowing green dot. A laser sight from a gun somewhere in the treetops.

"I'm in the FORESIGHT program!" I called out.

Judging by the army tent and the obvious tactical skill of their aim, I knew this person was military. Letting them know we were on the same side was my only card to play.

The leaves above shuffled, and a girl jumped down in front of us. Her boots landed hard on the soil. She was tanned, with long black hair pulled into a slick ponytail. She was in her early twenties, naturally pretty, but with harsh features. Her thick eyebrows were tense as she kept her assault rifle pointed at us.

She turned fast when Hound came back, barking.

"He's mine!" Archer cried out.

Hound stopped when she lowered her weapon.

"What are you two doing in the woods?" she asked in a husky voice.

"Hound was just looking for food. We don't want any trouble. We saw your camp and came to check if anyone was here," said Archer.

Hound was refusing to blink, waiting to see whether this newcomer was a friend or foe.

"Show me your FORESIGHT ID," she said to me.

Slowly, I unshouldered my backpack. From the small front pocket, I removed my identification card and handed it to her. She eyed my photo and credentials, then looked back up at me, her gun fully by her side now.

"Willa, huh? I'm Dame. And you are?" she asked, turning to my friend.

"His name's Archer. We met a few days back. He's with me now," I said, still not letting my guard down.

"You two shouldn't be walking around when it's dark. Teeth are way more active at night," she warned.

I only noticed then that the sun had completely set. The last glimmer of light came from a small solar lantern hanging from the canopy of her tent.

"We'll get back to our car," said Archer.

Hound was whining, still not having landed a meal.

"You can stay the night if you like," said Dame, her expression finally softening.

Archer and I traded looks. The prospect of a soft dirt floor under a tent sounded tempting. Plus, a trip back through the dark woods seemed unwise.

"We'll leave at sunrise. Thank you," I said to Dame.

She set her gun down near her backpack and sat by the extinguished firepit. While she used a firestarter to reignite the flames, I spotted a helmet of some sort among her belongings. It was mask-like, with a tube attached to a breathing pack.

She saw me eyeing it. "I'm in the EMBER Squad."

"I know of it. Where's the rest of your team?" I asked, half-knowing the answer.

She looked flustered. "They didn't make it. They were ambushed. I was on a supply run when it happened. Came back and they'd been massacred," she said, not making eye contact.

"Geez... How long have you been on your own?" Archer asked.

"A few weeks. I've continued my duties," she said, ducking inside the tent and bringing out her flamethrower to show us.

"Woah," said Archer. "You've got some heavy-duty weapons."

"Well, in EMBER Squad, we don't just burn bodies, we create them. Some of the best soldiers in the military are deployed into EMBER," she said. "We're the frontline. Pretty much the only military presence left out here to deal with the infected head-on... and things are getting worse every week."

"How so?" I asked, curious about her experience on the battlefield.

"The Phase Two Teeth are out of control. It's not just bites we have to worry about now. They can turn someone with their eyes."

I nearly snapped my neck with the speed of my double-take. "What... What do you mean?"

She nodded, confirming I'd heard her correctly. "Yeah. There's reports from all over that they'll grab you, hold your eyes open, and somehow turn you just by staring," she said, shuddering as she spoke.

"You've ... seen it?" Archer asked meekly.

She shook her head. "I hope I never do."

A part of me could not deny she was more in the know than I was, but the new information seemed so farfetched, I had to believe it was military legend. Stories soldiers told each other around a fire like this one.

I noticed a name tattooed in cursive on her forearm. Again, she clocked my curiosity.

"It's my grandfather's signature," she said, tracing it with her soiled fingers. "He served in World War Two. Runs in the family. Not that that kept my mom from crying for months when I enlisted."

"Wow, I thought my parents were bad. My mom only cried for two weeks when I got this piercing," I said.

She laughed. "You wouldn't want to witness my *mamá* and me going at it. Two Latinas toe to toe? It gets *heated.* The day I deployed was the day I cut ties with her and my sisters. I never understood why they were so devastated that I chose a different life than them. She said I was a crazy person for wanting to go to war. I told her people do crazy things when they want to be somebody."

"We have more in common than you know," I said, warming my hands over the flames. "My parents were always pressuring my brother and me to be 'the greatest we could be.' Our ideas of greatness weren't the same. They thought it meant a successful career that made a lot of money, end of story."

"Where's your family now?" she asked, gently.

"My parents are out of state, in one of the contained cities somewhere. I reentered to find my brother Malik. I think he's still out here. We're heading to my hometown to start looking."

Hound whimpered again.

"Okay, boy, go find something, but don't go far," said Archer, and Hound took off again.

"How about you?" Dame asked him.

"I was trying to make it to the border to find help for my ma. She's been infected," he said nervously. "I'm sticking with Willa until she goes back to the border camp."

She turned back to me. "You said you have a car?"

"Yeah, we found a van. We're gonna drive up the coast to my hometown, Seabird."

"Without my squadron, it's been difficult to get around," Dame said. "I can't return to basecamp until my campaign's over, anyhow. I can give you guys a little more protection if you give me a ride to the next city."

I thought about it. I eyed her jam-packed backpack, the flamethrower, the automatic, and her camping gear. Her energy was hard to read, but her supplies were undeniable.

Hound came back with a rabbit, joyfully digging into its furry ribs.

"If you don't mind sharing a backseat with a big German Shepherd, sure," I joked.

Dame looked ecstatic. "Don't mind at all. Anything to not have to walk any more miles with all this stuff."

Under the faint glow of the solar lantern, we talked for another hour. Dame got a kick out of Archer's homemade flamethrower. Hound was finally satisfied with a full stomach and sporting a bloody mustache. We shared a couple ration bars and stories before zipping up the tent for the night and burying ourselves under a large quilted blanket.

4.

A rough, wet tongue startled me awake. Hound stood over me.

"I'm up, I'm up!" I said, pushing his face away.

My groggy protests woke Dame and Archer, who laughed.

We broke camp and hauled the gear back to the van. Thanks to Hound, we found it with ease. Dame was baffled when Archer hopped into the driver's seat. She offered to drive instead, but he was adamant about pulling his weight.

With our supplies stowed in the cargo area and Dame and Hound settled in, Archer took the wheel with an air of pride. It'd be at least a few hours before we'd have to refuel again.

Our new ally turned out to be more well-versed in map reading than I was, so I handed off navigation duties to her. We made it to State Route 2 in less time than I had anticipated. The wide highway ran parallel to a gorgeous coastline for miles. A morning fog blanketed the ocean like a low-hanging cloud.

I fantasized about floating out there and staying lost in the silence, away from this poisoned world. Then my mind landed on Malik, and my parents. That family trip we took to a historic fishing village to celebrate his senior year in high school. It would be our last trip together...

The memories shifted to Tye and his friends. We didn't know that day, as we left the beach, that it would be one of our final moments as a group.

Radio static filled the car. Archer was turning the dial delicately to see if he could find a signal. Finally, he did: an emergency broadcast, declaring all civilians to evacuate to the nearest border facility. I'd heard those haunting words before. It was the very message that had driven me to set out across the state in search of my parents.

"Did you get a vaccine at the border?" asked Archer.

"Yeah, first thing they did when we arrived," I said, recalling the unpleasant experience.

"All military are given it too, but it only helps with airborne immunity," said Dame. "Won't save you from the rest."

The van followed the meandering coastal road for another hour. I took advantage of Dame and Archer's light-hearted debate over his distaste for spicy Latin food and entered some data into my tablet. I noted Dame's warning about Phase Two Morts spreading the virus through their eyes, but made an additional note that it was based on hearsay rather than personal observation. Still, the thought made the hair on the back of my neck rise.

Through the window I began seeing residential harbors and surf shacks, which eventually shifted into larger stores, marinas crowded with small boats, and further ahead, a mall.

The van was suddenly jolted by a violent impact. Dame had hold of her rifle in an instant as the car came to a stop. Archer and I scanned the rearview mirror to see if we could spot anything. There was nothing in view, but stopping in the middle of the freeway felt like we were asking for trouble. On one side of the road was a strip of commercial stores that was probably once a heavily populated hub for beachgoers. On the other, a cliff led down to the rocky beach.

Dame climbed out of the back. I watched through the side mirror as she circled around the van to assess. "Popped tire!" she said, irritated.

I slammed my hand on the dashboard. This was an unforeseen obstacle that could set us back for days. There wasn't going to be a set of car keys in every drawer we checked, and even if we found a spare tire, changing it on this hefty van was no easy task.

SLAM!

My passenger door shuddered. Hound barked as a Mort scratched ferociously at my window. Dame's gun went off. The Mort dropped. There was a moment of calm, but within seconds, a horde of undead flooded over the cliff's edge, slamming into the van like a wave of rot. The van tilted dangerously from the force.

Dame jumped back into the cargo hold and slammed the door shut. She was shaking. "Where the fuck did they all come from?!" she yelled over Hound's barking.

Both Archer and I readied our pistols as the van threatened to topple over. More of the creatures joined the frenzy.

"We can't let them surround us or we'll be stuck in here!" I shouted. "We need to barge through them and get to the mall."

"Get behind me!" said Dame, picking up the flamethrower.

Most of our stuff would have to stay behind. Anything that slowed us down was a liability to surviving the run.

"Ready?" she asked.

I nodded.

She kicked open the rear door and fire erupted from the nozzle of her flamethrower with a thunderous roar, scorching a path for us to sprint through the horde. She tossed aside the bulky fire gun and grabbed her automatic.

There was a burst of chaos as we blitzed the undead. I heard Archer's gun go off, followed by the distinct grunt of a fallen Mort. I shot another between the eyes. One grabbed Hound, but Dame was quick to blast it in the chest.

We ran towards town, my eyes darting to every possible escape route, but none were obvious enough to risk a detour. We sprinted towards the massive shopping mall up the road.

Even when we gained distance on the stampede, more undead crept out from the surrounding buildings. Three emerged from an underground subway stop ahead.

We finally reached the rear of the mall and I pulled hard on the exit door, but it was locked. In a panic, we ran for a second door further down.

The army of monsters was only feet away. I yanked on the handle. It opened!

A Mort grabbed Dame by the ankle a second before she made it inside. It pulled her forcefully, splitting her calf muscle open against the metal of the doorframe. She screamed as blood puddled on the floor beneath her. Archer grabbed her by the straps of her vest and heaved her inside, just as I put the barrel of my gun to the Jumbee's skull.

BAM!

The door slammed shut with all of us safely inside. I locked it fast.

Dame was wailing in pain, grabbing her leg like she was trying not to lose any more blood.

"Were you bit?!" Archer asked, panicked.

I answered for her. "Her leg tore on the door. We need to stop the bleeding."

Archer ran to the nearest store and snagged the first shirt he could find off a hanger. He threw it to me and I quickly tied it around her calf. Almost instantly, it was drenched in red.

Hound was barking persistently, which we ignored at first, until we realized he was pacing around a mall security golf cart. Archer walked over to check it out.

"Does it start?" I asked.

He flipped a switch and turned the fob near the steering wheel. The battery buzzed on.

"Help me lift her!" I said.

Together, we gently eased Dame into the backseat, Hound jumping in beside her. Archer and I climbed on and he drove us further into the sprawling mall.

This place, likely teeming with shoppers in the past, was now an eerie graveyard of stores. I wondered where all those people were now. The last time I'd been to a mall with friends, we had no idea how close the world was to ending.

The mall was airport-like in size. Even though we were driving at top speed, the stores seemed endless. Many of them had their security gates down, but a few had obviously been looted. Large skylights provided dusty light from above. We passed a grand water feature that must have been an elegant fountain in its prime. Now it was a stagnant lake of murky water.

With Dame's groans echoing throughout the first floor, I became increasingly aware that Morts could be lurking down these dark corridors. My eyes searched frantically for somewhere to bunker down and help tend her wounds. While I prayed for a pharmacy, the first convenient place I spotted was a mattress store.

"Stop here," I said to Archer.

After pulling up to the storefront, Archer and I carefully helped Dame onto one of the memory foam mattresses on the sales floor. Her shirt-bandage was saturated with blood. I ran over to the back wall and grabbed a pack of sheets, urgently ripping it open. Archer put a pillow under her leg while I removed the shirt and checked the wound. It was deep, but not large. If we could clean and properly seal it, she stood a chance. I tied the ripped-up sheet securely around it as she buried her face in her elbow, clenching a scream behind her teeth.

"You're gonna be okay. We'll keep changing it out as the bleeding slows," I said to her. "Archer, bag that bloodied shirt and toss it in the back room or something. Morts smell blood."

He winced as he picked it up with two fingers and carried out the task.

Dame was clearly in pain, but I was impressed that there was no sign of tears. She was breathing deeply to control the agony.

"Dame, will you be okay if Archer and I go look for something to help you?" I asked. "There's a lot of stores in this place. One of them could have a first aid kit or something."

"Yeah," she said with effort. "Just hand me my gun."

I picked up her automatic and placed it gently by her side.

"We can lower the security gate," said Archer, eyeing the entryway. "At least it'll give her some sort of barrier. We can leave Hound to keep watch. You stay put boy."

The dog instantly plopped himself by the entrance, on alert.

"Thank you, guys," Dame said, her face still lodged in her elbow, as if she was battling not to cry.

"We'll try to be quick," I said, and with loaded guns and the gate lowered, we set out into the dark halls of the shopping mall.

We decided not to use the golf cart. It was clearly battery-powered, and we had no access to a charging station. We wandered further and further away. My hope was to come across some sort of convenience store or pharmacy, but in my experience, those were always the first places to get ransacked. Still, it was worth a look.

"There's a store map," said Archer, pointing to a large square bulletin board.

It was four-sided. Two sides listed all the stores by category, and two had a labeled floor plan of the mall.

"This place is massive," I said, seeing there were three floors. Even more impressive was an underground subway stop built into the lower level for commuters.

We studied the different categories of retail: *Department Stores, Toys & Hobbies, Beauty, Jewelry & Watches, Home Décor,* and many, many others until Archer's finger landed on *Pharmacies.* Although this was great news, it denoted that the pharmacy was apparently inside a grocery store on the basement floor, within the mall's main *Food Hall.*

"This is gonna be more extensive than I planned," I thought out loud.

"The escalators aren't too far," said Archer hopefully.

"Just stay alert. It's a little too quiet," I warned.

We arrived at the escalators in the main atrium where the fountain was. It was only then that I spotted several large fish swimming slowly along the bottom. Their fins tattered from poor water conditions.

The escalator leading down to floor zero was shrouded in darkness. Archer and I clicked on our flashlights as we traipsed down the steps. I could almost hear Archer's heartbeat—or was it mine?

At the bottom, we came to a hallway that was blocked by two emergency fire doors, bolted shut. More sinister were the words spray-painted on them.

DO NOT oP3N

"Now what?" Archer asked, and although he'd whispered, something stirred behind the door and I heard the low growling of several Morts.

I weighed the risk versus the reward, and the risk far outweighed the small chance that medical supplies would still be available in a most likely gutted store. While it might become a necessary gamble in the future, it wasn't worth the risk yet.

I motioned to Archer to follow me back up the escalator. At the top, I turned to him. "Let's try a couple of these retail stores for a first aid kit."

We went into a clothing store and headed straight for the back room. It was very dark, but looked like mostly inventory storage. It didn't take long to comb through enough of the place to realize there wasn't a first aid kit anywhere.

Undeterred, we moved on to five other stores on our way back to Dame, even coming across the mall security office, which was disappointingly locked. Our mission was unsuccessful. We could, of course, continue on forever, but leaving Dame for too long was risky. She could black out from the blood loss at any moment.

Hound's tail wagged fervently when he spotted us. We lifted the gate and I was relieved to see Dame sitting up, her leg still elevated.

“It slowed a little,” she said weakly, pointing to her wound. “Any luck?”

Our faces must have said it all.

“*Coño,*” she said. “Well, I’m glad you made it back okay. I’m so pissed we had to ditch all my stuff in the van. I had a military medical kit in my pack. Of course I never needed it until I don’t have it on me ...”

With dozens of Morts roaming about, that was mission impossible, unless we could create some sort of diversion long enough to make it to the van and back. I’d left my stuff behind too. My risk-versus-reward meter was toggling again.

Archer could tell. “You’re not thinking of going back to the van, are you?” he asked warily, but not discouragingly.

“Dame’s got a medical kit and survival gear. My ammo and supplies are back there too. I know it’s risky, and maybe even crazy, but we don’t have a lot of options here.”

I walked over to the golf cart and lightly pressed down on the steering wheel. The horn blared for a moment, surprisingly louder than I’d expected from the small cart. I looked around. Not far away was a double-doored fire exit that must have led outside.

“If we can strap down this horn and put some weight on the gas pedal, every Mort in the area will chase after this thing,” I pitched.

Both of them stared at me with different degrees of shock, but I could tell they were digesting it.

Before responding, Archer went into the back room and came out with a sturdy-looking box. “Think this is heavy enough?” he asked with a smirk.

We drove the golf cart right up to the exit doors. Archer cautiously peeked outside to make sure the coast was clear before propping them open. I hurriedly tied a pillowcase tightly around the steering wheel. The horn blared, reverberating off the walls of the mall. I wedged the heavy box onto the pedal, propelling the golf cart through the exit and down the street. Archer quickly locked the doors again.

We had not a second to spare. We bolted to the other side of the mall where we'd entered from. Both our loaded weapons were raised, prepared to face whatever could still be lingering outside.

I cracked the door open, testing to see if anything would attack. We could hear the horn still screaming in the distance. I pushed the door open a little wider and dared to look out. I recoiled when I saw a group of the creatures out on the street, but they were facing away from us, racing towards the sound in the opposite direction of the van.

The van somehow seemed a lot further away than I remembered. This would be no easy feat.

"You ready?" I asked Archer. "Focus."

He nodded confidently, and we charged towards the van as if we were competing in a race. Even with our pattering footsteps drowned out by the horn, I tensed at every sound they made. My heavy breathing warmed my face in the brisk ocean air. Archer was slightly ahead of me. After two blocks of sprinting, we slowed down as we reached the graveyard of burnt bodies scattered around the van. Archer stepped around them like he was crossing a landmine field, while I scanned the streets frantically to make sure we were still alone. So far, we were. Without missing a beat, he jumped into the van's cargo hold, emerging a second later with both mine and Dame's bags.

"Got 'em," he said, his voice sounding unnervingly loud.

We both froze. My heart was in the pit of my stomach. It was suddenly dead quiet. The horn from the golf cart had stopped.

"*Run*!" I said, in a voice hoarse with fear.

We raced back the way we'd come, all the while looking in every direction for Morts. This time, I was ahead of Archer. I realized he was struggling with the bags and grabbed one from him.

"Willa!" he yelled.

I turned and fired into a Mort only a foot away. More were gathering in the distance. We were still a block from the mall, but our path was clear.

My optimism was short-lived. Morts began to emerge from every conceivable hiding place. Archer and I fought our way through the first wave, but a second threatened our course. I dropped my survival pack. We were surrounded. Archer and I stood back-to-back, unloading our cartridges into the heads of about fifteen Morts until we finally ran out of ammo.

I couldn't believe I had been so stupid as to think the risk was worth it. Dame was a life, yes, but I'd just sacrificed myself and getting to my brother for her needs and some trivial gains.

Archer punched a Mort as it made to bite him. I took the knife from my boot and drilled it into the skull of another. The growls and hisses from the horde were so loud now. I hadn't seen so many gathered since the Don Lux.

BAM. BAM. BAM. BAM. BAM. BAM. BAM.

Archer and I dropped and covered our heads as Morts fell by the dozen around us. A man appeared and grabbed Archer and me, pushing us in the direction of the mall.

"Go!" he yelled.

We grabbed the bags and followed him as he fired to clear a path. His precision and the distinct military gear left no room for doubt—he was a seasoned soldier.

I couldn't believe it when we made it back to the mall, the stranger ushering us inside the door. We plopped to the floor, touching the glossy tile as if to make sure we were really there and alive.

"First off, that was a *terrible* idea," said the guy, locking the door behind us.

He was wearing a fabric mask that covered the lower half of his face, and a helmet. He unstrapped it and set it aside, revealing hair that was so blond it looked white.

"Second, what the hell are you doing here?" he asked, lowering his face covering.

His tone was light, like he was addressing a friend. I looked up and took in the many familiar face tattoos that trailed all the way down his neck.

My jaw dropped. "*Maverick?*"

Even more shocked was Archer, who was looking incredulously from me to the new arrival, and back to me again.

"Holy shit," I said, still processing this twist.

"I mean, I'm in the military, it makes sense that *I'm* here, but you? Please explain how you got here from Seabird—weren't you evacuated?" he asked, almost parent-like, as if I had broken some sort of rule.

"Extremely long story," I said, still catching my breath after our sprint.

"I'm lost, for many reasons," said Archer.

"Sorry, this is Maverick. He's an old friend of my brother's... and mine," I said.

Maverick lived in the big city near Seabird, where I'd frequent the music scene with my friends. Our paths would cross regularly, and because of his friendship with Malik, he always kept a protective eye on me from a distance. He worked weekends at the shipping yard in Seabird. In town they called him Ghost, because of his white-blond hair. Eventually, he enlisted in the army and I never saw him again, but I'd always randomly think about him. My brother would say he was the scariest-looking nice guy he'd ever met. That his head-to-toe tattoos didn't match his demeanor at all. They were from his past, but he had turned over a new leaf.

Seeing him now gave a whole new meaning to his nickname. He was a ghost, from the past.

"Nice to meet you," Archer said. "And thanks for saving us."

"I heard that horn from way down. Lucky I came to see what was going on," said Maverick.

"I can't believe you're here," I said with a laugh.

He laughed too. "Back at you. We'll need a long catchup once we're safe. Do you have a camp?"

I told Maverick about Dame's injury on the walk back to the mattress store. When we lifted the security gate, she was sitting up a little higher than she could before. Spotting the newcomer, she quickly reached for her gun, but when she saw him holding her backpack she stopped herself.

"Hound, down!" Archer said as the dog jumped all over Maverick while he unzipped the bag.

I was surprised that Hound seemed instantly comfortable with him.

Maverick took out the small medical kit and laid it on the end of Dame's bed. "Dame, right?" he asked.

"Yeah," she said, looking half in pain, half in awe of him.

"I'm Maverick. I need you to trust me and let me help you."

She nodded.

While Maverick untied the sheet from around her bloodied calf, I laid out the peroxide, gauze, and a few other things I didn't quite recognize.

"Do we have any water?" Mav asked, his tone brusque.

I handed him the canteen from my pack and he poured a stream of water over the open wound. Dame tensed and groaned. When he switched to a stream of peroxide, she groaned even louder.

"I'm gonna need you to breathe through this. I'm gonna close your wound with this skin glue," he warned, holding up a tube of clear gel.

She gave him a weak nod, turning her head away as he took a piece of gauze and pushed down on the injury. Dame's hand clasped over her mouth as she screamed into her palm. He squeezed the fissure together and applied the glue over it. Dame's harsh breathing quickened.

"Hand me that bandaging," he said. I tossed him a roll of fabric dressing.

He waited a moment for the glue to dry, applied one final layer, then laid a patch of gauze over it and tied it around her calf firmly. I was impressed by his confidence and execution.

Dame's breathing was starting to even out. She looked down at the cleaned and dressed wound. "Thank you, guys," she said with emotion.

“Take this,” Maverick said, handing her a small pill from the kit. “Painkiller.”

She took it eagerly, tossing it back with a gulp from the canteen.

“Thank you,” I said quietly to Maverick. He smiled.

I would’ve been able to make do, with some improvising, but having his expertise at hand was a godsend. He’d saved all three of our lives in just the last hour.

“So, can you fill me in?” Dame asked, as if Maverick’s presence was a more pressing matter than her wound. “Who’s this?”

“Maverick was friends with my brother. I haven’t seen him since he enlisted. He just saved our asses out there,” I said, recalling our brush with death. “We were completely surrounded.”

“Wait, what? And you just happened to be there?” she asked, looking incredulous. “Was your unit deployed out here or something?”

“My unit’s long gone,” he replied. “I’ve been alone in the area for a week. We were part of the first wave sent in months ago when the outbreak got out of control. At first, the mission was to eliminate as many Teeth as we could and assist the evacuation... but we had no idea what they were sending us into. It was unlike anything we’d ever trained for.”

Dame scoffed. “I think I speak for all military when I say they fed us to the wolves,” she seethed. “We’re completely outnumbered out here and they’ve barely sent reinforcements. I was working in aviation before, helping with supply runs to heavily affected regions, when I was recruited into the EMBER program a few months back. We were the second wave. Our mission was to control spawning. Kill any Teeth we encountered and burn as many bodies as we could. A month in, we realized we were in way over our heads.

“We called for backup more times than I could count. No one came. And even when supplies started running low, radio silence. The government doesn’t care about us. I went out looking for supplies like a scavenger, to help my unit... and when I came back, my entire squadron was gone.

The only purpose we're serving out here is to be a human wall, keeping the Teeth from swarming the contained states."

I could feel the hurt in her voice. I already had my own distaste for enrolling myself in a government-affiliated program. I felt like a pawn, but I reminded myself I was doing it for my own benefit too.

"Even civilians are starting to get restless again," she went on. "I heard there's riots happening all over the nation in the safe cities. They want answers. When that first wave of flu was going around, the government had never been more vague. Now all those conspiracies about the sketchy planes are gaining traction again."

I couldn't suppress my questions any longer. "You guys are closer to the inner workings than I am—what do you make of all this? Why else would the government keep tight-lipped unless they were involved?"

"I don't know if it's our government," Mav replied. "It could be some sort of bioterrorism attack."

"The plane crash?" Dame asked, clearly referencing something I wasn't informed about.

"... Plane crash?" Archer echoed.

"There was a major plane crash the day before everything went to shit. Our aviation branch got the intel in briefings, but civilians never caught wind of it. By the time the reports reached the networks, the news was flooded with Teeth."

My blood pressure was rising. "Hold up. Every conspiracy leads back to planes, and you're telling me there was a plane crash big enough to be discussed in the military, twenty-four hours before the outbreak of the virus? There's no way the two aren't related."

Dame and Maverick exchanged a look. Neither denied my point.

"No one can get close enough to the crash site to get any real data. They're calling it 'Ground Misery,'" said Maverick. The name was spine-chilling. "The drones that've flown over it show the highest concentration of Teeth on record. At the end of the day, it's all just theories ... but let's just say the whispers among the people are definitely getting louder. I hope our government can step up whether they're involved or not. It's all out of control."

"Why are you two still helping the government if you feel like they've left you to die?" Archer asked of the two soldiers.

His question hung in the air like a haze as they digested the potent question.

"It's not about serving the government," Maverick said eventually. "It's about protecting civilians."

We looked to Dame for her response, but she was taking a prolonged sip from the canteen.

"More importantly," Mav continued, "I know you said it's a long story, but what are you doing out here? Is your family okay?"

I knew what he was really asking—if Malik was alive. I took a deep breath as my mind ran through the truly extensive circumstances, but I gave him the consolidated version.

"My parents had gone to visit Malik a few days before the outbreak. I was in Seabird without them when everything happened," I explained. "Took months to make it to the safe zone, but I did. I learned my parents and Malik were alive. Later, I found out Malik had reentered to go find me—so I joined FORESIGHT and came back out here to find *him*. We've been making our way to Seabird."

Maverick looked stunned. "Of course he reentered for you. I'm not surprised, but I'm impressed... "

"Every day that goes by, I get more worried that he bit off more than he could chew. But I'm confident he'll still be in our hometown if I can get there fast enough," I said, unable to keep my eyes from welling up.

Dame piped up. "Willa, you've done more than enough for me. You should get going."

I did consider it, but an even more pressing obstacle was the Jumbees surrounding the building. "We'll give it a few days and see how you're doing," I said.

She smiled weakly.

Maverick sat next to me on the edge of the mattress, putting a comforting hand on my shoulder. "Helping you find Malik and getting you all to safety is still within my duties. It's the least I can do after everything Malik's done for me," he said, and looked away.

Malik had told me in confidence about Mav's past drug use and how he was trying to help him stay clean, but Mav had never shared that with me directly. I just smiled in response. Having someone like him—a friend, but also a skilled comrade—would be more than I'd ever hoped for out here.

"He'll be so happy to see you," I said to him.

He nodded, looking wistful. "If we're staying put for a bit, we should plan on stocking up on food and water."

"We'll need energy for that. Let's get some sleep," said Archer, yawning. He plopped himself on a mattress towards the back of the store. Hound stationed himself at the foot of his bed, looking prepared to stay alert through the night.

After closing the security gate over the store entrance, Mav and I found our own beds. My aching body melted into the mattress like butter on a hot pan. Despite my turbulent mind, the comfort of having a protective energy like Maverick nearby allowed my thoughts to fade into sleep.

5.

A thousand waves crash over a small boat. It sways dramatically. I'm holding on, but I'm slipping. A voice is calling my name. Over and over, the distant cries echo. I can't see who it is. I can only feel them. It's a boy. His voice becomes more familiar with each call.

"Willa!"

"Willa!"

"Willa!"

I finally place the voice.

"Tye?!"

When my eyes opened, I expected to see him standing in front of me, but again, it was a dream. But not *just* a dream. These vivid, emotionally charged visions were different. They felt symbolic, important.

I'd had plenty of nightmares about Imani, but even in their brutality, the visions were fleeting. They would wane and I'd be left only with the anxiety they brought me. With these dreams about Tye, I could make out every detail, and remember them vividly even hours later. Strangely, it was just as difficult to see Tye's face as it was Imani's. Though in different ways, they were both great losses in my life.

Imani changed me as a person. In our short time together, we lived a lifetime. Parts of her were still sewn into me and knowing her had taught me not to be such a loner. Before our friendship, I would never have fit into a random group like I was able to now. I was always independent to a fault.

My first lesson in comradery was when we came to find some young survivors making do in an old bottle factory. Once we decided to stay, I had my guard up. It was tough for me to find my place among them. Imani, on the other hand, was open and warm, and had a way of being comfortable with everyone. In the long week that we made that place home, I dealt with all sorts of personalities. Eventually, I felt my energy gradually opening up to them. We didn't stay long enough for me to make friends, but Imani brought out the best in me. I liked who I was around her.

Months later, when I met Tye and his friends, I felt bonded to them in a way I hadn't experienced in the past. I was surprised I was open to them at all. After losing Imani, I remember wondering how I could ever be close to someone again. I carried tremendous guilt and pain over how it had ended for her. But the life of survival was chaotic and ever-moving, so I pushed forward. Part of me was glad I met new friends to keep my mind from pressing on the open wounds. The other part knew there was no way it was healthy to bury trauma like that. To never truly face it, or process it.

The soft flutter of flapping wings pulled me back to the present. A gray pigeon pattered along the tiled floor outside the security gate. Hound's eyes followed it. He whined when it flew off.

I walked over to him and patted his head as he fixated on the rafters near the skylights. A few more birds rested there. I opened the gate and let the black dog satisfy his curiosity, smiling to myself, until a daunting realization hit me: birds indoors meant that there was an opening somewhere to the outside. So far, we hadn't seen any Morts inside, but with the shopping mecca being so vast, it was possible we just hadn't come across them yet.

I grabbed my pack and sat leaning against the wall just outside the store entrance. Hound was chasing a black-and-white pigeon. I knew it was probably a good time to enter some observation data before the others woke up.

I powered up my tablet and typed some abbreviated notes, mostly annotating the sheer number of Morts I'd seen outside. Twice as many as I'd noticed when in the contamination zone the first time. I also found it worth noting that I was now in the presence of two military personnel, both of whom had lost their squadrons. A sure sign that the military was outnumbered. I clicked Send only a second before the radio beeped.

Holding down the button on the side, I said, "Good morning, Thirteen. You're superhuman if you read my notes that quickly."

"I can see when your tablet's in use, so I'm presuming that you're in a safe enough place," he said. *"I'm reading your observations now."* There was a momentary silence as he went through them. *"So, you're a party of four now?"*

"It was almost zero, twenty-four hours ago."

"As you noted, the military is becoming increasingly overwhelmed. Other FORESIGHT members have observed Host soldiers. They're much harder to take down with a gunshot while they're wearing protective gear. Stay alert."

The thought of a Mort wearing bulletproof armor made the skin on the back of my neck prickle. All these new versions of undead were getting out of hand.

"Do you actually care what happens to me, or is it part of the act?" I asked, even though I knew the answer deep down. The mention of other FORESIGHT members had reminded me that I was just a number in their system.

"Like you, I have a job to do. The longer you're alive, the better I can contribute to fighting this plague. But Willa, please do remember, also like you, I am human. I truly do hope you make it back to your family."

His sudden warmth caught me off guard. I was silent for a moment. "... Thanks, Thirteen," I said eventually. "If you have any family left, I'm manifesting a safe reunion for you too."

His slightly longer pause made me feel there was a real person behind this voice after all.

"Thank you, Willa. Talk soon." He clicked off.

In the quiet, I heard something move behind me and I jumped slightly. It was just Dame adjusting herself. She tossed and turned for a moment, then her eyes opened and she sat up. I went over to check on her.

She brushed her knotted hair away from her face. "How'd you sleep?" she asked me, probably noticing the bags under my eyes.

"Despite the comfortable mattress, pretty badly. I was freezing," I said, keeping my voice down so as not to wake the others.

"Same deal," she said. "That's those winter months creeping in. We'll have to stock up on blankets before bed tonight." She still had her leg propped up on a pillow.

"How's the pain?" I asked.

"You guys really came through. It feels a lot better." Her expression became thoughtful.

"Thank you for not leaving me. I know your brother's very important to you, so the sacrifice didn't go unnoticed."

I smiled faintly. I'd done what was right, but it was heart-wrenching to think I'd delayed my reunion with Malik.

When I didn't respond, she continued. "When we were all chatting yesterday, all that talk about how fucked this situation is, and how us soldiers are just pawns, and how much you love your brother... just had me feeling heavy. I sacrificed my entire family so I could take my own path and make a name for myself through the military. And was any of it worth it? Who's *really* gonna remember me?"

"Do you know where they are, your family?" I asked gently.

"Both my sisters and my mom were marked safe in one of the contained cities. My dad was a journalist. He was covering the story inside the outbreak zone. He didn't make it."

"I'm sorry," I said. "Look, I have a lot of regrets about how things stood with my parents before we were separated. One day, we'll both be back with our families and we'll take back all the dumb shit we ever fought about."

She mirrored my smile. “Well, first I need to relearn how to walk,” she joked, tapping her shin lightly.

“Morning,” said Mav, sitting up on the edge of his bed.

“Good morning,” I replied as he stretched.

He had shed all his gear the night before and was now redressing. I caught Dame taking in all the art on his defined body.

“Going somewhere?” she asked as he pulled down his shirt.

“We should move while there’s daylight,” he said. “Archer told me there’s a grocery store on the bottom level?”

“Did he mention the fire doors are locked down there? There’s Morts behind it. I can’t say how many, but it sounded like a handful,” I said.

Mav didn’t react to the nickname, *Morts.* I imagined there were many names for the horrific creatures and he’d heard a whole bunch of them.

“He did, but he said I could take them,” he replied with a smirk.

I rolled my eyes. If Archer was awake I would’ve shot him a look.

“Besides,” he went on, “there’s more of us now, we can handle it.”

“Probably, but why waste ammo? We should check the directory and see if there’s an alternate route,” I said.

He shrugged. “Alright. Lead the way, m’lady.”

Maverick, now in full combat gear, stood next to me before the large mall guide, focusing on the underground level where the grocery store and subway tunnel lived.

“Damn, the only other way to enter the grocery store is on the complete opposite side of the mall,” he said, irritated.

“Looks like we can get to a side entrance through the subway stop,” I suggested, my finger moving across the diagram to a large hall that led to the platform. “This is gonna be a long walk…”

“Ready when you are,” Mav said, cocking his assault rifle dramatically.

With my pistol held tight in my hand, I led the way.

We walked for ten minutes in silence, passing the koi pond. Our first hours together had been so hectic that this was the first real moment I'd had with Maverick—ever, really. Most of what I knew of him was through Malik's friendship with him.

Even when we'd run into each other in the city or at a concert, we'd exchange a few nice words but we never really got deeper than that. But even though our relationship was still green, having someone with any connection to my family and hometown was comforting.

"So, *Ghost,* in true ghost fashion, once you enlisted and left town, you disappeared. Fill me in a little," I said, curious, but keeping my voice low.

"Nothing exciting. I enlisted; few months later, I quit my job in Seabird and headed to training. Was there about two years, climbing the ranks fast, before my unit was deployed into the first wave of defense against the Teeth. Cut to, now," he said, busying himself with the scope of his gun.

"What do you mean, 'cut to?' I want to hear about how you ended up here," I said with a laugh. "I still can't process that I'm standing in front of the one soldier I know—who also knows my brother."

"The in-between part's bloody, full of trauma, and downright sad, so just accept the 'cut to' part," he laughed. His eyes got distant, as if he was remembering something fondly. "Your brother was a huge reason I even got back on track, you know. I'm sure he's told you about my past addictions ... When I left rehab, I kinda had to relearn who I was sober, and adjust to how people thought of me. It was awful feeling like no one really saw *me*. Because of my past, and how I looked ... When I got that job in Seabird and met your brother, I finally felt like someone was getting to know me, as if all that stuff never happened."

I felt my eyes gloss over. Malik really was so special.

Mav continued emphatically. "He was always so damn focused on his goals, and driven. Inspired the hell out of me. I mean, enlisting was never on my radar as far as my goals went, but I wasn't like Malik, with his scholarships and mega-brain. Figured at least the army would give me a path to something."

There was a beat where we were both probably thinking back on times shared with Malik, before he asked, "What did you want to do with your future? Before all this?"

I was caught off guard. Any goals I'd once had were so far out the window at that point, and before that, no one had really ever asked me about what I wanted to do in life. That question was always reserved for my scholarly brother.

I thought about it for a second. "I guess I imagined something in the music industry. Maybe artist development or something," I said, envisioning the alternative future that could have been. "You think things will ever go back to normal? In some form?"

He gave me a pained smile. "Things are definitely changed for good, but whether we adapt and thrive is still pending—"

His inked hand abruptly reached out to stop me from walking. He pulled me into a nearby beauty supply store and ducked behind a shelf.

"I see it," I breathed.

A deformed Phase Two Mort was limping down the hall in the distance. Its contorted face was turned toward the storefronts.

"It's heading for our basecamp. We have to take it down," said Mav, lifting his gun.

A clang made us both jump. The hilt of his bulky rifle had hit a can of hairspray off the shelf behind us. In a blink, the Mort turned its black eyes towards us and screeched violently.

We raced to the back of the store and ducked behind the checkout counter. The twitching Mort toppled over the shelf we were hiding behind only moments before. It sniffed for flesh, sensing we were near.

In seconds, the humanoid was too close for us to even whisper. From behind the counter, we could hear its steps getting closer as its raspy inhalations tried to pick up our scent in the air.

I spotted a small basket under the register containing some sample products. One of them was a small bottle of cologne and I reached for it slowly. Maverick watched me, looking baffled. I popped the cap off and sprayed the fragrance wildly in the air around us. Mav caught on to what I was doing and smiled.

Almost instantly, the Mort's steps grew frantic and further away. It seemed to be confused at losing track of our smell so suddenly; its sensors were probably going wild. Mav dared to peek his head above the desk, so I followed. Seeing the Mort's back turned to us, he fired a single round into its head. It let out a short grunt and fell onto a pile of makeup products, drenching them in blood.

"Guess mega-brains run in the family," he said to me with a grin.

As we passed it to leave, I looked down at the rotting body. It had obviously gone through many reanimations. Just like Thirteen had told me, the more times a Mort was bitten and revived, the more its human state would alter. I took a quick photo of it with my tablet. This one looked almost alien.

We set off on our way again. Mav consulted another mall guide to make sure we were still on the right track. The corridors of this shopping maze were all starting to look the same.

"Surprised we haven't seen more of them with how many there are outside," Mav said, surveying the area ahead with more concentration than before. "The reason I've been stuck in the area's because it seems like they're multiplying by the dozen every day. I can't even get near a car long enough to hotwire it."

"Seems like this part of town was popular. Probably tons of bodies around here to feed on," I said, feeling my heart rate going up. The thought of the imminent difficulty in leaving this place was daunting.

We walked a little while longer.

"Look," said Maverick, pointing up at a subway sign.

It hung above a set of escalators leading down to the lower level. Even more promising was the arrow pointing to the grocery store entrance in the same direction.

We followed it down to the dark platform. When the beams of our flashlights hit the subway, we both audibly gasped. It was a scene of destruction. The rail train looked frozen in time. Its doors were opened, and rubble and dust blanketed the ground. The ceiling had caved into a pile of concrete from some kind of explosion. Bullet shells, streaks of blood, and a few abandoned military helmets painted a horrific picture of an intense confrontation. The absence of bodies was a chilling sign that they had been fed on and turned.

Without speaking, Mav and I took up full defensive stances, inching slowly towards the pile of rubble.

Mav shined his light on a fallen plaque, wiping the dust from it. "*Food Hall*," he read aloud.

I sighed in frustration. The mountain of destruction before us was once another entrance to the grocery store, now completely cut off.

"Let's get out of here before we run into more trouble," said Maverick.

We walked in silence, retracing our steps towards the mattress store. We knew the failed mission was a massive setback, but we didn't need to say it out loud. On the way, we grabbed some heavy blankets and coats from a department store to make getting through the cold night more bearable. At least Dame and Archer would be happy to have some warmth.

We arrived at the koi fountain, a sign we were almost back at camp. I tensed when we heard barking and a gunshot echoing through the atrium. It was coming from the direction of the mattress store.

We picked up our pace, ducking behind a pillar once we turned the corner. Another gunshot ricocheted off the store's security gate with a spark, and we heard Dame yelling.

"I SAID I'M IN EMBER SQUAD! CEASE FIRE!"

"Name your unit!" came a woman's voice from the store opposite.

"UNIT 67!" Dame spat back.

Two soldiers emerged from the other store and approached our camp with offensive stances. Maverick jumped out with his weapon drawn.

“Stand down, soldiers,” he said with authority.

I joined him as he neared the pair. The woman kept her gun locked on Dame, the man’s aimed at Mav and me.

He eyed Maverick’s matching rank insignias. “Name your unit, major,” he said threateningly.

“Unit 4. I have two civilians with me,” he replied sternly. “I’m escorting them to the border. That’s my fellow soldier in there. She’s injured and we’re assisting her.”

“New orders,” the man snapped. “Civilians still in the contamination zone must be shot on sight. The border camps are over capacity.”

My heart fell to my stomach like a brick. With the amount of Morts in every city along the way, getting to Malik was already a near-impossible feat. Now the very people meant to protect us were told to turn on us? I looked at Maverick, feeling the blood drain from my face. Was he about to betray me?

“Anyone who hasn’t yet evacuated must be terminated and their body burned,” said the woman. “We can’t keep feeding the Teeth. You should’ve had updated orders through your lieutenants.”

“I’ve been separated from my unit for a long time. No radio. Same as my comrade,” Maverick said, his voice sounding dry.

“Well, you can’t harbor these civilians any longer. Step aside,” one of them said. Hound was barking wildly, and I was too distracted by the prospect of being shot to know which voice had delivered the condemnation.

“They’re on active FORESIGHT duties!” Maverick argued. “They’re subject to exception! You can carry on with your mission, but spare them. I’ll take full responsibility.”

The two soldiers lowered their masks from their helmets and, virtually in sync, tossed two small cylinders onto the ground. One landed by our feet and the other rolled between the bars of the security gate. Maverick grabbed me and pushed me out of the way as a massive plume of smoke clouded around us.

Tear gas.

Gunshots reverberated around us as complete chaos broke out. We couldn't see anything past the white wall of haze. I heard Archer yelling for Hound and Dame coughing. Shot after shot went off. I aimed into the smoke, but stopped myself from firing. I didn't want to hit my friends by mistake.

I heard the security gate rattle as it was lifted. Maverick followed me as I ran towards the sound. Deep in the thick smog, I could see flashes of gunshots. Hound wasn't barking anymore. I prayed he hadn't been shot.

"Dame?! Archer?!" I yelled into the smoke, nearly choking on the gas.

A bullet zipped so close past my face, it split one of my locs. I ducked behind a nearby bed. More gunshots rang in the air. Who and where they were coming from, I couldn't see. I heard a voice yell and a body drop to the floor. The haze started to dissipate.

The hilt of a gun slammed against my back. I turned and looked down the barrel of the woman's gun. I winced at the loud crack of a gunshot... but I was still alive.

When I opened my eyes, I saw her lying at my feet with a hole in her head. Maverick stood behind her with his gun raised.

My vision started to clear.

Dame limped to the edge of the bed, but looked unharmed. Archer was staring down at the male soldier's body before him, the window of his mask shattered by a bullet to the face. Hound came out from behind the checkout desk with his tail between his legs, whimpering. We'd all made it, but it had been a close call.

"Are you okay?" I asked Archer.

He finally peeled his eyes away from the soldier. "Yeah," he said softly, and petted Hound at his feet.

"What happened?" Maverick asked.

Dame sat back on her bed and started reloading her weapon. "Those *cabrones* snuck up on us. They saw Archer building the tent and asked what we were doing here. Barely let us explain before they started firing on him."

I hadn't noticed it before, but Dame's camper tent was now fully set up against the back wall of the store, all our supplies organized neatly inside.

"What's this mean for us, then?" Archer asked. "We have to fight Morts *and* soldiers now?"

Dame looked stressed. "Let's hope we don't run into many more. We can't be killing fellow soldiers like that…What do we do with them?" she asked, directing the question to Mav.

"I'll handle it," he said, kneeling down beside the woman's body.

Clearly troubled that he'd had to turn on his own kind, he stripped off her bulletproof vest, gun, and surplus ammo, throwing it onto a mattress. After doing the same to the man, he grabbed him by the ankles and dragged him towards the emergency exit.

As he did, Archer thankfully shifted the focus onto another topic. "Are you guys okay? How was the mission?" he asked me.

"The other entrance was demolished," I told him. "Some type of explosion caved the ceiling in. We got some coats from a store on the way, but no food. Back to the drawing board."

Maverick came back with some more ammo in hand. He set it down before dragging the woman's body to the exit.

"I know we're all running on fumes, but it seems like we'll have to have another night of ration bars," he said, coming back again and sitting on the end of a bed.

"Dame, you have a cooking pan, right?" I asked her, recalling her campsite.

"Should be in the tent with my other stuff," she said, looking confused.

"It is," said Archer, "but what are we cooking? You want to melt the bars down to a cake?" He laughed.

"There's that big fountain nearby. I saw some fish in there. Never eaten koi before, but if we can start a small fire and cook them in the pan, we'll at least get some calories in," I suggested.

No one argued, but they didn't seem too excited by the prospect.

"There's a kitchen supply store a few halls down. I saw it on the mall guide," said Archer. "Bet they have some seasoning and cooking tools at least. Worth a scope out."

"I mean, if it works, it works," Dame said, rubbing her stomach.

After a short lecture on why Archer and I shouldn't go alone, Maverick finally let up. Dame's wound had reopened slightly during the confrontation, so he stayed back to redress it while we embarked on the second mission of the day.

A quick glance at the map confirmed the kitchen supply store wasn't much further than the fountain, but it was on the second floor. We walked up the escalator and found it in no time.

"Should've worn one of the coats you snagged. It's getting cold fast," said Archer, rubbing his hands together.

"Hopefully we can start a little fire for warmth," I said, walking into the store with my guard up.

It was a high-end supply store, and I didn't know what half the contraptions were, but I could tell it was Betty Crocker's heaven on earth. Our flashlights illuminated the aisles as we ventured up and down.

A few minutes later, Archer found some silver salt and pepper shakers that came already filled. I grabbed a couple cooking knives and a cutting board. After scouring for a bit longer, we realized most of the store was baking accessories. On the way out, we landed a major score: a pack of canned ethanol gel. Archer was particularly excited, telling me he used to use it while camping. The extremely flammable contents would allow for a portable fire. The three cans were small, but effective. We bagged our goods and headed back down towards the fountain.

"Guess you could spear one with one of these," I said, taking out a sharp cooking knife.

Archer was looking into the shallow pool at the large orange-and-white fish. Their beauty made me regretful of what we were about to do.

"I think I can catch them with my hands. Water's shallow enough," he said confidently.

He threw off his sneakers and jumped into the fountain. The school of fish immediately sensed the disturbance and frantically swam away to avoid him.

"You sure?" I teased.

"Okay, maybe you're right. I could use a bag or a big t-shirt as a net," he said, hopping out of the water. He ran over to the nearest store and started to comb through a clothing rack.

I'd just sat down on the edge of the fountain's marble border when two Morts suddenly jumped down from the second-floor landing. I could tell one of them was the Mort we'd killed earlier in the beauty store. The second creature must have revived it.

One ran into the store after Archer. I sprang up and fired a round into the other's shoulder, but it sprinted towards me, undeterred. I barely had time to react. I got one more round into its neck before the weight of its corpse slammed against me, and we both toppled into the pond water behind me. I was fully submerged, pushing with all my might against it as its rotting hands grabbed at my face.

I managed to come up for air, gasping for breath. Staring into my eyes were two black orbs. I turned my head quickly and squeezed my eyes shut, remembering Dame's warning. Its long fingers tried to pry my eyes open. It was happening. It was trying to turn me with its glare.

I was dunked under water again. Through shut eyes, I saw a bright flash of light and heard a shriek. Coughing and pushing my hair from my face, I surfaced to see the Mort shrouded in flames. It toppled over the edge of the pond and crumbled like a sheet of paper tossed into a fireplace. Archer was there, holding his lighter and aerosol can. The other Mort's smoking body lay still on the floor behind him.

"Homemade flamethrower," he said, out of breath, but grinning.

I climbed out of the water and wrung out my locs. The murky water now turned a cloudy red from the bleeding Mort.

“No way we should eat these now,” I said to my friend.

“Ration bars it is,” he said.

We turned at the sound of frantic footsteps.

There stood Maverick, taking in the messy scene. He looked at us, disappointed. “Next time, I’m coming with … ”

After taking some notes on how I was able to throw off a Mort’s scent trail, I joined my friends around the small fire they’d set up with the ethanol cans. All four of us were wrapped in blankets, munching on ration bars for what felt like the hundredth time. Hound stared longingly at the snacks, but refused to take one when offered.

“He’s fine. He ate the other day,” said Archer, almost embarrassed.

“Well, he’s not missing out. These taste like chalk,” said Dame.

“Those pigeons are looking real tasty right about now,” Mav joked.

Everyone but me smiled.

“Between the birds, the cold, and the Morts roaming around, I’m almost sure there’s an open entrance somewhere,” I said. “If that horde outside discovers it, we’re done for. We should start thinking about our getaway plan.”

“Well, the good news is, Teeth are a lot slower when it’s cold out,” Mav told us. “Some of the weaker ones even go catatonic, as long as you don’t touch them.”

“That is good news,” I said. “But even if they’re slower, we’re completely outnumbered.”

“Is it just me, or are they getting scarier?” Archer asked.

“The more they’re bit, the more they change,” said Dame, wrinkling her nose.

“We saw one today, a Phase Two,” I told her. “It tried to force my eyes open.”

Her face paled. “So it’s true … ” she said, more to herself.

"It *is* true, I've seen it," said Mav seriously. "I'd rather get bitten. Phase Twos will force your eyes open and spill blood from their eyes into yours. It's another way they transfer the virus—"

"Okay, stop," Dame interrupted. "I really need to get some rest tonight."

He zipped an imaginary zipper across his mouth. Archer had turned even whiter than Dame. I rubbed his back to comfort him.

"Alright, let's call it a night," I said, getting up.

And with those nightmarish thoughts, we tried our best to settle in and sleep.

6.

A few days had gone by and winter had arrived with force. The coats and blankets had become permanent fixtures on our bodies, and we finally got around to putting sheets on our mattresses. Even a thin extra layer made a difference with this cold.

Dame was back on her feet. Although she still had a limp, she was doing her part in helping with our daily camp routine. She was remaking our beds—a totally unnecessary task—but she made a point to contribute as much as she could to make up for the days she'd been out of commission.

Every morning, Hound would lock onto the pigeons outside the store. His desperate whines became our daily alarm. He grew hungrier by the hour, and we were determined to finally get him a meal.

Archer and I watched Maverick aiming his scope up at the rafters. It was a shame the birds were so small. We were just as underfed as Hound.

"I got one shot," said Mav, aiming carefully. "Soon as this gun goes off, they're all gonna dart."

BAM. He missed.

"*Dammit!*" he cursed. "I hit the rafter. This angle's tough."

Just as he predicted, the small flock flew away in a frenzy. Hound looked distraught.

"They'll be back tomorrow," I said to Archer, sensing his stress.

"You guys are the best for trying. Usually he can hunt for himself, but this place ain't no woods," he said.

Hound's demeanor completely changed at the word *hunt.* He wagged his tail and paced back and forth.

"I don't know, boy, it's dangerous out there." The dog jumped up and down. Archer looked to me for assurance. "What do you think?"

"Well, if he needs to eat, there's not much else we can do. Just tell him not to go too far," I warned.

Archer went over to the Shepherd, patted him on the back, and told him to be back quick. With a big lick of Archer's face, Hound darted off energetically down the dark hall. Archer stood there for a few beats before following Mav and me inside the store.

Mav began his daily weapons check while I took my tablet to the back room and called up Thirteen on the radio. I had something on my mind. He connected within seconds.

"Good morning, Willa."

"Morning."

"I was just doing research on the P2 Hosts using alternative means of transferring the virus. It's an interesting annotation."

"Interesting? I'd call it horrifying. Did you get my notes about the cold weather slowing the Hosts down?"

"There have been reports of that. Instead of the Hosts dropping dead again, they've been observed going into a state of hibernation. Almost as if they're conserving energy until they're disturbed."

"What happens if they're disturbed?" I asked warily.

"A handful of reports have noted a burst of intense rage. But their senses are muted if they're left alone."

Of course there was a catch.

"Well, we haven't seen any inside for a couple days. Hoping that means the theory's accurate. The area's completely surrounded."

"Stay safe."

And just like that, he disconnected. I paused in the whiplash of his curt dismissal, trying to digest the conversation. Despite the challenges it brought, the cold was getting more intense by the day, and if we could stay put long enough, the horde outside could become manageable. I was brimming with anxiety. With each passing day, the chances of catching up to Malik diminished.

When I came back onto the shop floor, Archer was cleaning his pistol. He'd grown very fond of it, like it was a special gift that meant a lot to him. I joined him on the edge of his bed.

"Our weapon starts to feel like it's the last thing we own in the world, huh?" I said.

"That's a good way to put it. I do kinda feel that way."

He dug into the box of ammo next to him and put a few more rounds into the cartridge. Dame laughed from across the room and I turned to see Mav lending his shoulder to help balance her as she limped. He had his other arm around her waist.

"I'm ticklish! Let me just use your shoulder," she said with a giggle.

"You don't even need me! You're doing great," he said as she made it across the room.

"Couple more days and I'll be sprinting," she boasted jokingly.

She joined Mav again on the edge of a mattress. I watched her point out one of his tattoos, a word I couldn't make out. She lifted her sleeve and showed him her grandfather's signature. Mav was always nice to everyone, so it was no surprise he seemed interested, but the way Dame acted around him seemed to carry different intentions. She looked and spoke to Maverick in a totally different way than the rest of us. With a lot more interest and enthusiasm.

It didn't bother me. Maverick was subjectively a very attractive guy. I'd watched many a girl swoon over him at parties, and although I was drawn to Maverick, Dame would be a far better match for him than I would. Guys always wanted one thing at the end of the day, and that was something I couldn't give.

For as long as I could remember, my sexual needs and desires were pretty nonexistent. There were times in my life I'd felt very close to someone, maybe even in love, but I'd never felt the ambition to get physical with them. It was something I thought so little about, I didn't even see the need to label it.

Archer put his hand on my shoulder and I flinched, realizing I had completely spaced out watching Dame resting her feet across Mav's lap.

"I'm getting a little worried about Hound," he said.

"Has it been longer than usual?" I asked.

"Well, I know we're not out in the woods, but he's always pretty quick about it."

"Pigeons are hard to catch..." My words trailed off when I saw how much worry was on his face. "Should we try calling him back?"

We headed out past the security gate.

"Hound! Come on, boy! Time to come back!" he called into the void.

His voice echoed loudly. I half-expected to hear a bark answer back, but nothing.

"Maybe it's best we take a walk to look for him. I don't want any Morts following your voice."

Dame and Mav came over.

"What's going on?" Mav asked with concern.

"Hound hasn't come back. He never takes this long. I think he might've got lost or something," said Archer, but I could tell he didn't believe that.

"Want me to scout ahead and see if I can spot him?" Mav offered.

"I can go with you," Archer said.

"I'll go. You stay here in case he comes back," said Dame. "Our training covers tracking."

"Are you good to walk?" I asked, wondering which of them would be more of a liability.

"I need to practice walking on it. Can't be on bedrest forever," she said, limping back into the store to gear up.

Maverick joined her while Archer watched anxiously.

"Thanks, guys. I don't mean to be paranoid. I just wanna make sure he's okay," he said.

"Hey, buddy, don't sweat it. He's one of us," said Mav, and Archer and I waved them off.

Archer stayed there for several minutes, his foot tapping with unease. I took him by the shoulder and led him back inside.

"I bet he'll have two birds with him when he's back," I said with a smile.

"Hah. Hope so, I could use one myself...I mean, he always comes back."

"Yeah, and this time won't be any different."

"Willa?" he said suddenly. "You think we'll make it out of here?"

I took a longer beat than I meant to. "If it gets cold enough, there's a chance."

"After seeing how many are out there, and with the army turned against us, I feel like even *if* I find a way to help my ma, it'd be impossible to get back to her..."

When I didn't respond, he continued.

"Besides Hound, she was the only one who was ever nice to me. Maybe she felt the same about me. I took care of her more than anyone else did. Rest of my family treated her like she was a burden and turned their backs on us. I can't lose Hound. I've always been on my own. He's the last family I've got."

"That's not true, Archer. I told you, the friends you make out here are different," I said matter-of-factly. "You're like my little brother now."

His face completely lit up. I could tell how much that meant to him.

"So does that give me full rights to bug the shit out of you?" he laughed.

I shoved at his shoulder. "If I get full rights to smack the shit out of you," I shot back, and we both laughed for a full minute, rough-housing on the mattress.

It was almost an hour later before Dame and Maverick returned empty-handed. Archer was on the verge of panic, but they assured him there was still a big part of the mall they hadn't reached, and without being able to shout Hound's name, it was no easy task. We agreed we would try again at first light.

We spent the rest of the evening sharing funny stories around our small fire, hoping to keep Archer's mind at ease until morning.

Archer shook me awake. It truly was first light, but as promised, I got up and dressed in my gear and coat. Under his, he wore one of the bulletproof vests Maverick had stripped off the soldiers. He looked focused and ready.

Dame and Maverick awoke shortly after us.

"If there's any trouble at all, come straight back," Maverick said firmly. "We can't get comfortable just because there haven't been many Teeth around."

"Deal," I said as I cocked my gun.

Archer pulled open the security gate and I followed his lead down the hall.

We passed the koi pond in no time. The bloody scene of our encounter was a reminder to keep our guard up. I could see the fog from my breath in front of me.

We walked slowly past each store, shining flashlights inside and hoping Hound would reveal himself when he picked up our scent. We must've passed thirty stores with no sign of him.

With each passing failure, Archer deflated. I was starting to feel major guilt for encouraging Hound to embark on a hunt.

When the temperature dropped further, and with still no sign of Hound, it became obvious we should turn back. As we retraced our steps, I started to mentally prepare for the worst. It was very unlikely Hound had survived out there that long. I wondered if I had the emotional stamina to console Archer when that devastating truth hit him.

A noise made us both turn quickly, our flashlights and guns raised in its direction.

"*Hound?*" Archer whispered, but only silence answered.

My flashlight swept across the corridor slowly, but I saw nothing. After a moment, we pressed on, but I couldn't shake the sense that something was following us. I caught myself looking over my shoulder more than once. I was usually very attuned to other energies, and I definitely felt something. What it was, I couldn't place.

We made it back to camp in one piece. Mav eagerly lifted the security gate, visibly glad to see us alive.

"No luck?" Dame asked, looking rather surprised. "*Coño ...*"

Archer looked sick to his stomach. Without a word, he sat on his bed and began to strip off his heavy vest in defeat.

"You guys looking for your dog?" came a voice that made the four of us jump.

We were up and armed in a blink. Standing outside the store was a group of three guys. They were almost cartoonish in appearance. The man in the middle who'd spoken was tall and fit. His hair was discolored, somewhere between brown and faded red, like it'd once been box-dyed. The two flanking him were less intimidating, but equally outlandish. They all wore crisp-looking clothing and diamond jewelry that glistened like strange ornaments in the dim light. All of them were heavily armed, two guns each.

Archer approached them and they raised their weapons. I pulled him back.

"Have you seen him?" asked Archer, desperate, but his voice carried a hint of suspicion.

The middle man smiled, revealing another diamond embedded in a silver toothcap. "Yeah, we have him! We're really looking forward to dinner tonight," he said with a laugh.

Maverick took an aggressive step forward. "If you touch that dog, I will hunt you down and—"

"Calm down, bad boy. I'm not heartless. I'm willing to make a trade. I'm Jett," said the guy, lowering his weapon and approaching Maverick confidently with his hand out.

Mav eyed it for a full beat before shaking it forcefully. "Trade for what?" he asked through a clenched jaw.

Archer grabbed our bag of gas station snacks and tossed it at Jett's feet. "If you're hungry, we'll give you some food."

Jett prodded the bag with his foot, uninterested. "Junk food over fresh meat? Nice try," he snarled. "How about that tent and some ammo too? Then we can talk."

My blood simmered. They were asking for most of our vital supplies. The tent we could do without, but ammo was undoubtedly our biggest asset. I stepped forward this time.

"Look, if you're stuck here like us, we can band together to make it out of here," I suggested. "Between the seven of us, that's a lot of firepower."

Dame shot me a look that I ignored. These guys would of course make a terrible match for our group, but I was trying to put out the flames.

Jett and his friends laughed. "Stuck? We love it here!" he said. "Our lives were shit before all this. We can have whatever we want now. Fancy clothes, luxury, we've even bounced from mansion to mansion. We have everything we could ever want, besides food... See why the dog's so valuable now?"

A darkness clouded over his face. Archer's lip quivered like he was holding back tears.

I tossed a few ration bars into the plastic bag. "Okay. Take the food, and we'll give you some ammo and the tent," I fired back. "But we want Hound here first."

It was Maverick who shot me a look then.

"That's more like it," Jett said, with an obnoxious bow. "We'll be back in an hour with the mutt. Have our shit ready."

And with that, the three of them took off, laughing down the hallway.

Dame slammed the security gate behind them. "You realize this'll put us in a tight position, right?" she scolded.

"We don't want trouble with them! Even if we got Hound back without a trade, they've seen our camp and know about our supplies," I retorted. "Let's give them what they want and be done with it."

Archer couldn't hold back anymore. He cried into his arm, turning away to try to hide it from us.

Mav pulled him close. "We can ambush them when they get back. We'll be ready this time," he said confidently.

"Mav, no," I protested. "They're heavily armed. One injury to any of us can set us back weeks."

"They're clearly low on ammo, though," said Dame.

"Let's keep this clean," I said with finality. "We'll figure it out once they're off our backs."

We rolled up the tent, gathered as much ammo as we could possibly spare, and set it all aside with the small bag of food rations we were going to sacrifice. Archer couldn't sit still for a moment as we waited for their return.

We heard them before we saw them. In complete contrast to how silently we moved through the halls, they laughed and stomped around with no care in the world.

Archer nearly buckled at the knees when he spotted Hound through the gate. He lifted it immediately, calling Hound to him, but Jett held him by the collar. A piece of twine was wrapped tightly around his muzzle.

I pushed the pile of supplies towards the gang. "Okay, you got what you wanted, asshole. Let him go," I said, resting my hand on my pistol's holster.

There was a very tense pause. Jett's next move would determine everything. Finally, he let Hound go. The dog ran over and jumped into Archer's arms, whining and wagging his tail. Archer untied his mouth and toppled over as his friend licked him in a frenzy.

"Pleasure doing business with you," said Jett as his two cronies grabbed the goods.

Dame and Maverick were ready to pounce, but surprisingly, the clan walked away without another word.

I let out the deep breath I was holding in. Hound made his rounds, jumping onto each of us with uncontrolled glee.

"Thank you, thank you, thank you!" Archer said to us, his tears now those of joy.

I was unbelievably relieved that the ordeal was over, but the reality of what I'd sacrificed was hovering over me.

Dame was the only one not smiling. It was most of her supplies, after all.

"Hey," I said to her, "I'm sorry. I had to ..."

She made a noticeable effort to push down her disappointment. "You saved my life, so let's call it even. We'll find more."

"What's that sound?" Maverick cut in.

We stayed quiet and listened. At first I heard nothing, but then—

Tick. Tick. Tick.

Mav followed the sound around the room, closer and closer to the hall outside the store.

"Get down—"

BOOM!

A forceful shockwave knocked me off my feet. The wall across the store exploded in a fiery crash, a gaping hole appearing where the emergency exit once stood. Jett had left us an unexpected gift. A bomb that now left us completely exposed to the outdoors. The sound alone would have alerted every Mort in the area.

After the heat came a wave of cold wind from outside. Through smoke and dust, I ran for the security gate, slamming it shut.

"Jesus!" said Mav, his face filthy with ash.

Several Morts crawled through the opening, spotting us instantly and attacking the gate.

Dame let off a few rounds, but every time a Mort fell, another came to join the fray. I recalled the time Tye and I were similarly trapped inside the pharmacy.

"Archer! Where's your flamethrower?" I called to him.

He brushed the dust from his eyes, rummaged through his satchel, and approached the gate. Maverick shot down a few more Morts before Archer sprayed a stream of fire through his lighter and torched the fiends. A handful screeched and dropped before another wave was on us.

"The gate won't hold!" I said to Mav, watching the remaining Morts shake it violently.

I looked frantically around the store. We were cornered.

"Willa!" called Mav, pointing up at a vent above the checkout desk.

Instantly, I caught onto the plan. The two of us shoved the desk closer to the wall and called to Dame and Archer.

The vent was relatively large, but there was no way any of our bags would fit through. Mav and Dame stripped a few pieces of their military gear. I clipped my flashlight to my belt and shoved the map, radio, and tablet into the pockets of my cargo pants. Archer swiped up the last of our ration bars before pulling Hound over to the desk.

I climbed up into the crawl space. Mav followed in front of Archer, who pulled Hound up by the collar. Dame made it up a fraction of a second before we heard the security gate crash to the floor.

"Everyone good?" I called, straining to turn my neck in the tight space. Only Hound was able to stand normally.

"Sure ... " said Mav, crawling on his forearms.

"What's the plan?" Dame called from the back.

"The subway tunnel," I said, the idea only coming to me at that moment. "Part of the ceiling's caved in. If we keep to the vents long enough, we should come across it."

"We can follow the tunnel to the next subway stop and get outside to street level," said Mav.

Though a bit premature and unorganized, the moment had arrived. We were getting out of that place.

We crawled aimlessly for some time, periodically looking through store vents to get any clue at all of where we were. My knees and elbows were bleeding by the time we were halfway across the mall.

"I feel a draft," Dame said.

I felt it too. A cold breeze swept over us. We crawled more eagerly. Eventually, the ventilation shaft tilted dramatically downwards.

"This has to be it," I called out. "I'll go first."

I pushed myself towards the drop and slid down into a pile of rubble, adding another gash to my elbow.

"Found it," I called up to them, raising my weapon to be safe.

The others joined me as I pointed my flashlight across the scene. There was no sign of any Morts, only the aftermath of the violent confrontation.

"Ready?" I asked, turning to the group.

They followed my lead down onto the railway. The tunnel ahead was a wall of black, the thin beams from mine and Mav's flashlights our only guide.

7.

The tunnel stretched on endlessly, and the bone-chilling cold seemed to seep through my multiple layers. The tunnel was so wide, even two flashlights weren't enough to walk safely. We clung together, keeping a careful pace in the dark.

"Where we goin' once we get outside?" Archer whispered.

"Depends where we come out," I muttered.

"What about the harbor?" asked Mav. "There's too many Teeth on land to travel far. It's why I've been stuck in the area. I was thinking about taking a boat before I ran into you."

I pictured the map in my head. Seabird was a port after all. Getting there by boat would actually be faster than land under the circumstances. "You know how to sail one?"

"I know the basics. Used to sail with my parents as a kid, and we covered basic naval skills in training."

Being out at sea would undoubtedly be safer than on land. I'd never heard of a Mort swimming. If Maverick was confident in his skills, then so was I.

"Alright, I'm into it," I said.

Hound growled. I stopped short and the others bumped into me.

"What is it, boy?" whispered Archer.

The shivering beam of my flashlight skimmed the tunnel. It revealed a terrifying silhouette: a tall, Phase Two Mort, alien in appearance.

Our weapons were aimed, but the Mort was frozen in place. It was hibernating, unaware that we were only feet away.

"Don't touch it," I warned. "It'll sleep until we touch it."

We slowly stepped around the creature, but only took a few steps before we stopped again. My light had caught two more in front of us, their obsidian, orb-like eyes staring blankly into space.

"Oh, man," came Maverick's voice from behind me.

His flashlight now shined on ten more Morts scattered up ahead. Some were wearing military gear, others completely bare. We were in a minefield of undead. Any wrong move could awaken them all.

"Hold onto each other, and stay in a straight line," I said, leading the pack.

Even Hound followed the order, staying glued to my heels.

We snaked around the pillars of flesh, walking even slower than before. It was rare I got to see one that close. It was hard to look at them, but hard to turn away. Though the sight was disturbing, I couldn't help but analyze the differences in their appearance. Some were still close to human; others were so distorted, I couldn't even tell what gender they once were. I took out my tablet carefully and snapped a couple photos for Thirteen.

A faint light in the distance caught our attention.

Mav squeezed my shoulder. "That's the subway stop ahead—"

"*Coño!*" Dame's voice cut loudly through the quiet. With a clatter, she tripped over a metal track with her weak leg. Directly onto a Mort.

A guttural wail echoed down the tunnel. Her gun fired with a flash and the body dropped heavily.

"Go!" she said, as movement stirred all around us.

The horde had awakened. The tunnel filled with primal, warlike screams as they all sprang to life, instantly rabid. Chaos ensued. Shots fired at random as both mine and Mav's flashlights tumbled to the ground. All we could do was sprint for the subway stop ahead.

A Phase Two grabbed me by the arm, baring its teeth. Someone shot it before it could sink its fangs into my neck. I ran, my limbs numb from the cold.

At last, we came into the light. I pulled myself up onto the platform, Archer and Maverick right behind me. Hound jumped up after us.

I couldn't wait to see if Dame had made it. There was only a short window of time before the swarm would reach us. I ran up the stairs towards the exit. With huge relief, I heard Dame cursing in Spanish behind us.

Up ahead, two turnstile gates led outside. I rushed through, my comrades close behind. The Morts slammed against the gates, unable to figure out the mechanism with their rotted minds.

Even the winter sun was blinding when we made it to street level. I looked in every direction, finding the streets eerily deserted.

My gaze landed on the harbor across the freeway. "There!"

As a unit, we sprinted past the storefronts toward the road. Amid the frantic footsteps, a distinct engine hum reached my ears. My pace didn't falter, but I cast a quick glance in the direction of the sound, half-expecting to spot a military vehicle. To my disbelief, a vibrant green sports car screeched around the corner, skidding to a halt as it blocked our path. The window lowered and a familiar diamond smile flashed our way. *Jett.*

"I'm impressed!" he jeered. "The Teeth were supposed to take care of you so we could take the rest of your stuff, but I guess we'll just take it now—"

Mav didn't even let him finish his taunt. He showered the Lamborghini with lead. The windows shattered and bullet holes pocked the glossy paint job. The car revved and spun around us as we jumped out of the way. This time, it was Jett's bullets raining down from a machine gun aimed out of his window.

Down the street, Morts marched towards us, drawn to the sound of gunshots and rubber on asphalt. Maverick aimed at Jett, who leapt out of the passenger-side door. Maverick jumped over the hood just as Jett fired a bullet directly into his combat vest. Mav barely recoiled before grabbing him by the neck and slamming him hard on the pavement.

"Go!" Maverick yelled to us.

I stood there for way longer than I meant to. The throng of undead were closing the distance between us. If it was any warmer, they would've reached us by now.

Jett grabbed Mav around his chest and the two wrestled fiercely among the shattered glass on the ground. It was so hard to leave him behind, but my thoughts were with reaching my brother.

"Come on!" Dame yelled at me.

Even her injury didn't slow her as we raced towards the docks.

We tailed her across the freeway, making it to the harbor just as the Morts were on us. Archer quickly heaved Hound over the dock's entry gate and the three of us climbed over with haste. The Morts snarled, clawing at the fence.

I scanned the helm of every boat for any sign of keys left behind. I spotted a medium-sized sailboat tethered to the end of the harbor, a set of silver keys dangling from the ignition. I thanked the universe out loud.

The three of us untied the ropes in a hurry. I only stopped when I heard the whining engine of the sports car growing louder by the second. Jett's Lamborghini crashed through the horde and mowed down the gate, screeching to a halt just inches before it could plummet into the water.

I couldn't believe Jett was that persistent. He'd completely lost his mind. I raised my gun to end it there and then, but when the butterfly door swung open, it wasn't Jett at the wheel, but Maverick.

I lowered my gun, a laugh of desperation escaping me. I was so relieved to see him.

"Hurry!" he said, ushering me onto the boat.

Hound was barking as some of the Morts began to rise up from the wreckage, but Maverick kicked us off the dock and our boat began to drift away from the shore.

Without missing a beat, he climbed up to the helm, taking hold of the steering wheel. He clicked a few buttons on the navigation dock and turned the keys. I could feel the motor start, vibrating beneath my feet. I watched gratefully as he guided the boat smoothly into the open water.

Our group took a moment to look back to shore, the Morts splashing clumsily in the shallows. The massive shopping mall loomed over the aftermath of a town destroyed. I felt an unbelievable relief as the skyline slowly vanished behind ocean mist.

"Help me open the sails," said Maverick, toggling a few levers.

We didn't hesitate. Maverick was the only one with any knowledge of how to sail, so that made him captain of this ship.

After some very specific instructions and a few complex knots, the mainsail was up and our speed significantly increased, despite Maverick shutting off the engine.

"It has basic autopilot so I can leave it be for now, as long as we stay in open waters," he said. "I'll just have to check on it now and then."

I uncrumpled the map from my back pocket, holding it down firmly so it wouldn't blow away in the chilling wind. He looked it over with me.

"This is the route we were following to get to Seabird by car," I explained, tracing my finger along the coast. "It's a straight shot to the port if we stay heading south."

Dame and Archer joined us at the helm.

"It'll take about four or five days, depending on weather conditions," Mav told the group.

A heavy knot formed in my lungs. Another week seemed so long, considering how delayed I already felt. I tried to remind myself how many obstacles were waiting for us on land. This would be an easier route, after all.

With the sun setting, we finally succumbed to the cold and headed down to the cabin. It was only then that I was able to take in the ship's details. It was an older model, but probably considered top-of-the-line in its heyday.

Below deck, there was a small seating area around a table, across from a tiny kitchenette. Dame went through the cabinets and found some spices, a few canned goods, and some cookware, all major scores.

An even more welcome surprise was the two small bedrooms towards the back. One had a queen-sized bed; the other, two bunks. I spotted Dame eyeing Maverick, probably hoping they'd share. Whether he clocked it or not, I couldn't tell, but he turned to me instead.

"I don't mind crashing with you," he said simply.

A micro-flash of disappointment came over Dame's face.

Surprised by his offer, I nodded shyly. Hound jumped into the bottom bunk of the other room, claiming it on behalf of Archer.

We explored for a bit longer, happily discovering some extra blankets in the cabinets next to the tiny bathroom. The boat was named *La Sirena*—'The Mermaid,' according to Dame's translation of the plaque in the galley.

I voice-recorded details of our encounter with the catatonic Morts on my tablet while Mav checked on the steering. Soon after, we all gathered at the small table. Dame had opened a can of beans and split it among the four of us. Even Hound licked up a few that fell, unable to fight his hunger.

"This beats the mattress store any day," said Archer, shoveling half his portion into his mouth at once.

"Remind me to never visit a mall again if things ever get back to normal," Dame quipped sarcastically.

"Dame, you said you were in Unit 67, yeah?" Mav asked through a mouthful.

"I was," she said. "I heard Unit 4 was badass."

"Well, I don't wanna brag," he said with a smirk. "My buddy Sable was in 67. Best snipe in the game."

"Definitely," she said. "Wish he made it, man. Great guy."

"The greatest. Where were you stationed for training?"

"After aviation training—"

A chime from the bedroom interrupted us.

"Be right back," I said, going to grab my radio.

I slid the door shut behind me and answered the call. "Hey."

"I see you're on the water. Everything alright?"

"One of the soldiers I'm with, Maverick, knows how to sail. Way too many Teeth on land for us to travel safely. We're taking a shortcut to my hometown, so should be there in a few days. Really hoping my brother's still there."

"I do too," said Thirteen, sounding genuine. *"Your notes and photos have been astronomically useful. Thank you for your contribution."*

"Just doing my job ... You never told me, do you have any family out there?"

"... I have a son."

It was the first time he'd actually revealed anything personal.

"A son. Makes sense why you're trying to help find a cure."

"It's true that there's very little I wouldn't do to ensure his safety, but I want one for the people. I do hope he can inherit a much better world."

Thirteen seemed to be in an open mood, so I decided to take my shot. "Have you heard of Ground Misery, and the plane crash there?"

There was a pregnant pause. *"That's not my area of jurisdiction or expertise."*

The overuse light started to flash.

"Is this a secure line?" I asked.

"It is."

"Well, you've at least heard about it. What do you know?"

The light continued to flash, quicker now.

"Why do you ask? Have you gathered any intel on this crash?"

"No, I don't even know where it is, but you said you're researching every aspect of this virus. A major one is where it originated from—the source of it. Wouldn't that tell us a lot?"

The line disconnected. I threw the radio onto the mattress, cursing under my breath at the timing. It'd be the very first thing I brought up the next time we talked. Thirteen definitely knew about the plane. What he knew, I still had to find out.

There was a knock on the door.

"Come in," I called.

Maverick entered. "You good? You didn't even finish your food," he asked with concern.

"Yeah, just anxious. A lot on my mind."

"Fair," he said, sitting on the bed and removing his boots. "Well, I'm gonna try to crash soon. I have to check on the steering every few hours."

"Brutal. You'll have to teach us tomorrow so we can take shifts."

He started stripping off his clothes, then stopped. "Sorry, used to being around the guys," he laughed.

"Oh, you're fine. I didn't expect you to sleep in your gear."

Both of us peeled off the multiple layers we had on and organized them neatly at opposite ends of the room. I definitely caught Maverick looking for a second, but he did his best to be respectful. With how many tattoos he had on his skin, it almost looked like he was still wearing a shirt when he got under the covers.

I'm sure that for him, it was weird to be in our underwear in the same bed, but despite the situational intimacy, it was fully platonic on my end.

"What do you think of Dame?" he asked randomly, his voice lowered.

I shrugged. "Why?"

"Back at the mall, some things she told me about her campaign weren't adding up. Just now, I told her my friend Sable was in her squad and she acted like she knew him. Sable was in squad 22, not 67."

"She lied about knowing him?"

"I'm saying, I don't think she was in 67 at all," he clarified.

I was staring up at the ceiling, but I turned to him then. "Why would she lie about what unit she's in?"

"Not sure," he said. "But just something to think about."

Dame had been hard to read since day one. Maybe that had to do with her covering for something. It was an interesting detail to note. "Great. Remember when I said I had a lot on my mind?"

"Rest easy. I'm gonna figure it out."

And with that, he rolled over and flipped off the overhead light.

8.

Snow falls all around me. Or is it ash? I stand before the wreckage of a massive plane. Cries of misery ring out. Thousands of Morts pour from the ruins. One of them's Imani. I scream her name, over and over. There's a bullet hole between her eyes and she can't hear me.

Tye's with me now. He takes me somewhere safe and the screaming fades. I can finally stop running.

I was grateful Maverick had already left the room because I wasn't sure if I had yelled in my sleep. I wiped the sweat from my face—or maybe it was tears. Eager to get some fresh air, I grabbed my coat and headed up to the deck.

The sun was high in the sky, making the waves glitter magically. Archer was adjusting the mainsail, Hound watching dutifully by his side.

"He's already got the basics down. Perfect weather to learn," Mav said to me as I joined him at the helm. "Were you able to get some shut-eye?"

"Barely... I keep having dreams about my friends."

He clicked on the autopilot and gave me his attention. "From Seabird?"

"No. A lot of them are of my friend Tye."

"Are they bad dreams? I can't remember the last time I had a good one."

I stared out at the calm sea. "I keep having these vivid dreams about him. I met him and his friends near the end of my travels to the border. Didn't know him long, but I'd be dead, or at least still out there alone, if it wasn't for him. He was really special."

A smile stretched across my face. Even I was surprised by it.

"Where is he now?" asked Mav. I could see there was a slight hint of jealousy in his gaze from the way I spoke about Tye, but his voice remained casual.

"I don't know. We were separated at the border."

"He ever try to contact you?"

"No. He had a fever when we arrived. They took him and I don't know what happened after that... but I feel him out there, like we're connected. I know he's still alive."

"How so?"

"It's just a feeling," I said simply.

"Well, he sounds like a hell of a guy. I hope you find him again. It's not easy to find that kind of connection with someone."

He was right, but somehow, I'd been lucky enough to find two familiar souls on my long journey through no-man's-land, and both had been ripped away from me suddenly. It was no wonder I couldn't shake the thought of them. I hadn't even had time to process their absence because survival was my constant priority.

Imani and I bounced from place to place, never staying long enough for the Jumbees to sense us. It was me who came up with the idea to break into a food bank after seeing that raiders had stripped almost every obvious place. I'd volunteered once in the past and I knew these shelters had large pantries of donated canned goods.

Imani was hesitant to go out in the open, but we not only knew the houses we'd been searching through were running dry, now that time had passed and things had spoiled, but also that homes without undead were becoming harder to find. So I planned the raid... and it was a decision I would regret for the rest of my life.

We were ambushed by the infected who were still inside, once the very people who'd sheltered there. One managed to corner Imani and bite her shoulder. Seeing her hurt turned me animalistic. I massacred as many as I could, but even when they were all dead, it would not undo the fatal bite.

Imani was so scared. Not scared of dying, but of what would happen when she turned. What it'd feel like. Losing her mind was her biggest fear.

I cried and cried like I'd never done before, feeling guilty for having pushed the idea in the first place. We stayed in that shelter for days while I tended her wound, until she started to become delirious. She got a fever, and I insisted it was just her body fighting it off, but we knew. Her nose wouldn't stop bleeding. We had to stay far apart, but we sobbed together for hours before she started to forget how we'd met, and when she realized she was fading, she asked me for the darkest favor anyone could ask. To end it for her.

BAM!

I was yanked away from my torturous thoughts.

"I got it!" yelled Archer from the starboard side.

He'd shot a seagull that dropped to rest on the bow. Hound immediately went at it, feathers flying everywhere in a chilly gust.

"Nice one, bud!" Maverick called to him.

Dame came out to see the commotion. Her look of concern quickly shifted to one of approval. "Oh, wow," she said, eyeing the mess of feathers. "Could've left some for us to cook, Hound."

"Sorry if I scared you. Had to take the shot," Archer said, grinning.

"I'm cleaning and reloading all the weapons, if you guys want to give me yours," Dame said.

Maverick reached for his rifle on the navigation dock, then stopped. "Actually, I think mine's good."

Archer and I handed her our pistols. In any other circumstances we'd never part with our weapons, but the open ocean was probably the only place safe from Morts these days.

"I'll go down with you, it's freezing," I said to Dame.

Below deck, she'd laid out our arsenal on the table and was cleaning it all with a cloth, then refilling the clips with their respective ammo. It was obvious we were on the last of our rations after the exchange with Jett. I debated confronting her about her unit while we were there alone, but she spoke before I could.

"Maverick taught me how to keep the ship on course, so I can do a shift tonight."

I sat on the small bench behind the table. "I thank the universe for him every day."

"So, what's his deal, anyway? I feel like he's so mysterious," Dame said.

"Honestly, I really don't know a lot about him. He was more my brother's friend."

She threw me a subtle smile. "Have you guys ever ... ?"

I shot back a much less humorous look. "No. I'm not into him that way."

"How?! He's so sexy," she laughed. "Jealous you get to share a bed with him."

I'd been in this position plenty of times, where girls would tap me into these kinds of conversations about boys and I'd contribute very little. "I don't really find people sexually attractive."

She put down the rifle she'd just loaded. "Wait, what do you mean? You've never had sex?"

I laughed. "I have, and it was fine, but I just don't really have the desire to."

She looked perplexed by the concept. "Have you had a boyfriend before?"

"Kinda," I said. "But it was more emotional than physical. Probably why it didn't last very long."

"Ugh, of course. Men ... "

We shared a knowing laugh. She seemed to accept my preferences, and probably felt placated that she still had an open lane to Maverick.

On our third day out at sea, the sails required a little more attention as the cold wind picked up and the waves grew choppy. I'd picked up a thing or two thanks to some patient lessons from Maverick. I sat beside him at the wheel, eyeing the mainsail as it billowed. When I turned to him, I caught him looking at me admiringly.

Unsure what to make of it, I just smiled back. "What're you thinking about?"

"I'm just still mind-blown that we ran into each other out here," he explained. "I always felt like we were passing ships when we were out at the same place. Malik talked so much about you, I felt like I knew you from afar."

"Oh...Sorry if I ever seemed distant. It wasn't on purpose. I just thought of you as Malik's friend, so I just let you be."

"I get it, but I always thought we'd vibe," he said. "We had more similar interests than Malik and me if you think about it."

"Definitely," I said with a grin, remembering how odd they'd looked together. The bookworm and the bad boy.

"Crazy as it's been, I've been enjoying getting to know you. Just can't wrap my head around finding you when I did."

"I don't think it's a coincidence," I said. "Everything happens exactly how it's meant to. You found me exactly when I needed you, and the universe sent me someone that cares about my brother to help me find him. If that's not fate, I don't know what is."

"Well then, fate's on our side," he said, smiling out to sea.

The rest of the day, we switched shifts at the helm. The temperature plummeted brutally, and combined with the ocean spray, it was challenging to spend more than an hour at a time out in the open.

At one point, we found some netting on board and used it to catch a handful of small fish off the side of the boat. Dame was confident in preparing them for cooking, excited to not only get a proper meal, but also to show off her cooking skills. With just a small gas grill, a pan, and some basic spices at her disposal, she managed to feed us an incredible meal, even by normal standards.

Maverick's suspicion was still somewhere in the back of my mind, but there was no denying that Dame contributed a lot to the group. I just couldn't help but shake the feeling that there was more to her than she was letting on, and that wasn't a good feeling when we were all relying on each other for survival.

Hound was sleeping heavily on Archer's lap, filled to the brim with protein these last few days.

"Where'd you learn how to cook like this?" asked Mav while chewing.

"My mom. Me and my sisters were complete opposites, but cooking was the *one* thing we had in common. It was the only time we got along. *Las tres hermanas.*"

"They older or younger?" I asked, almost hesitant to talk because I was enjoying the food so much.

"Older, but prettier. And smarter. And better at everything..." She looked pained.

"Prettier? You sure?" Archer asked charmingly, clearly disarming her.

Her cheeks flushed, and she busied herself with the pan at the sink. "Trust me."

"Do you have any siblings, Mav?" Archer asked.

"I don't, no," he said. "You?"

"One older sister. If you could call her that."

"Yikes," said Dame.

Mav forked at his food. "I always thought it'd be nice growing up with siblings. Malik was the closest thing I had to a brother." He glanced over at me. "So we'll have to share when we get him back."

We laughed.

"You guys were really that close?" asked Dame.

"Yeah. He was probably more important to me than I was to him, but I felt like he was a big reason I found myself again. You know, I had a serious drug problem growing up, and everyone always thinks if a kid's getting into that stuff, their home life's probably shit... But no, my parents loved me so damn much, and I did everything possible to push them away."

I couldn't help but think of my own parents. Despite their years of micromanaging and pushing me to be and do better, I did miss them. I'd never thought it possible.

"And over time, I proved I couldn't keep my promises of getting back on track, so they eventually gave up. I don't blame them, but it left me with no family. People kinda wrote me off my whole life. Hell, I started writing myself off. And when I finally got sober, I felt like I was back out in the world alone. Malik just really motivated me to rebuild myself."

Every time his name came up, I got emotional, but I felt like when these positive thoughts about him arose, I was somehow reconnecting to him from afar. Like he could feel me getting closer.

"Probably another reason I joined the military. It's kinda a built-in family," Mav mused.

"Well, if I learned anything out here, it's that you can make your own family," said Archer, smiling at me.

I messed up his hair. "That's right."

"We're gonna find Malik," Dame said, clearing away some of the plates.

I managed a smile.

After dinner, the best part of my day arrived: getting to shower in the small bathroom below deck. The water was nowhere near hot, but compared to the frigid air, it was such a nice treat to indulge in. It was funny how things I'd never thought twice about in the old world were now luxuries.

I walked into my room to find Maverick already in bed, his white-blond hair still wet from his own shower. He turned away as I slipped on my underwear underneath my towel.

"Such a gentleman," I joked.

He rolled his eyes. I got under the covers and as I was tying my locs into two buns, one of Maverick's tattoos caught my eye—the name *Connor,* in scarlet letters across his toned chest.

"Who's Connor?" I asked curiously.

His face dropped, and his hand instinctively went to his heart. "My best friend, growing up. He, um ... he ended up taking his own life, so I got this in his memory."

"Oh, Maverick, I'm so sorry," I said, taking his hand in mine. "I didn't mean to pry."

"It's okay, not your fault. I mean, it's not exactly subtle. After he passed, I went downhill ... That was the start of everything."

I kept my hand tight around his. "I know what it feels like," I said quietly. "I lost one of my best friends, Imani. I'll never be the same."

I felt the tears coming, but tilted my head back to try and stop them.

"I'm sorry," he said, squeezing my hand. He was tearing up too. "We're both tough motherfuckers, so you know it's heavy if we're crying."

We laughed through the tears, but it was hard to see his normally stoic façade crumble. I had the urge to hug him, so I did.

He was caught by surprise, but returned the embrace. He knew about my intimacy preferences, and I could feel his appreciation that I'd offered him affection. I felt unusually comfortable with him. So much so that I found myself not pulling away. We held each other until our breathing synced and we faded into sleep, still holding one another.

At sunrise, I woke to the sound of laughter and footsteps running down the stairs. Maverick and I had been intertwined pretty much the entire night, and strangely, it was the best night of sleep I'd had since reentering. But when I rolled over, I realized I was alone.

There was a knock at the door.

"Come in," I said.

Archer peeked his head in. "You have to come see this! There's *whales!*"

His enthusiasm was contagious. I dressed in a hurry and followed him up to the deck.

Dame and Mav were already there, admiring a rainbow that had formed in the mist exhaled by one of the whales' blowholes. I sat with them quietly, Archer and Hound beside me. We watched in awe as the two giants swam alongside our boat.

It dawned on me how resilient Mother Nature was. How the earth had gone through so many shifts and cataclysmic events, and she always prevailed. Even if humans were on borrowed time, it comforted me that these creatures would remain despite this apocalypse. If anything, they would thrive once we were gone.

"Sorry I woke you. It was way too cool to miss," said Archer.

"Happy you did. Thanks for looking out, little brother."

We watched the whales make a final dive, their huge tails waving above the surface before they disappeared.

Mav was still staring into the water in admiration. "Insane!"

"Reminds you how little we are," Dame said, walking over to the helm to begin her shift. "Mav, can you show me how to do that reef knot again?"

"No problem," he said, joining her at the wheel.

"I'm gonna go shower," Archer said to me, heading back downstairs.

I watched Maverick retie one of the sail ropes, showing Dame the steps. She put her hands over his as she rehearsed the proper form. Maverick looked focused, but it was clear to me she was enjoying their closeness. The disconnect in their intentions was hard to watch.

I followed Archer's lead and headed to the galley below, filling up a cup of water from the faucet. As I sipped, I took a second to ask myself if there was any jealousy in me towards Dame. Although I had no sexual interest in Maverick, there was something there I couldn't yet pinpoint. The more I thought about it, the more I became convinced it was just Maverick's distrust of her that was leaking into my own read.

My eyes followed Hound as he wandered into Archer and Dame's bedroom while the boy showered. It was otherwise unoccupied for the moment. I could faintly hear Maverick and her chatting above me.

Impulsively, I strode into the room. Hound looked up as I entered, no doubt sensing I was up to something. I put the cup of water down in front of him and he drank, as if showing me he'd mind his own business. I then looked over Dame's military vest sitting at the corner of her bunk.

It felt wrong to go through her things, but something in me was compelled to find out if there was a wolf among our herd. With every pocket I opened, I kept hoping I wouldn't find anything, but the bottom-right zipper revealed a silver dog tag. I turned it over in my hand and immediately saw the number 51 engraved between her full name and military ID number.

As if the chain had stung my hand, I quickly shoved it back into the pocket, terribly disappointed that Maverick's intuition was correct. She'd lied.

"What's up?" Dame suddenly asked from the doorway.

I turned unnaturally quick. "Was just giving Hound some water," I covered, nodding toward the Shepherd still tonguing at the cup.

Her gaze held on me for a beat, but then she knelt down and petted Hound, seemingly buying my answer. I picked up the empty cup and headed back into the galley, keen to avoid any further exchange with her. Partly so she wouldn't pick up on my investigation, and partly because I couldn't help but look at her with some suspicion now. Why would she lie about which unit she was part of? Was she hiding something significant, or was the reasoning something unimportant?

I avoided Dame for the rest of the day, counting down the hours until I could tell Maverick in the confines of our room.

When he walked in from his shower, I immediately jumped to the point.

"You were right," I said, my voice low.

He sat on the bed in his towel, his own silver tag dangling in the center of his chest. "I'm always right... but what about?"

"Dame. I found her old dog tag. She was in Unit 51, not 67."

"How did you—"

"You're a soldier. What would be a reason to lie about what unit you're in?" I probed.

"Well, she might have a reputation she's hiding from. Maybe something on record we could find out if we knew her actual unit."

"How would we find out?"

"You can look up any soldier's record in the database by their name or ID. Would need a computer, though."

"Maybe my contact can help." I reached over to my radio and called Thirteen.

Maverick watched as the dialing tone repeated a few times.

"*Good evening, Willa,*" came Thirteen's voice.

"Since you won't tell me about the plane crash, can you look up something else for me?"

"If it's in line with your duties, I'm here to help."

"It's someone in my party. Can you look up Dame Moreno, Unit 51? I need to know if she's who she says she is."

There was silence on the other end. Maverick eyed the radio as if it might explode at any moment.

"Thirteen? Please."

I could sense him debating whether he should help me or not. There was another beat before he spoke again.

"*With the exception of a few names, it says Unit 51 are all missing in action or presumed dead.*"

Mav and I traded a look.

"Thanks, Thirteen. We're meant to hit land sometime tomorrow. I'll have more updates for you soon."

"I look forward to it. Be safe."

And with a click, he was gone.

"So, she somehow outlived her comrades, but doesn't want anyone to find out," Mav thought out loud.

"Why don't we just ask her about it?" I suggested.

"I mean, I would. I just didn't want to cause any issues while we're focusing on getting to Malik."

"We don't need to make it heavy, just ask her for the truth. Maybe it's not a big deal."

"Your call. We can ask her in the morning," he said, yawning.

There was a brief moment where we looked at each other, and I silently wondered if the previous night's embrace was circumstantial or a new normal.

Maverick got up to change and hang up his towel, and I pulled up the covers and turned over. When he crawled back into bed and shut off the light, I caught myself waiting for his arm to settle around me. It never did.

Archer took his morning shift at the helm, but that day on the sea was the roughest yet. The boat rocked back and forth dramatically, making it hard to walk about, and rain pelted the deck like tiny hands on a drum. Mav checked in on him periodically, reassuring him that a little rain was nothing to be concerned about.

He came back down into the galley, hair dripping from the rain, and Dame handed him a cup of tomato soup she'd warmed in a pan for breakfast. As I spooned mine, I caught Maverick's eye across the table. With Archer up top, it was ideal timing to finally confront Dame.

She joined us in the dining nook. "You sleep alright?" she asked us. "Boat was like a rollercoaster all night."

"Could've been better," I said. I looked to Mav, hoping he'd initiate.

"Dame, we want to ask you something... Don't want you to freak out, but we just want to all be on the same page," he started.

She lowered her spoon from her mouth. "Well, you're definitely freaking me out talking like that," she said, her face getting serious. "What's up?"

"Why did you say you're from Unit 67 when you're in 51?" I asked directly.

Her expression went through a Rolodex of emotions.

"We can't be hiding stuff from each other," Mav said gently.

"First of all, why did you go through my stuff?" she shot back at me suddenly.

She was clearly deflecting.

"Maverick asked you about his friend Sable in Unit 67 and you said you knew him," I replied. "He wasn't in that unit. So I felt like you were hiding something. I just want to know what it is—"

"So now you guys are teaming up on me?" she snapped.

"Don't try and turn this around," Mav insisted. "We're asking you point blank and giving you a chance to be upfront with us."

Her demeanor changed when it was Maverick confronting her. She visibly softened. "My unit... My *real* unit, 51, was ambushed. I went on a supply run, and when I came back they'd been swarmed by Teeth. I didn't lie about that part."

"You told me that," I said, "but that doesn't explain why you'd need to hide what unit you were in."

"I was embarrassed! I didn't want other soldiers finding out I survived an attack because I was out on a supply run while my brothers and sisters fought for their lives!"

I looked to Maverick to see if he was buying it. He was having a hard time looking at her.

"What do you want me to say? That I'm some secret spy sent here to sabotage your mission?" she demanded, her tone sharpening.

The conversation had escalated to a point I'd never meant for it to go. The ship tilted and creaked, mimicking the mood of our words.

"Dame, we're not accusing you of anything," I said slowly. "Trust is the one thing we have, and that I need. If you can look me in the eye and give me your word that what you're telling me is true, then we're good."

She took a step closer and fixed her eyes on mine. "I'm telling you the truth."

Maverick and I stayed quiet.

"I feel like you guys don't believe me—"

"We believe you," said Maverick.

I wasn't sure if I did, but I followed his lead. "We're good," I said. "Are you?"

She took a deep breath. "I'm good if you're good."

Our eyes stayed locked until Archer opened the hatch and came down the steps, dripping wet and shivering.

"It's getting rough out there," he said through blue lips, then looked at Dame, who was sporting dewy eyes. "Everything alright—"

Suddenly, the boat lurched with such force, all of us fell backwards, slamming hard into the wall. The kitchen cabinets flew open and their contents crashed to the floor. Hound was barking madly from the other room. I grabbed at my shoulder. It'd scraped against the round window frame of the galley.

We swayed back and forth, trying to regain our footing, until the ship finally seemed steady enough for us to stand again.

"What was that?!" Archer asked, panicked, rubbing the back of his head.

"A rogue wave," Mav said worriedly. "I'm gonna check the steering."

He pushed open the hatch and climbed out. The howling wind whistled past the opening as water dripped down the steps onto the cabin floor.

Nearly everything had flown from the cabinets, and now lay strewn across the floor in a broken mess. Archer was petting a whimpering Hound while Dame and I gathered up the wreckage, avoiding eye contact.

Moments later, Maverick came back down the steps, his face almost as white as his hair.

"... It took out our mast," he said with difficulty.

"What's the mast again?" I asked, stressed out by his expression alone.

"The sail! It snapped it. It's dragging overboard."

I pushed past him to see the damage for myself.

There it was, hanging off the side of the boat like a kite that had crashed into the ground. The towering pole had snapped near its base, leaving the ship with irreparable damage. Maverick walked up next to me, keying some settings on the navigation dock.

"We can still use the engine. There's enough gas for one more day or so, but we'll be a lot slower than we planned—"

"We can't go slower! Malik's been waiting for me!" I burst out. "There's only so long he can stick around before he'll move on to look for me somewhere else." I turned and stormed back below deck.

I paced around the cabin as Maverick rejoined us. He watched me like I was a stick of dynamite.

"Every time I feel like we're getting close, something else sets me back!" I yelled, punching the small porthole above the sink. The inner layer of glass cracked under my knuckles, but I was too angry to feel the pain.

"Willa, we got your back. We're still here," said Archer.

His tone was so genuine, it disarmed me. I took a deep breath. "I know... I'm sorry... I'm just getting worried I'll miss him."

"Your hand's bleeding. Let me help," Mav offered.

I looked down and saw the red dripping over my ebony skin. Mav walked me to the dining nook and sat me on the bench. "Archer, bring me that first aid kit you found."

"Yes, captain," Archer said, obviously trying to lighten the mood.

He brought over the small green box, and Mav set about gently wrapping my cuts with gauze. He spoke in a low voice.

"Look, I know you're anxious to get to him, but if he's there, he's not gonna leave without you. He loves you to death. Even if he's moved on from Seabird, I can say with every part of my soul that he'll be looking for you just as hard as you are him."

My heart was still beating fast, but his words were settling my rising blood pressure.

"We're still on course," he reassured me.

I nodded.

"I'll take the first shift," said Dame. Without looking at us, she threw on her coat and blanket and headed up to the deck.

9.

When we finally made it to bed, I was only able to calm myself down because Maverick had put a comforting arm around me. There was such safety in his energy, and yet that feeling scared me. Getting close to someone like that was my danger zone. Not only because I knew men's nature, but because I couldn't bear the thought of attaching myself to someone, only for it to be ripped away from me again. I scooted away from him, masking my discomfort by readjusting the pillows.

In the middle of the night, Dame came to wake me for my shift. She spotted Maverick sleeping on my side of the bed and immediately turned away.

"You're up," she said flatly, then went to her room.

This new tension between us was palpable, but I had much more pressing things to mentally prepare for now that we were approaching Seabird.

I threw on my gear and wrapped my wool blanket around me like a shawl. This would be one arctic night watch.

When I lifted the hatch, I was relieved to find that at least the rain had stopped, but the wind was sharp. I headed to the helm, and though the navigation was still on course, a small, red blip on the radar immediately caught my eye. I walked to the bow, straining my eyes to make anything out in the curtain of darkness around me. There was nothing there.

I ran back up to the helm. The blip still showed, getting closer. I tried shutting off all our lights, looking out to the horizon again. This time it was much clearer, and I could just make out what looked like a vessel headed towards us. I stared for a full minute at the floating lights, making sure my lack of sleep wasn't making me hallucinate. Just as I was about to go wake the others, a loud, booming horn pierced through the night and beat me to it.

I heard Hound barking and before long, the others were next to me, up and armed.

"What was—Holy *shit,*" said Mav, spotting the approaching boat.

He shut off our engines as the medium-sized cruiser slowed and drew parallel with us. It towered three stories above *La Sirena*. Its floodlights illuminated our deck like an artificial sun.

One passenger leaned over the side and eyed our broken sail. "Are you young'uns alright?" he asked.

I looked at the others, wondering what answer would be safest. These strangers could be dangerous, but the man's weathered face looked friendly enough.

"We're fine, but we took some damage in the storm," Mav called out. "Heading to Seabird, running only on the engine."

"I see that. Looks like a bad hit. We're headed in that direction, but we can't let you aboard. Everyone in our colony's been vetted for infection. We could offer a tow, though, if you need it."

"Colony?" asked Mav.

A few more passengers peeked over the edge of their top deck.

"There's a whole fleet of us. We're an independent sovereign," the man explained proudly. "The sea is our nation now."

Maverick lowered his voice to us. "What do you guys think? We'd make up a ton of time if they can get us a bit closer to Seabird."

I had no time to be overly cautious. "Let's do it."

"If it means we'll get there sooner, definitely," seconded Archer.

Dame eyed the colossal ship doubtfully. "Your call," she said.

Maverick shouted back up to the man. "If you can get us near enough, we'd be very grateful."

The man disappeared for a moment before throwing down a set of thick ropes towards our bow. Maverick sprang into action, tying a bunch of complicated knots to multiple parts of our boat until we were linked to the back of theirs.

With another blare of the horn, the bigger vessel turned its nose south and we rode its wake into the night. I looked up at the stars, thanking the universe for this turn of events. Finally, something was going right.

The four of us high-fived, smiling at our sudden stroke of luck.

"Go get some rest, guys. I'll keep an eye on things up here," said Maverick.

"Let us know if you need us," I said with a smile.

It was the first time in forever that I felt Malik was within reach. I lay in bed, picturing his kind eyes and bright smile once we reunited. It was daunting to think just how much time had passed since I'd last seen my brother. Did his face even look the same? Even before the world imploded, he'd been at school for almost a year. We'd video call when he had free time, but it wasn't the same as hanging out in person.

Our time together was always the best. We'd try new food spots, show each other music, debate topics through different lenses: his book smarts, and my street smarts. We'd even made a plan for me to come visit him without my parents, but that time never came. We said a thousand times we'd be in each other's lives forever, and I planned on keeping that promise.

Memories of him swam around in my shallow sleep, only interrupted by Maverick getting into bed at some point in the night. I was excited that, come morning, we'd be close enough to Seabird to see it. Probably the only time I would ever be happy to be back in my hometown.

The sunrise had just started creeping through the small porthole when I opened my eyes to a knock at the door.

Archer came in, sounding urgent. "Mav, can you come look at something?"

"What's wrong, bud?" Mav asked, getting up quickly to dress.

"It seems like we're not heading south. Maybe I'm reading it wrong."

Maverick quickened, following Archer upstairs. I dressed urgently and followed a moment later.

We were still surfing the wake of the cruise boat, but the navigation confirmed we were in fact heading west.

I realized right away what was happening.

"Cut the lines!" I said in panic. "They're not taking us to Seabird—"

As if in answer to my call, the cruise ship's horn blared, and in response, another sounded from the distance. We turned to see an even larger naval ship approaching.

Archer's eyes were wide with confusion. "What's going on?"

Hound growled at the approaching vessel, as if he could scare it off.

"They're turning us in," I said in horror.

"It's a military ship. Let me do the talking," said Mav.

Dame joined us, weapon in hand. She was visibly anxious when she spotted the ship. "This could be bad," she said under her breath.

The military ship landed portside, leaving us sandwiched between it and the cruise ship at starboard. We were trapped. A wide ramp dropped from the naval ship onto our sailboat, tipping us slightly to one side. A bulky, silver-haired man walked halfway along the walkway. A few younger soldiers flanked him, all of them masked. His vest was heavily decorated and there was something about his presence that commanded authority. In contrast, his guards seemed nervous, almost novice. My guess was they'd been recently drafted as the tides had turned in the contamination zone and older soldiers succumbed to the virus.

The older man eyed our drawn weapons and Dame and Maverick's military uniforms.

"General," Maverick greeted him, respectfully.

"Name your units," he ordered.

"Unit 4," Mav replied.

"67," said Dame. "I'm in EMBER." There was less confidence in her answers now.

"I'm in FORESIGHT," I interjected.

He eyed Hound and Archer. "And the boy?"

"I'm—"

"He's my cousin," said Maverick quickly.

"Is he listed as family in your file, major?" asked the general. "You can't harbor any civilians unless they,ve been registered. You know this."

"And what about them?" I challenged, pointing to the cruise ship. "They're civilians. Why are they okay?"

"They're sea nomads. As long as they're not heading to land and feeding the Teeth, our arrangement's good. They bring us strays, we give them supplies," he said with a smirk. He turned to his soldiers. "Take them."

I raised my weapon, but Maverick put a hand out.

"They're just following protocol. Do what they say."

Resentfully, I let the soldiers take me by the arm. They escorted our group up the ramp and on board the naval ship. Almost immediately, they pointed thermometers at our foreheads and pricked our fingers to draw small samples of our blood into some sort of hand-held mechanism.

"You three will be in isolation until we vet you," said the general. "As for the boy and dog, they'll be in a holding cell until we can look into his files."

We were forcefully stripped of our weapons and belongings and escorted inside the vessel, down a few fluorescent-lit hallways, and into a cold holding room with two bunks on either side and a toilet against the back wall.

The minute the soldier shut the door behind us, I looked to Maverick desperately.

"I know. It's all protocol. I *will* get us out of this," he insisted.

"We're moving away from Seabird now! I'm gonna lose it!"

"Once we're cleared, they won't hold us. The three of us are technically on active missions right now," said Dame.

"*Are* you?" I retorted, the words escaping before I could stop them.

She stared at me and I looked away. "And Archer? He's a civilian with no family. They're gonna kill him," I said, sick to my stomach.

"He's a minor. He's gonna be okay... Let's try to get some rest," Mav suggested.

Dame kicked off her boots and climbed up to the top bunk. "We'll be fine," she said, but it almost sounded like she was trying to convince herself.

I sat on the edge of the other bunk, resting my head in my hands. I felt so out of control of the situation, so off course from my path. If my exhaustion wasn't so severe, I'd be panicking until the next morning, but when I rolled my head back onto the pillow, sleep came fast.

Blinking lights. Maroon liquid moving through tubes. Monitors with endless readings of indecipherable data. Tye lies on a bed in a stark white room. Shadows move around him, watching, waiting. His hand reaches out to me. I try to grab it but it slips away. Blood floods the room like we're on a sinking ship.

I shot upright so quickly, I bumped my head against the metal underside of the bunk above me. Maverick climbed down the ladder a second later.

"What was that? You okay?" he asked, half-concerned, half-laughing as I rubbed my head.

"I'm fine," I lied, still reeling from the dream.

"Tye again?"

"...Yeah."

He sat on the bunk beside me. "What do you see when you dream about him?"

"That's the thing. I keep seeing him in danger, or scared, but I don't really know what I'm looking at. All I know is these dreams of him feel different, like premonitions. They're more vivid than my other dreams... like they're trying to tell me something."

As I explained, I recalled how I'd dreamt about being on a boat before the prospect of sailing to Seabird was even a thing. Was I seeing glimpses of what was to come? I hoped not, because every time I'd see Tye in these nightmares, he was in some kind of trouble.

"You're under a lot of stress right now. Try not to read into it too much," said Mav. "I'm sure Tye's out there somewhere."

The door to our holding room slid open and two soldiers entered.

"Your results were negative," one said. "You're clear to move about the ship. We're still tracking the boy."

Dame sat up in bed. "Can we go see him?"

"Not at the moment. Neither his nor Maverick's files have each other listed as family, and we're still locating your files, Dame. We're awaiting orders on the next steps," said the man.

Dame visibly swallowed.

"And you. You've been getting calls all afternoon," he said, handing me my tablet and radio.

Both men then left, leaving the door ajar.

Maybe Thirteen could help. Getting off this ship was in his interest. There must be some way he could prioritize our release. I dialed his line on the radio.

"Willa?"

"It's me. Look, we've been picked up by a military ship, but they won't let my friend go. Can you do something?"

"It's not within my jurisdiction to do so. But you are in FORESIGHT, so they should allow you to continue your duties."

"They are, but I'm not leaving Archer behind."

"If he's not military or affiliated with any programs, I'm afraid he isn't protected—"

"Really?" I interrupted. "Well, then, you won't be getting any updates anytime soon, because we're moving away from Seabird, and I'm not getting off this ship without my friend!"

I smashed the button to disconnect the call. Dame and Maverick were looking at me, seemingly concerned by the level of anxiety I had displayed over the last twenty-four hours.

"I'll go talk to the general," Mav said. "You two go get something to eat."

Dame and I looked at each other. There appeared to be an unspoken understanding between us that we could set our issues aside, for now.

Once we'd split up with Maverick, it took us a while to find the cafeteria. I noticed the crew seemed disproportionately small for a ship this size, and there was no one around to ask for directions. Even inside the cafeteria, there was only one person serving food and one other young soldier eating alone. I must've counted only a handful of people since our arrival.

Dame and I made small talk over the bland food on our trays until Maverick finally rejoined us.

"Any luck?" I asked.

"None. The general says if we can't show proof that Archer's related to me, he'll be transported to a foster camp. I'm already on thin ice considering the current orders on civilians."

"Oh, that's bullshit," said Dame.

My face grew hot. "Why don't we overthrow them?" I asked, keeping my voice low. "I've only counted twelve people on this ship, including the commander. Half of them are new recruits. We can take them."

Dame was taken aback by my suggestion. Maverick looked concerned.

"That type of treason will have the entire military against us."

"Seems like they already are," I pointed out.

We broke up our huddle when two young soldiers stomped into the cafeteria. For a moment, Dame locked eyes with one of them, but then turned away as if she was hiding. I could see the blood drain from her cheeks, like she'd seen a ghost.

"Dame, what—"

I jumped back as the soldier threw a drink over her, prompting Maverick to jump up and push him away. The other soldier held him back.

"Bold of you to give another unit's name!" the man yelled.

"What's going on?" I demanded, stepping between the two.

"She's a fucking traitor! She was in *my* unit, not 67! We were ambushed because of her! She was on night watch, and abandoned her post in the night!"

I speared her with my eyes.

"You've got PTSD, *hermano*," she said.

He lunged at her, but Maverick stopped him.

"Calm down, man! Tell us what happened," he said, holding the guy's arms down.

"Unit 51! Almost all of us are *dead* because of her. She ran away and left us open to attack. And what happened to your night watch partner, huh?! You killed him! Deserter... *traitor!*"

"You don't know what you're talking about!" Dame spat back. "I went on a supply run, to *help* us, and when I came back—"

"A supply run in the middle of the night?!"

"What's happening here?" came a deeper voice.

The general walked in, a few more soldiers by his side.

"Sir, this woman committed treason!" the man proclaimed. "She even lied about her unit when coming aboard! That's why we couldn't locate her files."

The commander approached Dame, scanning her face like he was reading her thoughts. Her hands were trembling, but she stood her ground as we held our breath.

A ship's bellowing horn broke the silence. The soldiers darted away, hustling to their stations outside.

The general leaned in to take one final look at Dame. "I'm not done with you," he said in her ear before turning his back. "Stations! We got another shipment!"

Maverick and I looked at Dame. She looked unrecognizable to me. If what this man said about her was true, it was unforgivable.

We spared her any words, joining the others outside to see what all the commotion was about.

The cruise ship that had delivered us the night before was back, this time towing a smaller fishing yacht. A young man and a frail-looking woman were aboard, trembling in the shadow of the naval vessel. Like us, they must have been hoodwinked into thinking help had come.

The ramp lowered onto their boat. Routinely, the general and his brigade approached, readopting their masks and weapons.

"And what do we have here?" demanded the general, keeping distance between him and the new captives.

The man was shaking. He was wearing enough layers that I knew it wasn't from the cold. "I'm j-just heading to the border to find help for my family."

"How many of you are aboard?" asked the general calmly.

The man stayed quiet.

"Do you have any credentials?"

The man nodded. "No, but we—"

BAM. BAM.

The general fired two shots to their heads and the civilians tumbled off the ramp into the water with a splash, a bloody plume forming around them.

"Search the ship," he said without missing a beat.

I watched in disgust as the soldiers raided the boat.

"This door's locked, general. Want us to break it open?" asked one of the soldiers, standing before a small cabin door on the deck.

"Make sure no one else is on board."

Two men fired a couple rounds into the hinges and the door came crashing down. There was a silent beat as they peeked inside, and then a scream. One of the soldiers was thrown violently backwards. A group of

Morts burst from inside, tossing more men overboard with ease and ravaging another two who were within reach.

The general and remaining soldiers retreated, shocked to receive such an unexpected surprise. These Morts must have been the young man's family. Though distorted, one was smaller and I could tell it was younger than the rest. Tattered remnants of its lavender blouse still hung from its body.

They ran up the ramp towards us, screeching and flailing wildly.

"Come on!" Mav urged us.

We followed him inside and down the hallway. He brought us to an unattended back room, where we found our weapons.

I grabbed my pistol and loaded it just as a Mort turned the corner. One shot from each of us blasted through it. It fell hard to the ground, dark blood oozing from its wounds.

"We need to find Archer!" I said, swiping his gun off the table.

"This way," said Maverick. He'd clearly been on a ship like this before.

We heard the growling of another Mort tailing us. Gunshots and screams echoed throughout the halls. Then came another distant sound: barking.

"Here!" Dame called, shoving us into a smaller hallway.

A Mort sped down the corridor moments after we did. We opened the cell door and slammed it behind us a fraction of a beat before it could snag us. It smashed its deformed head into the door's viewing port, gnawing ineffectively at the glass for a minute before turning its attention to another soldier now firing at it from down the hall.

Archer looked too stunned to even celebrate our arrival. We all froze, listening to Hound howl over the agonizing wails of people being eaten alive for a few minutes before the ship fell silent again.

Finally, Archer hugged me tight. "What's going on?" he asked, taking his pistol from me with shaking hands.

"Another boat was delivered. I think the guy held on to his infected family too long," Dame explained, straining to look through the porthole for any danger.

Hound whimpered. The silence outside was eerie.

"You guys stay here," said Maverick. "I'll check if it's clear."

"I'm coming with you," I said, grabbing the handle of the door. "Dame, stay with him."

She gave me a nod. The look in her eyes assured me that she could at least be trusted with that task.

I pulled the door open and Maverick followed me, both our guns at the ready. Every corner we turned could be our final step. We passed three dead men and a lifeless Mort. I strained my ears for any sign of movement, but all I heard was waves.

I stepped out onto the deck, noticing the delivery ship had fled. Blood dripped from the ramp and off the sides of the smaller boat. We walked cautiously around the corner, where another Mort was sprawled limply over a storage container. I turned into the cafeteria, stepping over the general's lifeless body.

Maverick's gun went off. I hadn't even seen the Mort spring out from behind the door. It fell back, twitching on the ground where it lay.

"Thanks," I said, my heart pounding.

Just then, the child Mort exploded into the cafeteria, flipping a table and charging towards us. I fired a few rounds before turning to run. It chased us through the hallways until Mav and I were able to duck into a divot. In its frenzy, the monster missed us and ran past the opening. With a forceful kick, Maverick shoved the smaller creature into the wall, giving him a split second to fire a round into its misshapen skull.

We stayed frozen, straining to hear any other sounds, but it seemed we had the ship now.

"Let's get back to the others before the bodies wake up," I said, walking past a dead soldier with a massive bite in his ribcage.

Back in the holding cell, Archer was visibly distraught.

"Thank you, guys, for not leaving me," he said with a pained smile.

"Never, little bro," I said, reloading my clip.

Dame busied herself with her weapon. "We should probably throw the bodies overboard."

Our previous dispute came back to mind, and I turned to Mav to hide my disdain from her. "Can you steer this thing?"

"It's pretty much on autopilot if I enter the coordinates for Seabird. You guys start with the bodies and I'll get us back on course."

Without waiting for Dame, I took Archer by the shoulder and we headed out into the hallway. Hound followed.

As we dragged the first body outside, Archer gave me a look. "Everything okay with you and Dame?" He'd clearly noticed a change in our demeanor towards her.

Together, we tossed the cadaver overboard.

"She lied about what unit she was in. We found out she turned on her own squadron. Her whole group ended up dead because of it."

Archer's eyes widened with every word. "*Dame?* But she ... So what now?" he asked, rolling another body over the edge as he processed it.

It was a valid question. No part of me felt comfortable around her anymore. Whatever the true story was, my trust in her was broken.

A splash in the water made us turn. Maverick had just pushed another body into the water.

"I got us on course. We're about half a day away. Good news is, this ship's much faster than the sailboat."

"Half a day ... " I repeated. Getting closer to Malik felt like trying to hold water in the palms of my hands.

In silence, I walked over to collect another body, this time with Hound helping me by dragging it with his teeth. The dead soldier was the man who'd accused Dame. If only he'd survived to elaborate. I recalled his words and the venom behind them.

Dame turned the corner, wiping her bloodied hands on her pants. She spotted the man and turned away for a moment as I toppled him over the edge. She turned back to us with glossy eyes.

"Can I talk to you guys ... ?" she asked, looking from one of us to the other.

Archer and Mav both looked at me, as if to let me know it was ultimately my call. When I didn't say anything, she went on.

"Look, I'll tell you the truth. I ran away from my squadron during my night shift because I was scared, okay? Things were getting worse and worse and it was obvious we had no chance of surviving very long out there with how little the government was supporting our forces. So yeah, I'm a deserter, but if you saw what we were up against, you would've probably done the same. I hid my unit because I was ashamed that I left them vulnerable, and my actions cost them their lives—"

"You're still dodging," Mav cut in. "What about your night watch partner? Where were they?"

She stuttered a little, then stopped herself.

"You killed him," I said.

" ... I will never get over that night," she admitted. "I enlisted to make a name for myself and be honorable, and my fear got the best of me. I would *never* turn on you guys!"

My cheeks flushed with heat. If she could do something like that to her *brothers and sisters,* who could say what she'd do when things got serious? As far as I was concerned, she was no longer reliable, nor trustworthy.

"Back on the sailboat, I told you to look me in the eye and tell me the truth. That trust was all we had, and you lied. When we get to Seabird, I think it's best we go our separate ways."

Her face went white. For a moment, only the sound of waves and gulls picking at the floating bodies could be heard. I waited for a response, but she stared at her feet. I was suddenly aware of the assault rifle she was holding.

"I understand," she finally said, crestfallen.

"I appreciate everything you've done for us so far—"

She turned and stormed off before I could finish my sentence. I glanced at the others to gauge their reactions. Archer looked floored by the sudden change in our group dynamic, but Maverick nodded assuringly at me.

"Let's gather some stuff together before we port. We don't know what'll be waiting for us."

The naval ship was rich with supplies. After washing up, we managed to harvest new tactical packs, heavier jackets, ammo, and a few medical supplies. We hadn't seen Dame at all during our gathering.

As the sun set, Maverick monitored the navigation cabin while Archer and I sat along the edge of the bow, dangling our feet over the waves and watching the amber horizon. Hound's head rested on his owner's lap.

"When I have a house one day, it's gonna be on the water," said Archer, looking pensive.

I smiled at him. It was nice to hear someone talk about the future like there was still hope that all of this would eventually be resolved. "After growing up in Seabird, I hope mine's nowhere near."

We laughed.

"Thanks again for sticking up for me," he said.

"Get used to it."

He smiled.

The unmistakable chime of my radio sounded. I walked over to my pack leaning against the steel wall, dug out the device, then stepped into the cafeteria to answer.

"Thirteen."

"Thought I'd check in to see how things panned out."

I tried to keep my tone calm. "Thanks. The ship was ambushed by infected. We're the last ones standing. While you're on, here's an observation for you. I've seen more Phase Twos than normal Teeth out here. I even saw a child one."

"A rare sighting indeed. It's possible you'll continue to see other iterations of the infected as you spend more time in the contamination zone."

"If I live long enough. The Teeth aren't our only problem. Things are out of hand with the military. They're after civilians now."

"As long as you continue your duties to the FORESIGHT program, you're protected."

"Well, they're getting in my way." I checked to see if the overuse light was flashing. It hadn't started yet, so I spoke quickly. "Thirteen, you said this was a secure line, so just help me out on this one. Tell me what you know about Ground Misery."

"What have you heard that has you suddenly so interested?"

"A plane crashed the day before everything changed. I've heard tons of rumors and theories about suspicious planes flying over the U.S., dropping chemicals on us ... I can't be the only one that thinks the two are related."

For a moment I only heard white noise on the other end.

"... There's a plane crash on record. I don't know much about it other than that it's been the subject of whispers here. We've had reports that there are hundreds of the infected surrounding the crash site. No FORESIGHT members or soldiers have ventured over there yet, so we've only seen aerial shots."

The light began to flash.

"Where is it?" I asked.

"That's classified, Willa—"

"Thirteen, do you want to help the world or not?!"

I heard him taking a deep breath right before the line dropped. I tried to dial him again, but the signal didn't connect.

It seemed ludicrous that he'd be involved in a program that gathered info on the effects of the virus while discouraging me from finding out important, if not crucial information. Was Thirteen not who he said he was? Was he masquerading as a concerned researcher, when he was actually just protecting the very people who may have caused this? Dame had rattled my confidence in anyone at that point.

I needed to know more about this crash than Thirteen was telling me ... but Malik was more important right then.

10.

Maverick had anchored the ship just a few miles offshore from Seabird. I could see it in the distance, dimly sunlit through heavy morning fog. We'd finally arrived. My lungs were tight from a mixture of cold air and anticipation.

The four of us climbed into an inflatable combat raft secured to the side of the ship—the fourth being Hound, as Dame was still nowhere to be seen. We'd searched the ship earlier that morning, but wherever she was, it was clear she didn't want to be found. Part of me felt bad that our story had to end like that. I knew that loneliness was a terrible fate out there, but I couldn't leave any room for setbacks to completing what I needed to do.

We'd have to take the smaller boat through the thick mist to get to shore. As we untied the raft from its fastenings and lowered it into the water, the only thing on my mind was seeing Malik again.

Archer was staring regretfully up at the ship. He'd taken the decision about Dame the hardest. Maverick followed his gaze up for one last look before switching on the engine at the back of the raft.

We zoomed over the water towards the shoreline, closing our jackets as the wind picked up. It was slightly warmer than where we'd come from, something we'd have to account for when dealing with Jumbees.

I could see the shipping factories up ahead. Just like the ones my parents used to work at. I recalled the few times they'd told me to come visit them. An invite I'd always declined. Now I wished I'd taken them up on every moment they'd wanted to spend with me. As unpleasant as it would inevitably turn out to be, I could've made more of an effort to get along with them. I wondered where they were and what they were doing. Probably frantically trying to get any updates on their kids. I could imagine my mom telling us we'd thrown our futures away after finding out we'd both decided to reenter.

The amount of trash in the water increased the closer we got to shore. The currents there had pushed debris from the shipping yards all along the coast. My hand reached for my gun when I saw movement on land, but as we cut through the fog, I saw it was a harem of a hundred or so seals. I let out a sigh of relief. I'd never seen one in Seabird before. After it was abandoned, the pod must have claimed it as their home.

As we reached the sand bar, we lifted our bags over our heads and jumped into the shallow water. Hound sprinted for the beach and the seals dispersed in a frenzy. The three of us laughed as he wagged his tail.

We walked up the littered beach, past the machinery and shipping containers, until we reached street level.

"Keep quiet and keep your eyes open," said Maverick, scanning the hazy streets ahead with the scope of his gun.

We walked slowly into town. Signs of past military presence were prevalent. Every few blocks, an abandoned army vehicle reminded us that although the town was evacuated, many had lost their lives. The eerie graveyard feel clashed with the quaint nautical shops and bodegas. These were the same streets I'd wandered when I first left home, hoping to find help or any familiar face at all. Now, I was back, but I was hardly the same person.

We walked for some time, signs that people had been through there more recently giving me hope that Malik could be among the survivors. Our local market was shattered and ransacked, and the pharmacy was almost empty.

We walked past a small ice cream shop that I'd frequented as a kid, now rank with the smell of spoiled dairy.

All three of us raised our weapons when we heard rustling. A large pelican had landed on a bike rack, and was staring at us like it hadn't seen another human in ages. Hound chased it off, his tail wagging in victory.

Further in the distance, a heavy military Humvee was left in the middle of the road, doors flung open. It was similar to the one I'd reentered the contamination zone in. My companions followed me as I made my way over.

The smell hit me before I saw it: a dead soldier, hanging out of the driver's seat. He looked decayed, but I kept my weapon aimed at his head. It was shocking to see a human corpse that old, considering almost all of them had turned and mutated. As I took a closer look, the reason for his preservation was revealed. His left wrist was handcuffed to the steering wheel.

"Made sure his body wasn't going anywhere," said Maverick, as if the idea had crossed his mind before.

"My house is about a fifteen-minute drive from here. It'll take too long to walk," I said, aiming my gun at the cuff and blasting the chain off. "Help me."

Maverick pushed the body to the pavement and with a jingle, the keys fell from the soldier's vest. Braving the smell, we climbed into the Humvee, waiting to see if the engine would start once Maverick took the driver's seat.

A wheezing rumble brought the vehicle to life.

"Lead the way," said Mav.

With my directions, we drove through Seabird. A handful of Morts paraded the streets along the way. More jarring were the smoking pyres that EMBER had left behind. An intense anxiety rushed through me, picturing Malik being added to one of the cadaver piles.

In the spirit of optimism, I shifted my thoughts to more positive scenarios. The small plazas I'd ride my bike to after school, the park where I'd smoke and listen to music with my friends, the place I bought my septum ring, the bus I'd sometimes take into the city.

"Make a left, then a right on Beaufort," I directed.

Maverick did as asked, and we soon pulled onto my street. My heart pounded in my ears. Partially from adrenaline and partially from PTSD, as it was the site of the nightmare that changed my world.

"That one there!" I said, pointing at a light blue, Cape Cod-style home on the corner. Maverick pulled into the driveway, but before he could even bring the car to a full stop, I jumped out and ran for the front door.

"Willa! Careful!" Mav called after me.

I ignored him, only stopping for a beat when I pulled the door open and realized it was unlocked. If Malik was there, that would've been a terribly dumb thing to forget.

But just as that thought formed, another detail beyond the threshold caught my eye. Used candles, all over the small wooden coffee table in the living room, melted down almost to their stubs.

Someone had been there since I'd left!

"Malik?!" I called out.

No answer.

My hand was still on the trigger of my dad's old pistol, but my muscle memory had me walking around downstairs like I still lived there.

I stepped into the tiny galley kitchen. A few emptied cans of food were in the sink, gnats swarming in a small cloud above them. "Malik?" I called again.

I heard footsteps and sprang back into the foyer, but it was just my friends. They looked at me with concern in their eyes, but I ignored them and sprinted up the stairs.

"Malik? I'm here, it's Willa!" I called, pushing open the door of his bedroom.

His bed was unmade, but the rest of his room looked like a dusty version of how I'd left it. His rows of books, his neatly organized trophies. I ran across the hall to my own room. Like his, it was pretty much as I remembered; unlike his, it was cluttered with band memorabilia and a small collection of crystals on the mantel.

I felt a tear run down my cheek. I wiped it away aggressively, as if to erase any sign that I was admitting he wasn't there. I called his name at least ten more times as I made my way over to my parents' room.

I hesitated before the door, knowing that if I opened it and he wasn't there, everything I had worked towards in the last year had been a waste. The trauma I had reopened, the hardships I'd invited back in, the loss, the pain—it would all be for nothing. I grabbed the knob and turned it.

My gun clattered to the floor. There was Malik, lying in my parents' bed!

My teary smile was short-lived when I noticed the pool of blood soaking the sheets around him.

"Willa...?"

"*Malik!*" I ran over and knelt at his bedside. "What happened?!"

Despite the state he was in, he smiled up at me. "I thought I was hearing things. I waited for you for so long..."

"I'm so sorry. I tried everything to get here as quickly as I could. I knew you'd come here," I said through my tears. "What happened to you?"

Maverick and Archer stepped into the room. Malik's face lit up even more at the sight of his friend.

"Mav? What are you... I'm sorry you guys are seeing me this way," he said through a rattled breath. "I was shot by some soldier who thought I was infected. It only hit my shoulder, but I'm not feeling so hot."

Maverick pulled the bloodied sheets back, revealing my brother's open wound that was riddled with maggots.

"We need to help him!" I said to Mav desperately.

"We have medical kits! I'll bring up the bags," said Archer, running back downstairs.

Maverick looked at the wound, then back at me. "This might take more than we have." He put his hand on Malik's forehead. "You're burning up, my man. How long ago did this happen?"

"About a week..."

My insides turned over. If I'd made it there sooner, this would've never happened.

"I'm so glad I got to see you two, at least. That's a happy ending," he said weakly.

"Malik! Shut up! We're gonna save you," I said, resting my forehead on his arm.

Even with a festering wound, I could smell his skin. The scent I'd grown up smelling every time he hugged me. The smell I'd breathed in when I slept in his empty bed those few times, waiting for my family to return while the world crumbled around me.

"Willa," he said, lifting my chin so my eyes met his, "I'm not coming back from this... It's okay."

I cried harder. "Malik, please stop saying that—"

"All I wanted was to know you were okay."

Maverick's lips were trembling. My sobs were uncontrollable now. Malik spoke over them.

"Maverick... promise me you'll take care of her? Please, whatever it takes."

"Of course I will. Promise," Mav replied firmly.

"Malik, we're gonna help you!" I insisted.

The moment Archer walked in with the packs, I snatched them from his arms and dug inside for a medical kit. I tossed it onto the bed and opened it, but all we had were bandages, some pain meds, and a small tube of ointment. Nothing useful. I threw it at the wall, its contents scattering over the floor.

I dropped to my knees beside the bed and held my brother's hand tightly. He could hardly maintain eye contact, his lids heavy as he slipped closer to unconsciousness.

"Drink this," I said, taking the canteen from my pack and dribbling some water between his lips. "Have you eaten?"

"Few days ago."

"Maverick, can you find him something?"

He nodded, looking reluctant to leave Malik, but he turned and took Archer downstairs with him.

Malik was slipping. I wanted to keep talking to make sure he stayed with me. It wasn't hard; I had so many things to say to him.

"Malik... what happened when Mom and Dad went to visit you? Are they okay?"

"They never made it to me... When I realized they were a few hours late, I kept calling them. I started hearing stuff around campus about the outbreak... Everything was so chaotic. When I got to the safe zone a few weeks later, I found out they were alive and we talked on the phone. They're with Aunt Solana in a safe city."

A small laugh escaped my quivering lips. My mom's sister was incredibly warm and kind, and would've loved having the chance to provide a safe haven for them. My heart felt some momentary relief, but my brother's paling face brought me back to my panic.

He continued when I squeezed his hand tighter.

"When I found out you'd stayed home, I did what I had to do to go get you..."

"I know you did. I love you, Malik."

"I love you too..." He looked at me with half-closed eyes. "Willa, I need you to listen to me carefully," he said in a raspy voice.

My vision blurred as I watched him. I concentrated on his every movement, his every word. These could be my last moments with him. I'd need to remember every detail.

"Something's not right. All the stuff about the planes, it's true."

Like a vinyl coming loose from its turntable, my brain stuttered. They were the last words I'd expected from him. "What do you mean?"

His eyes closed and he took a painful-sounding breath. "I wrote it all down for you. Everything my chemistry professor told me in confidence..."

"Where?" I asked, picking up on his urgency.

The hand of his good arm unclasped from mine and his finger pointed to some loose-leaf papers on the dresser. I walked over, slowly preparing myself, as if they were some tome of ancient knowledge that could potentially change everything as I knew it.

I picked up the handwritten notes. They were nearly illegible, like they were written in a hurry.

Willa,

I don't know how much time I have left. There are so many last words I want to write to you and the fact that these next few pages are none of those things should be proof enough of their importance and urgency.

My chemistry professor, Dr. Keagan Slate, used to work for a pharmaceutical tech company called Zenith. He was part of their developmental team and working on a confidential project for them. They were trying to find a way to widely distribute basic treatments and medications for common illnesses through the atmosphere. It was meant to be a tactic to combat potential future pandemics. They were using planes to distribute the treatments.

He said the small-scale tests were proving successful, but when the company was purchased by a private buyer, things started getting strange.

The trials started showing negative effects on wild animals, and a lot of the employees expressed concern. A few even quit when company protocols weren't being followed by the new higher-ups —all of them were silenced by gag orders.

My professor stayed, trying to figure out what was going on until Zenith ended up doing a mass layoff and his contract was terminated. They claimed they were "going in a new direction."

I did some research, and there were tons of ex-employees that spoke out on record about Zenith. None of them were taken seriously. People wrote them off as disgruntled or conspiracy theorists. A few even got huge lawsuits by Zenith's powerhouse legal teams.

There was even an FBI investigation to look into the company, but "nothing abnormal was found." My professor gave up trying to take them down. He swallowed his suspicions for years, listening to all those rumors swirling about weird planes spreading chemicals...until the breakout.

There were still a few more pages, but my mind was already swimming with questions. I looked up to ask Malik some of them, but his eyes were closed and he was breathing deeply, resting.

Maverick came in, holding a bowl of soup. "I mashed down a can of chickpeas, made some soup for him," he said, kneeling beside my brother.

He tenderly brought a spoonful to Malik's lips.

"Thank you, Ghost," he whispered.

"Probably the only time I'll be able to save your life the way you saved mine."

Another tiny smile cracked through Malik's withered face.

I held the first page out to Maverick. "Read this," I said.

He took it from my trembling hand. I fed Malik a few more spoonfuls as Maverick read in silence.

After a few moments, he said, "It all makes sense. I've heard a lot of theories, but this one adds up."

I nodded. "I knew there was something to those planes ... I *knew* it."

After a light knock on the door, Archer came in. "Hound's keeping watch. How's he doing?"

"He's hanging in there," said Mav, keeping his tone light, but his expression gave away his true feelings.

"Why did your professor tell you all this?" I asked my brother.

"We were very close," Malik muttered. "He was my mentor. I think he knew I'd believe him when no one else would."

"Where is he now?" asked Mav.

"He didn't make it ..."

I didn't need to ask what happened. The tension in my brother's face painted a picture of a gory ending for the doctor. "Did you report all of this to FORESIGHT?"

"No ... I don't know who to trust."

Maverick and I traded a look. "So it was one of their planes," I said to him. "The crash must've been a plane Zenith was using to distribute the virus. But why would they want the world to turn to this?"

"... There's a lot of possibilities, but regardless, Zenith needs to be looked into."

Archer was looking over the pages now. "I know of Zenith. They're on the packaging of all my mom's MS medicines. That logo's burned into my brain."

Malik had closed his eyes again. I shook him lightly. I didn't think it was a good idea to let him doze off.

"I'm okay. It's not hurting that bad," he said weakly. "I just need to rest."

Despite that seemingly good news, his lack of pain had to be a bad sign. I could almost feel his presence fading, like the volume was being turned down on his frequency. My tears came again quickly. My body was starting to mourn before I could even process the thought of it. What happens to someone's mind when they lose the most important person in their life?

I dropped to his bedside, adjusting his pillow behind his head. A handgun lay underneath. I placed it on the bedside table, along with the papers. The first page glared at me, the words repeating on me like my head was an echo chamber. I decided it was worth having on record. Almost absentmindedly, I snapped a photo of it with my tablet. I didn't have the strength just then to even dive into the remaining pages.

"Can I have some time with him?" I asked quietly.

My friends nodded and left the room. I climbed into the bed next to Malik, ignoring the bloodstains and focusing solely on the fact that I was there with my brother again. It wasn't at all how I'd imagined our reunion, but I made it. I found him.

My mind toggled between processing everything I'd just read and mentally preparing for the worst. I recalled Imani saying her biggest fear was losing her mind...I shuddered at the thought of who I'd be without him.

The name Zenith kept interrupting my train of thought. Had anyone taken these allegations seriously? All those silenced employees were vindicated now...but at what cost? Whatever happened behind closed doors at Zenith had destroyed our nation as we knew it. Maybe Thirteen did need to see this and finally open his eyes to the fact that the virus did not need to be researched as much as the source of it did. The plane crash *had* to be investigated thoroughly, especially if it was done on purpose.

I reached over for my tablet, pulled up the image of Malik's note, and held my finger over the green submit button. I exited out and messaged Thirteen in a separate tab, typing: *Can I trust you?*

I sat there for a full minute before a response came through.

Yes.

I stared at the screen, debating if that was a genuine answer. I was rarely wrong about my intuition, and although I felt there was more to him than he'd let on, I did trust Thirteen somehow. He'd want to solve this as much as I did. For his son.

I clicked submit and sent him the first page of notes. I listened to Malik's agitated breathing while I waited. The familiar chime from my radio made me jump. I answered.

"You found your brother—"

"Did you read that carefully?" I interrupted. "Zenith is who we need to be looking into. The plane that crashed is where everything started."

The silence from Thirteen was so long that I almost thought he was just running the time out so the light would flash.

"Thirteen, why are you—"

"I worked with Doctor Slate. Before I joined this research team, I was working under Zenith. I was part of the mass layoff."

My head spun. "What?! So you knew all of this? Why were you hiding it—"

"Willa, once I left the company, I was no longer informed on anything happening within. I never spoke out after that because I had to think of my son. Everyone who blew the whistle was aggressively silenced, and the official investigation was closed. There wasn't much left to do."

"Well, do you know anything about the crash? Like where it is? We need to look into this! If they were messing with chemicals or viruses, knowing the cause could help find a cure! Fuck your virus research, this is the key to everything."

The overuse light was flashing.

"Are you alone?"

I looked over at Malik. "Yes."

"I'm going to put my faith in you that you will remember I am doing this for my son." There was a heavy pause. *"There's a group of us here working outside of the government's research program that are gathering intel to build a case against Zenith and the man behind it. If we're exposed, it could all come crashing down. I have a feeling the government is more aware of Zenith's doings than they're admitting. Everything we've put together is independent and off the record."*

My ears started to ring. "Where's the crash site?"

Another pause, and then a *ping*. I opened my tablet and saw a drop pin on an image of the state. Huntersville ... eight hundred miles away.

The call finally dropped.

The sun had burned away the morning fog, and sunlight beamed through the window and cast soft shadows around the room. I took the deepest breath I'd been able to take in hours. For a moment, I felt like the world was back to normal and I was just a kid again, lying in my parents' bed. And that everything I'd just learned never happened.

Malik coughed, and I was brought back to reality. I rolled over and put my arm around him gently.

"You did good, brother. Zenith's gonna pay for this."

My head rested against his. I closed my eyes and saw the two of us, as kids, hiding under my mom's covers in our makeshift fort. And then I remembered us a little older, staying up late in his room and talking about life. The first time he played me a song from what would become my favorite band. How we were the only ones who understood each other.

And then I felt a pain shoot through my soul. A stabbing tear in my heart that nearly made my insides reboot. I knew before I knew.

"Malik," I whispered, opening my eyes and looking at him. " ... *Malik*?"

I took his hand in mine and squeezed it. It was ice-cold. I slid my head slowly down to his chest and pressed my ear against his heart. I heard nothing inside.

I lay there for a long time, with not a single thought in my head. I shut off.

Suddenly, the stabbing pain came back, tenfold. So strong that something actually broke within me.

Malik was gone.

11.

I didn't know how long I lay there and cried next to him, but the room fell dark. It could've just been how I saw the world then, or I'd been there for hours and the sun had waned.

My body was completely numb. I couldn't move. Not that it mattered; I wanted to lie there next to Malik forever. The thought of leaving that room and never seeing him again was excruciating. I felt sick to my stomach. How would I ever be able to tell my parents that Malik was gone, and I'd survived? They'd almost certainly wish it was me over him… They'd never say it out loud, but Malik was their everything. I didn't blame them, though. He was my everything too. I would have given myself to death one hundred times over if it meant Malik would live.

All that I believed about how the universe worked told me that Malik wasn't truly gone. His physical body was, but he'd be with me forever. His energy was part of me. Still, it did little to alleviate the overwhelming grief I felt.

That sadness boiled within me until it churned into rage. A rage that filled me with hate. And suddenly, I felt compelled to stand. To get up and kick the nightstand nearest me. It toppled over, the porcelain lamp shattering on the floor with a satisfying crash.

I wanted to break everything in sight—the way this world had broken me. I punched the mirror above the vanity across the room, cracking it down the middle. I ripped the curtains off the bedroom window. I walked over to the shelf near my parents' closet and overturned it, screaming at the top of my lungs.

Maverick burst through the door. His eyes widened with dread when he spotted Malik. He knew from my reaction that it was over.

I kicked a hole in the closet door just before Maverick grabbed me from behind. I thrashed with my arms, unable to control my exasperation.

"Willa, I'm here! You're okay. You're okay."

I wasn't, and yet his embrace made me feel that it was possible I eventually would be. Malik was important to him too, but he held me tight, as if I was the only thing that mattered in that moment.

I felt his chest rise as he took a deep breath. "You're gonna be okay. I'm here," he kept saying.

Slowly, my breathing synced with his. He had that power. To make my energy match his. In a way, he was the closest thing I had to family out here now.

We held each other for about a hundred breaths, only breaking apart when we heard Hound barking wildly downstairs. Both of us ran to the window.

Filling the driveway was a pack of Morts. I spotted more in the distance, limping in our direction.

"They must've heard me," I said weakly, my voice hoarse from screaming.

Maverick took me by the hand, and together, we ran downstairs to find Archer in the living room. Hound was standing on the couch, looking out the window and growling. Archer held him by the collar, his gun raised with his free hand.

"There's at least fifteen that I can see. Came out of nowhere," he said in a hushed tone.

"There's more down the street," warned Mav. "What do you want to do?"

The question was directed at me. My mind was swimming. The last thing I could do right then was make a battle plan. And leaving Malik there unceremoniously felt cruel.

The chance to choose was lost. A window shattered near the kitchen. A Mort burst into the house, screeching as it ran for us. Mav blew a hole through its neck in a flash.

Two more windows shattered and gunshots rang out as we rushed up the stairs. Maverick turned right at the top, but I took a left, back to my parents' room.

"Willa!" he called after me.

In the doorway, I stared at Malik, trying to memorize every feature. I knew this was the last time I would see him as I heard the growls of crazed Morts coming from the first floor.

"*I love you,*" I said under my breath.

"Willa, come on!" Maverick shouted behind me.

Tears rolled down my face as I grabbed my pistol off the floor, took Malik's gun and letters off the dresser, and threw everything into my pack. The creatures were upstairs by then. Out in the hall, I slammed the door behind me. I wouldn't let them turn Malik.

I heard Archer fire a few rounds as I rushed after Maverick, who shot a few outside my brother's bedroom. I then cleared a few more blocking the bathroom door with a round from each of my guns.

"In here!" I called to the others.

Hound ran in first, then the boys. Four frenzied Jumbees wrestled with each other to get to us before I slammed and locked the door.

Maverick was already ahead of me, sliding the bathroom window open and punching the screen out. Archer lifted Hound onto the rooftop outside and the rest of us followed. The door of the bathroom shook violently.

We leapt down onto the grass of the backyard below. The Morts downstairs pounded violently on the sliding doors from inside, splintering the glass. I ran along the perimeter fence to get to the side gate that led to the neighboring yard. Just as I opened it, the horde crashed through the glass. Maverick sprayed a handful of bullets into the frenzy, but was forced to turn and run. There were too many.

I ran around our neighbors' yard, frantically looking for an escape route. There was no obvious exit, so I jumped up and grabbed the top of the wooden fence. We'd have to climb—but then I remembered Hound. I dropped back down, just in time to fire my dual pistols into the heads of two advancing Morts. Hound barked as Archer and Maverick flanked me.

The yard was filled with them and we were cornered. There was something poetic about dying on the same day as my brother, in the neighborhood where we grew up.

Malik's gun clicked, and shortly after, so did my extended magazine. I lowered both guns in defeat.

Hound jumped and grabbed a Mort by the jugular, dragging it to the floor. Archer used that moment to break away from our corner, some of the Jumbees in pursuit.

"Archer!" I yelled after him, watching him make his way over to the barbecue grill.

He ducked behind it as he shot off a couple more rounds. What in the world was he doing? Trying to get himself killed?

More and more were flooding into the yard, arriving from every direction. Suddenly, Archer kicked over the barbecue, causing the propane tank to roll out from underneath.

"Duck!" he yelled, aiming his pistol at it.

Mav and I dropped to the floor, shielding Hound with our bodies as a rumbling boom followed by a heat wave slammed against our backs.

I was scared to look up, but when I finally did, the yard was ablaze in a roaring firestorm. Within the inferno, the Morts were melting.

I could hardly see through the thick black smoke and my face burned from the scorching heat. We coughed as we edged carefully along the fence, finally spotting Archer through the haze.

He was covered in soot, but his bright smile was vivid within his blackened face. I hugged him, and Maverick grabbed his face and planted a fat kiss on his forehead.

"Fire's so cool," the kid said jokingly.

"Well, you had your fun. Let's not stick around any longer," said Mav, and we followed him past the flames and over the singed remains of the fence.

Back on the street, we walked quickly, knowing more monsters would follow the sound of the explosion. We threw our bags into the backseat of the Humvee and took up the same seats we had on the way over.

I looked up at my house against the smoky backdrop. I saw my parents' bedroom window, and my lip started to tremble as I struggled to swallow the wave of emotion that was swelling up again.

Maverick grabbed my hand. "Take all the time you—"

"Go," I said, and he turned on the ignition.

I couldn't look at it directly, but through the passenger mirror I watched my house grow smaller and smaller.

Night had come. We drove through Seabird for twenty minutes in complete silence. I never wanted to come back here. I'd never been a huge fan of my hometown, but now it was forever tainted with grief and suffering.

Maverick placed his hand over mine on the center console. "Where do you want me to drive?" he asked softly.

"Anywhere ... Away from here."

He just nodded. The engine's hum picked up as he put more weight on the gas pedal.

Hound rested his head between the seats, whimpering and looking up at me. I didn't smile, but I patted him on the head. His gesture was appreciated.

After some time, Archer asked Maverick, "Where we headed?"

"There's a military safehouse I have access to in Waterboro. Few hours' drive, then we can rest there for a bit."

Past winding coastline, through a few marshy towns, and just beyond a city I couldn't place, we approached a countryside house at the end of a long road. We were surrounded by woodland. The closest house we'd passed on the way was several minutes down the street.

Maverick drove up to a callbox outside a large metal gate, rolled down the window, and punched in a long code before the gate slid aside.

It closed behind us as we parked out front. Other than the hefty fence surrounding it, the house looked pretty ordinary. I'd been anticipating a fort of some kind. But maybe these safehouses were just used for respite.

We followed Mav to the front door, bringing our stuff with us. I half-expected him to pull the welcome mat up to find a key, but to my surprise, he grabbed hold of the sconce above the doorbell and lifted it. It opened on a hinge, and underneath was a hidden keypad. He typed in another code, then hit the doorbell. After an audible click, he pushed open the heavy door.

Inside was very spacious, although ordinary and lacking in furniture. It looked as if someone was in the process of moving in or moving out. The living room had a large couch, but was otherwise empty. The entryway table was decorated with picture frames, but inside them were generic black-and-white pictures of different people and families, like the ones you'd find in the frames when you purchased them.

We followed Mav into a dining room that had nothing but a very long wooden table under an old light fixture. Hound chased a small mouse that bolted in our presence. He caught it and swallowed it in one bite.

Just when I thought we were only scoping out the space, Mav grabbed one end of the table and lifted it. Even more surprisingly than the sconce outside, the legs of the table were bolted into the floorboards, lifting a large piece of the floor with them.

"Woah," said Archer, looking down at the staircase that appeared.

Maverick led the way. Small lights along the walls illuminated the steps as we descended.

Down below, the space was industrially modern. It was similarly laid out to the first floor, with a kitchen, dining room, living room, and hallway leading to some bedrooms. The walls were dark gray concrete and motion-sensor LED lights popped on as we passed them.

Archer was in awe, walking around with his jaw dropped. I, on the other hand, was walking around like a Mort. My body was moving, but my mind was gone.

Maverick must've noticed, because he put his hand on my back and led me to one of the bedrooms along the hallway. Inside was a simple setup: a bed at one end of the room, a small desk with a lamp, and a tiny bathroom. Of course there was no window, but despite that and the stale smell, I was happy to have somewhere to rest.

I collapsed onto the bed. Maverick took my pack and weapon holsters and placed them on the desk.

"We have nowhere to be. Take your time," he said, and gently closed the door.

My body melted into the sheets. I imagined myself next to Malik again. But now, he was alive and breathing. His smile flashed through my mind. And then, Imani's. The gap-toothed beauty. I pictured them together in the afterlife. They would've loved each other.

Every time my mind touched on a happy thought, reality came crashing down. The flood of sorrow was relentless. My entire body ached. I was drained to my limit, yet the prospect of sleep seemed impossible.

The last time I'd felt anywhere near that way was when I lost Imani. I still had to do mental gymnastics to justify what I did to her. It's what she wanted, and I saved her from suffering a horrible transformation, but *shooting your best friend?* How could you ever recover from that? You couldn't. So my best defense was to bury it.

I'd only been able to bring myself to commit such an inconceivable act because of the immense love and respect I had for Imani. I sacrificed all of my screaming doubt, my sanity, to fulfill her last wish. To put her out of her misery.

A darkness consumed me after that. After the outbreak, it was the biggest shift in reality as I knew it. And now, with Malik, it was another.

I'd distracted myself from mourning over Imani by hyper-focusing on getting back to my family. I dedicated my day-to-day efforts to becoming a better shot, learning and practicing every skill set I could. Gathering useful tools, strengthening myself. Nothing would stop me. Some days, I walked so many miles, I would have to plant myself for two days just to rest my cramping legs.

After weeks on my own, I'd had no idea where I was going. Signs meant nothing to me. I was so far from home.

It was only when I made it to a City Hall and heard the broadcast that I rerouted and found what would be the first group of people I'd trusted in years.

Tye had felt so familiar to me. His soul was like an old friend. I recognized that immediately, but I remember being hesitant to admit it to myself. I wrote it off, telling myself I was just projecting what I'd lost in Imani onto him...but it was different. A unique bond we shared, even without spoken words. Maybe that connection was what kept him so vividly in my dreams.

I couldn't bear another lucid vision. My psyche was being brutally badgered by an onslaught of my past traumas and losses. There was a throbbing shard of glass in my temple. My skin switched between boiling hot and freezing cold. My insides were in full-body mutiny.

This mutiny continued ruthlessly through the night. I did not sleep a wink, and time seemed endless. The windowless room didn't help. There was no sunlight to suggest it was morning, although I noticed the lamp on the desk had progressively brightened to mimic the time of day.

It was only when Maverick knocked and entered the room that my toxic stream of consciousness was broken.

"Morning," he said gently. He was holding some ration bars. "Brought you some food. The kitchen supplies are gone. This camp must've been occupied recently."

When I didn't take them, he placed them on the bedside table and sat beside me.

"Sorry. I'm not hungry," I said. "Didn't sleep at all."

"I understand. Neither did I. No dreams about Tye at least?" he joked feebly.

It was the first time in what felt like ages that a small smile lifted the corner of my mouth.

When he saw it, he continued. "None of your other friends know where he could be?"

"Not while I was at the camp. And now, even if I wanted to ask them, I doubt my radio works for friendly catchups..."

We smiled at each other, but it was short-lived. Malik's absence came over me again.

"I know he was important to you too, Mav," I said. "Thank you for being strong for me."

He turned away, but I could tell how my words had struck him. After a moment he said, "Of course. I promised him I'd take care of you. That's the best way I can honor him."

Even though I wanted to lie there forever, and had no will to do otherwise, I was happy I didn't have to suffer alone. There had been points in my journey where loneliness was more frightening than any of the creatures I'd come across. When I had lost everyone and everything, and didn't know if any of it would ever come back.

My thoughts briefly landed on Dame for the first time since our parting. I hoped she wasn't suffering alone. Maybe she'd make her way back to her sisters and they'd mend things.

"Do you want to get some fresh air?" Maverick asked, standing.

"I'm gonna stay put for now."

He rubbed my back for a moment, then left the room.

Mournful thoughts trickled in again, but another knock on the door stunted them. Archer came in, holding a glass of water.

"At least have some water," he said, handing it to me.

I sat up, with some effort, and took a few sips.

"This place is so cool," he said. "There's tons of rooms and gadgets everywhere."

I stared at the floor, unable to share his enthusiasm.

"I would ask how you're doing, but I already know," he said. "It took me a long time to get my head on straight after I accepted my mama had turned. I just didn't want to admit to myself that she wasn't there anymore. Been thinking a lot about it lately. If there's no known cure for her, what's the point of anything now?"

I looked up at him. "Hey, look, we don't always know our purpose in life. And we can have many purposes in our lifetime. I don't know what mine is, now that I found my brother. My parents are still out there, but it'll be a whole different storm when I get back to them ... when I have to tell them ... "

"Maybe my sister's still out there somewhere," he mused. "But I feel like you're more my sister now than her."

I took his hand and squeezed it, to let him know I was okay with being that for him. "Archer, maybe our purpose right now is just to get through all of this together."

A genuine smile spread across his face. "Well, I'll let you be, but shout if you need anything at all."

With that, he left the room.

Some hours passed. It felt good to lie still, with nowhere to be. No driving force pulling me manically anymore. I dozed in and out of a shallow sleep.

I was pulled awake when I heard my radio chime. It was inside my pack on top of the desk. I stared at it. It felt a million miles away. It chimed a few more times before going silent. It was unlike me to miss a call.

It rang again. Thirteen would probably only try a few more times before thinking I was dead, so I took a deep breath and rolled out of bed. My body ached as I reached inside my bag.

I answered flatly. "I'm gonna be out of commission for a little."

"Why's that?"

My reply caught in my throat. I paused for so long that he continued.

"Where are—"

"My brother didn't make it."

This time, the long pause was on his end. *"... Willa, I am so, so sorry. I know finding him was very important to you."*

"So I'm dropping the program, okay? I know I'll lose the reentry perks and contact with you, but I'm done, Thirteen. I hope your group can get to the bottom of all this."

"Willa, wait. I called you to ask... what if you helped me with something bigger than the program?" I noticed the overuse light wasn't flashing on the call. As if he was using a different line. *"Part of me thought you'd be well on your way to the crash site by now. What if you went and gathered proof? Photos, samples—you may even be able to locate the flight recorder."*

"What's that?"

"It records the flight's history and even the pilots' conversations in the cockpit. It's used in investigations all the time. If we got our hands on that, it would change the course of our entire mission."

"If the military couldn't even get close, I'm sure I'll be killed long before I see the actual plane," I pointed out.

"It's not that the military couldn't. It's that no one was brave enough after the first attempt failed. I would send you backup, and supplies."

"What sort of backup?"

"Give me some time to reach out to the others in my network and see what I can pull."

"I'm kind of dealing with something right now," I reminded him. "I'll think on it."

"Okay. Willa, again, I am genuinely very sorry for your loss. Take care of yourself first."

The call ended. I stared up at the smooth concrete ceiling. My recent conversation with Archer about purpose resurfaced. Was this my new purpose? I could blow the lid off all the conspiracies and make whoever was behind Zenith finally pay for the hell they created.

Finding the flight recorder would be an undeniable game changer, but something deeper within me was calling me there. I'd dreamt about the crash site before. Was it premonitory, like my visions of the sailboat had been?

Everything Malik had heard from his professor added up with every rumor and conspiracy I'd ever read. It wasn't farfetched to think a huge biotech company could have ties to a world-ending plan. The world was filled with all sorts of dark happenings behind the closed doors of billion-dollar enterprises.

I sat on the chair at the desk, putting my radio aside and taking out the sheets of Malik's notebook paper. With the flood of new information and possibilities, I hardly remembered there were still two more pages I hadn't read. My hand started to tremble. I wasn't sure if I was ready for more, but I couldn't stop myself from laying the papers flat and reading.

My professor spent more time trying to piece together all the possibilities than he did on his own personal research. He believed that before Zenith was sold, the project was for a good cause. But when the new owner took over, everything went south. After his deep dive, he learned that the new buyer was a business magnate named Midas Rothfield, who apparently has ties to all sorts of *sketchy, powerful people. It's not clear why he orchestrated it all, but whatever was being dropped from that plane and into the air, it was laced with something sinister.*

Everything we knew ended the day that plane crashed so all of this makes sense to me! But my professor's gone. It's all going to be written off as a conspiracy, as everything else has been. I'm trying to figure out if there's a way to prove any of this. I'm not in the best shape right now, but I'm hoping to find out where their facility is, or where this Midas guy is now.

Willa, this is not how I ever pictured life would turn out for us—

I stopped myself from moving onto the next page. It was too painful to read anything beyond the facts on Zenith, but I read the name Midas Rothfield repeatedly, going over it countless times like I wanted it tattooed on my brain. With trembling hands, I folded the last sheet into four and put it in the pocket of my cargo pants, then tucked the others away in my pack.

My face dropped into my palms as my mind raced. Now that both Malik and his professor were gone, I felt like I had this massive burden bestowed upon me. Information that could change the course of history if it proved to be true.

Malik said it himself. He wanted to prove it to the world... just like Thirteen and his secret group. Meanwhile, I was running from what really needed to be done. I had to do this. For him and for the world.

I knew I'd most likely die trying, but somehow, that part didn't scare me. What scared me was leaving my friends behind. Maybe they'd be relieved to be on their way. Not to have to take care of me in this state. Archer could have a nice life with Hound in the halfway camp and beyond. He was smart. And Maverick could finally get back to his duties, or even leave the military and finally enjoy his sober life.

I stood up slowly, breathing deeply to pull myself together. I walked out into the hallway and turned into the living area, where Hound instantly perked up on the large gray couch where he lay. Archer was there, looking surprised to see me up and about.

Mav walked in behind me. "Everything okay?"

I nodded, then sat on the couch. Maverick joined me. I took another deep breath. "I'm going to Ground Misery. I know it sounds crazy, but Thirteen's gonna send me supplies and stuff—"

"Willa—"

I kept on, not even registering which of my friends had interrupted. "I'll miss you guys a lot, but I need to help prove that Zenith's behind this. I don't know what I'll find, but I just know I need to—"

"Willa—"

"You guys should stick together. I know what I'm doing is a risk, but everything Malik wrote makes sense—"

"Willa!" said Maverick, this time with his hand on my shoulder. "I'll go with you."

"Me too," said Archer quickly.

I gawked at the two of them. Hound barked, as if to say he was on board as well. "I can't ask you guys to do that. I'll probably end up dead."

"You didn't ask, we're telling you," Mav said. "I want to get to the bottom of this just as much as you."

I nodded. "So did Malik. And this doesn't leave this room, but Thirteen's working with others, secretly, trying to expose what happened with Zenith. He's in on this too."

There was a beat as they registered just how complex the situation was.

"There's a weapon room here," said Archer. "We can stock up."

I looked at his young face. "Archer... Maverick's trained for stuff like this, and as good of a shot as you are, I don't think you should put your life on the line. You should head back to the border."

"For what? To be thrown in some orphanage camp? Have Hound taken away from me? I'd rather die fighting with you."

Maverick and I exchanged a look. Archer's words were so certain, there was no real rebuttal.

"I love you guys, you hear me?" I said.

Hound jumped onto the floor in front of me and licked the palms of my hands.

I felt a fire reignite within me. This was what I needed. A driving force to pull me out of the darkness. What better way to make it all worth it than to be able to provide evidence that could lead the world in the right direction? Even if I could just manage a few photos and videos of the crash site, it could spark an avalanche of new interest in Zenith.

They couldn't silence the whole world.

12.

We spent the next two days heavily planning and preparing for our excursion to the crash site. Maverick hadn't exactly seen anything with his own eyes, but he'd heard that there were at least a hundred Morts at Ground Misery, maybe even more now that time had passed. Our plan would have to be airtight.

We took every last bit of ammo left at the safehouse and upgraded our arsenal. I had my dad's and my brother's pistols, one for each hand and each with an extended magazine now in the clip, plus a newly adopted assault rifle to strap on my back. Maverick had a handgun in his leg holster to pair with his assault rifle, and Archer had the same.

Laying out the map, I drew a big red circle around Huntersville, where Thirteen had revealed the crash site was. We were roughly six hundred miles away from it. There were plenty of gas tanks in the safehouse storage, but it would still take about two days if we accounted for some stops and reroutes along the way.

I hadn't heard anything from Thirteen since our last call. I tried him a few times, but he didn't answer. I was starting to get anxious, thinking that maybe he'd changed his mind. Or maybe he just didn't want to talk on the main line anymore. Or, maybe, he'd been caught. Whatever the reason, I'd made up my mind about going, and I had to do it while the adrenaline was still running through me, whether he sent support or not.

Archer and Maverick were being incredibly attentive and caring with me, making sure I ate the little that I could, and talking with me about anything at all to keep my mind off Malik.

The safehouse provided a calmness I hadn't felt in a while. A strange feeling, considering what was to come. While Hound had a field day catching mice upstairs, the three of us shared fond memories of the old world. Archer told us some great hunting stories. Maverick shared a sweet memory of how his mom would call him her "little old man" because he was born with a head of white hair. And I shared some funny stories about sneaking out of the house and getting caught.

After we piled our bags and weapons at the foot of the stairs, I went to take a shower. When I caught my reflection in the mirror, the dark circles under my hazel eyes reminded me of how my mascara used to look when I'd get back late from concerts.

I let down my locs from their fastens, turned the lukewarm water on, and stepped into the shower. I closed my eyes and let the water take me far away.

We'd planned on leaving in the morning. It had the very real possibility of being my final day on earth, the climax of my life. I was comforted knowing that if I did fall tomorrow, I'd see Malik and Imani again soon.

I never wanted to be ordinary. And what could be a more extraordinary way to leave a legacy than to be the one who braved a contaminated warzone, all for the chance to send back any clue that would help millions of strangers?

The thought of contamination made me shiver. Surely that would be covered by the supplies Thirteen suggested he'd send? We'd have to have some sort of ventilation masks to get anywhere near the plane.

My hand reached out to steady myself on the wall when, suddenly, the floor underneath me shook. An explosion somewhere? An earthquake?

I shut the water off, but the rumbling vibration didn't stop.

I grabbed a towel and ran out into the hallway. Out there, over Hound's barking, I could hear the distinct sound of a helicopter. Maverick was already making his way upstairs, gun in hand.

I quickly ran to my room and changed back into my uniform, then ran barefoot for the stairs, still tying up my sopping hair. I grabbed my two pistols from near our bags and Archer followed me up to the first floor.

The three of us stood in the front doorway, looking up at a huge military helicopter landing in the street beyond the gate. I'd never seen a helicopter like this one. It had wings on either side that curved upwards and ended in two huge propellers. A massive artillery gun protruded from its nose.

Maverick stepped forward protectively, but I grabbed him by the shoulder.

"Wait, I think—"

I was interrupted by my radio's ringtone, drifting up from the bottom of the staircase. I ran downstairs and grabbed it, rejoining my friends before answering.

"Thirteen!"

"I've sent some help and supplies. They don't know anything about what I'm doing behind closed doors, so keep it between us. But with some support, I was able to greenlight this operation to assist you at Ground Misery, off the record. Their orders are to aid you as a FORESIGHT operative."

We all looked at each other, eyes wide with surprise and adrenaline.

"Thirteen! You're a legend," said Mav.

"Thank you, friend," I said. "I mean that."

"Let's make this count. Be safe."

The call ended just as the chopper blades shut off. We opened the gate and approached the aircraft with our guns at our sides. A diverse handful of soldiers jumped out from the center cabin. All of them were heavily armed and clad in black uniforms.

A tall, well-built guy stepped away from the others and approached me with a smile. "Long time no see," he said.

I frowned at him, confused, but when I properly took in his features, I nearly jumped out of my skin. "Holy shit... *Dustin*?!" His smile stretched even wider. "I didn't recognize you with the buzzcut! What are you... ?"

He hugged me tight. "You have no clue how happy I was to hear I was going to see you. I joined the Special Forces. They knew we arrived at the border camp together, so it made sense to assign me to lead the support team."

"Dustin, holy shit! I... I have so much to ask you!"

He gestured to my companions. "We'll catch up in a bit, but before I introduce you to everyone, who's this?"

"Sorry, this is Maverick and Archer. That's Hound over there."

He shook Maverick's hand but Maverick only nodded in response, his eyes darting from me to Dustin as if to question why we were so familiar with each other.

"Dustin was friends with Tye," I clarified.

Again, Maverick only nodded. Dustin looked unfazed.

Archer was staring in awe at the huge helicopter. "So badass..."

"Our unit's called *The Ten*," Dustin explained. "We were all drafted into the program and we finished top of our class in Special Forces. I go by One."

The other nine members lined up as Dustin went down the list, two through ten.

Two was a lean beauty with cropped, highlighted hair. She was holding a lit cigarette in one hand and an assault rifle in the other. She greeted me with a gesture.

Three and Four were two tanks of men, one dark-skinned and the other pale and freckled with a reddish buzzcut. The two of them held flamethrowers.

Five carried a long-barreled sniper with a scope on top. She had jet-black hair that was pulled back from her face.

Six looked a bit out of place at first glance, being so lanky and wiry, but a closer look at his utility belts revealed a row of multi-shaped explosives.

Next to him was a man wearing glasses. Dustin introduced him as the mechanic. Where Six had explosives, Seven had tools. Strapped to his back was a hefty machine gun.

The handsome man next to him, Eight, could've been Maverick's brother. He had gelled-back, white-blond hair.

I did a double-take when he introduced Nine. She was the tallest woman I'd ever laid eyes on. As if one wasn't enough for her size, she had two machine guns, one in each hand.

And lastly, Ten was an Asian man with a handgun strapped to his thigh and an intimidating assault rifle at his side.

"Quite the group. Nice to meet you guys," I said. "I can't tell you how much your help means to me."

Some nodded, some saluted.

"Let's move inside?" Dustin suggested. "Morts would've heard the chopper."

Inside, some of the squadron set down in the spacious living area of the first floor, shedding some of their gear. Others found rooms throughout the bunker or gathered in the common areas like the kitchen.

There was an ease about how they interacted with the space, as if they were there just to wait out the night and the real work began the following morning. Maybe they were faking it a bit, but they all seemed to be calm and chatting normally among themselves. Most of them were eating canned goods that they'd brought with them.

I watched Dustin help Archer open a can with a combat knife. When he offered another to Maverick, he said "No thanks."

When Dustin offered it to Three instead, I pulled Maverick aside.

"Are you okay?" I asked him in a whisper.

"Yeah, why?"

"Just making sure."

Dustin walked back over. Another look was exchanged between the two guys. "Willa, which room are you in? You want to catch up?"

"Of course," I said, leading him down the hall.

We walked into my small room and Dustin took the chair at the desk while I sat on the edge of my bed.

"I really can't believe you're here," I said to him, almost laughing.

The last time I'd seen him was when we parted ways at the halfway camp once I began my training, back when his head was still a mess of shaggy, dirty-blond hair.

"You and me both. You look like you're surviving pretty damn well."

"Not really. Barely, actually… I just lost my brother out here."

His face dropped. "Damn. Willa, I'm *so* sorry. I know you really wanted to find him."

The wound was still too raw to touch. I changed the subject. "So, catch me up. How'd you get here?"

"Well, shortly after you joined FORESIGHT, I started thinking about what I was going to do next. I wasn't able to get in touch with any of my close relatives, so it got me planning my next steps. When I heard they were recruiting people, I applied and passed all the initial tests with high stats. Long story short, I climbed the ranks quickly and made my way into special ops. We're the ten best they could send out here… or the ten most disposable ones at least..."

He tried to laugh the last part off, but I could tell he wasn't joking.

"What did they tell you was your mission here, exactly?" I asked.

"All we were told was that we're to do whatever it takes to help you gather intel and samples at Ground Misery."

"Do you know much about the crash site?"

"I know we're going to have to fight for our fucking lives. We have ventilation masks, at least."

That was a relief to hear, although the more I thought about it, breathing was the least of our concerns. If there truly were hundreds of Morts out there, I would choose airborne infection over a bite any day.

"Dustin," I began, "I know I can trust you, but what I tell you, I don't want you to tell the others, okay? Only Mav and Archer know."

"Of course. Shoot."

"My contact at FORESIGHT is onto some crazy leads that could expose who started the virus. He's working with a whole undercover group trying to gather evidence to prove it. That's what me going to the crash site's all about." I took a deep breath. "This is really big, Dustin. All those conspiracy theories we used to throw back and forth could be real."

He was silent, rubbing his temples as if to squish the outpouring of information into his brain.

There was a knock at the door and Maverick's head peeked through. "All good?" he asked.

Dustin hadn't looked up at him. I gave a tight smile and nodded.

"Yeah, just catching up," I said.

Maverick smiled awkwardly and left.

Dustin looked up at me once the door was closed. "He your boyfriend or something?"

"No, he's just protective. He was friends with my brother."

"Gotcha. Makes sense."

I leaned further forward on the edge of the bed. "Where's everyone else? Have you heard anything from Tye?"

"We all got a bit scattered once our release process started, but everyone was good last I saw them. Ava actually found her mom. I think she and Otto ended up staying with her. Riley moved in with her dad who was helping her with the pregnancy. Tye... We tried everything to get an update on him, but nothing."

I stared at the ground, my eyes unable to focus, as I dissected each word like I'd just learned the language.

"We started to think maybe the virus took him, but his status on the board stopped updating," he went on. "It was only after a few weeks at the camp, once we started making more friends, that we heard he'd made a run for it back to the otherside—"

"Wait, wait, wait. Tye? Tye's out here, on the *run*? In the contamination zone?!"

"According to records I found, yeah. After I joined SF, I got more info. Willa, Tye has some weird shit going on with his blood. It keeps him from turning, and now they've made it top priority that he's found and brought back. Every military personnel has him on their radar. Even Maverick should know about him."

I blinked to clear my head. My ears were burning and it felt like heavy lead was filling my stomach. "Maverick? He never mentioned... He was cut off from his unit pretty early on. I don't think he was getting updates," I reasoned.

The leaden feeling started to fade when the realization hit me that Tye was at least, very possibly, alive. All those dreams of him, the energy I felt from afar, all seemed so much more significant now. But this new information also made them all the more frightening. The visions were never of Tye at peace. He had so much pain and fear surrounding him.

"Well, your friend should've at least heard about it. The boy with 'god's blood' is a prime target."

I took a long, deep breath and lay back on my bed. I'd talked about Tye with Maverick multiple times and not once had he mentioned it.

"It's a lot to take in, I know," said Dustin, "but try to get some rest tonight. If tomorrow will help solve all these theories, I am even more in on this than I was before."

"Thanks, Dust... Yeah, I might just need some alone time. I'll see you in the morning."

"Right on. Sleep tight." And with that, he left the room.

I was reeling. I lay there and listened to the low hum of everyone chatting quietly in their rooms.

So, the whole damn military was after my friend Tye. What an insane notion that was. How was he surviving out there? Where was he? I wished he was in this room with me right then, just so I could protect him.

The boy with god's blood echoed in my head. Were they after him for a cure? I couldn't imagine Tye would run from a good cause. Something had to have scared him to make him leave the safety of the border wall and reenter this hell. I just hoped he was okay, wherever he was out there.

Had Maverick really not known about Tye's status? He seemed so mission-oriented and focused on his duties, it was hard to imagine why he would play dumb about it.

These thoughts along with a cacophony of others kept me at a surface-level sleep. I knew I wasn't going to rest well the night before my potential death, but the evening moved slow and my anxiety heightened as morning crept in.

Just as the simulated sun from the desk lamp brightened, I drifted a bit deeper into sleep.

Heavy breathing, rhythmic and urgent. I'm running, but it's not my breathing. Someone is following me, frantically. It's Tye. He's with someone I can't place. He's happy to see me, but we can't stop running. We run and run, endlessly. Nowhere to turn, no destination in mind. We run for ten thousand years.

Almost as if I sensed it before it happened, my eyelids parted only a second before my radio chimed. I reached over to the bedside table and answered.

"Morning," I rasped.

"I just wanted to go over some things with you before you leave. Is now a good time?"

"I'm listening."

"You'll have a new pack prepared for you. Inside will be a handful of sample kits. It's imperative you take swabs inside the plane. Photos and videos of anything you can capture will be very useful, but the flight recorder box is our highest priority."

"Got it."

"It's always located in the tail of the plane and usually painted neon orange. They're nearly indestructible, so you'll most likely locate it quickly. The Ten will

have your back, but be prepared for anything. Keep your ventilation mask on at all times, understood?"

"Yes."

"And most importantly... be safe."

I nodded to myself, even though he couldn't see me. His tone was genuine and kind. The reality of it all was sinking in. "Thank you, Thirteen. We got this."

The call ended just as I heard a knock and Maverick entered. He put my new backpack on the ground near the desk.

"Everyone's gearing up. Meet upstairs when you're ready."

"Thanks," I said.

"... Willa?"

"What's up?"

"I'm not gonna let anything happen to you today, alright?"

I smiled the best I could. "I'm happy you'll be with me."

I saw him smile just before he closed the door.

There was a lot on my mind. I busied myself with my gear, tied up my locs, and threw some cold water on my face. The longer I took, the longer I'd be alive. I kept my breathing slow and even as I tried to subdue the anticipation boiling deep in my stomach. I took one final deep breath before stepping out into the hallway.

There were noises all around the house: weapons clicking, low chatter, bags being zipped up. I tossed a handful of magazines into my new pack.

"Maverick taught me some rifle pointers," said Archer from nearby.

"Nice. I'm sure you'll be able to put them to the test today," I said. I looked over at him, fully clad in weapons, a sight that seemed so out of place for someone of his age. "Archer... are you *sure* you want to do this? You don't have to come."

He shrugged. "Look, you said we all got many purposes in life. This is one of mine. So stop trying to get rid of me."

He put his hand out with a smile. I shook my head, but smiled too, then grabbed his hand to shake it.

Upstairs, Dustin stood before The Ten in the living room. Half of them sat on the couch and the rest were lined up against the back wall, Maverick among them. When Archer and I walked in, all eyes landed on me.

"Speaking of," Dustin said, grabbing me by the shoulder. "The goal is the plane crash. Whatever it takes to get her in there long enough to retrieve the flight recorder, we do it."

There were murmurs of agreement.

"Seven, what's the weather report in Huntersville?" Dustin asked.

The man in glasses quickly referenced the tablet in his hand. "Says there's some light snow. Clear skies for the chopper, though."

"Day's starting off good!" Dustin said enthusiastically. "So, with the cold, it's likely the Teeth will be catatonic. We'll have to land a few miles away to not risk waking any of them. A sneak attack will be to our advantage if we approach on foot."

"So we're going in blind? Shouldn't we do a flyover to know the numbers we're dealing with?" Maverick cut in.

All heads in the room turned to him.

Dustin kept his tone even. "Why wake a sleeping hive? If they're at a standstill when we get there, we have the advantage. Six can plant enough explosives around them to knock out a chunk of them before we move in."

Maverick let it drop, but I could tell he wasn't used to taking a back seat in military operations.

"Three and Four, you move in once those explosives go off. They'll storm us once they're disturbed. You cover us with a flamethrower wall 'til we can push far enough into the battlefield, then we take our positions to cover Willa. Got it?"

His comrades confirmed.

"What are we doing with the dog? He can't turn, but infection could kill him," Dustin told Archer. "We don't have a ventilation mask for him."

“He’s coming.” Archer immediately put his hand on Hound’s head. “He’ll stay with the chopper when we land, right, boy?”

I wasn't convinced that Hound would, but Dustin moved on. “Let’s load up,” he ordered, and The Ten got moving towards the helicopter. “How you feeling?” he asked, turning to me.

“I’m ready.”

“Good,” he said, flicking my septum ring lightly. “Look alive!”

Out on the street, Nine and Ten provided cover as the rest of us climbed into the chopper’s cabin. It was spacious, with two parallel benches that faced each other. A few members were already strapped in. Maverick sat across from me and Archer beside me, Hound between his shins. The blonde soldier, Eight, took the pilot seat, while Dustin was co-pilot.

Once we were all buckled up, Nine and Ten joined, sliding the heavy cabin doors shut. When they gave the signal to the pilot, the engine’s tone shifted and the roaring propellers kicked on. The massive aircraft lifted off into the sky. Through the small portholes, I watched the safehouse get further away with each passing second.

I didn’t know how long the ride would be and I didn’t want to ask. There was no use in trying to brace myself. Nothing would fully prepare me for whatever was to come.

I looked around at The Ten. Most of them wore focused expressions, some harder to read than others. They were complete strangers to me, but I knew they all had a story. Just like Dustin, each of them once had a family, a life, and a path that had led them to the program. And now here they were, throwing themselves into the very heart of hell itself, all to be of service.

I wondered what each of their motives were for even wanting to be in the military, knowing death was very likely. What were they gaining? Glory? A feeling of belonging? Or maybe it was just direction and purpose. I guessed that, for each of them, it could be one or all of those things.

I noticed Archer's knee was anxiously bouncing up and down. I put a hand on it and spoke into his ear. "We'll stick together," I told him.

"I know. Just trying not to picture what's out there."

"We've already seen some wild shit together, little brother. We're gonna be okay."

He smiled and I felt his energy calm. I didn't even believe my own words, but it helped saying it out loud.

I noticed my own energy was swimming around chaotically. I closed my eyes and tried to center myself, focusing on my breathing. I pictured our mission being completed play by play, everything going smoothly. I imagined our group embracing, roughed up a bit from the fight, but all alive and well. Despite the positive imagery, my heart pounding in my chest reminded me that reality was far more brutal than my hopes.

For half the flight, no one spoke. The chopper blades were the only thing louder than my heartbeat. I could see outside that the towns below had disappeared and there was nothing but woodland for miles on end.

Maverick's eyes met mine across the aisle. He was looking at me like he was memorizing my features. He smiled, but there was pain in it. I knew he was worried about what the day's outcome would be. I smiled back, trying to look more confident than I felt.

Dustin pressed a button on the panel in front of him and a series of ventilation masks dropped from above. He signaled for us to put them on.

I grabbed the one hanging in front of me, looking it over for a minute. It was shaped for the bottom half of my face. A small red light blinked on the side of the transparent thermoplastic. Copying the others, I held it up to my face and pressed it against my skin. I felt the edges seal it like a suction cup, the red light in my peripheral turned green to signal it was activated. Additionally, a small wired earbud hung from the corner of the mask. I tucked it snugly into my ear and could hear Dustin speaking clearly from his com.

"We're landing. We're about a two-mile walk from the crash site. Biohazard gear stays on from this point forward," he said, handing us all safety gloves.

I felt my stomach drop as the chopper lowered. Everyone's faces tensed. It was time.

13.

We landed in a clearing the size of a football field within the woods. A rush of cold air filled the cabin when the doors slid open. I followed The Ten outside, stepping down onto a thin layer of snow. The chopper blades shut off and we were greeted by dead silence. No birds overhead, no sounds of life anywhere.

Everyone was on high alert, taking in our surroundings before moving away from the safety of the helicopter. My breath fogged in front of my face in random puffs, exposing my uneven breathing through the mask.

Dustin was the first to step forward, turning to different corners of the clearing to listen for any activity. When he deemed it safe, he motioned for us to gather around.

"We walk slowly, and silently, as a unit. If the Teeth are asleep, we'll have a brief window to take advantage. I want everyone covering everyone, but remember, Willa's our priority and she *must* get to the plane. Got it?"

The Ten confirmed their tasks. Maverick nodded a beat later, clearly trying to shrug off the fact that he was being given orders by him.

Dustin's watchful eyes moved from him to Hound, who had just leapt from the chopper's cabin.

Archer ran over to him. "You *stay here,* boy. Do not leave here, okay? It's not safe for you. We'll be back. *Stay.*" He spoke slowly so his companion would clearly understand, but part of me felt like Archer was trying to convince himself too. The dog whined but hopped back into the aircraft, displaying his understanding.

"Love you, bud." Archer gave him a loving rub behind the ears before rejoining us.

Dustin gave a quick nod, and signaled with his hand for us to follow him.

Together we moved into the woods, automatically taking our positions. Maverick and I flanked Dustin, Archer close behind. The Ten strategically fanned out around us, providing cover from all angles. Despite Dustin clearly being an adequate leader, you could see in his walk that he wasn't trained the way Maverick was. Their strides were different. Maverick's were precise, his formal training apparent, whereas Dustin's were focused but unseasoned.

Animal bones were scattered all along our path. We walked briskly, but carefully. Tye's face kept flashing through my turbulent thoughts. I imagined him hiding in isolation in woods like these. Cold and hungry and alone. If I made it through the day, I would do anything to find him again.

I bumped into Dustin as he stopped short. We all raised our guns higher in response.

"What is it?" I whispered into the com.

I followed his gaze to an overturned military vehicle up ahead. It was so dented and beat-up that it was hard to recognize whatever it originally was. We walked past it, now even more cautious than before.

A hundred feet further on, we ran into a pile of abandoned hazmat suits, strewn across the snow in contorted positions.

Two knelt down to analyze one of them. "These aren't military," she said, a British accent revealing itself.

Dustin and I joined her. The pale green biohazard suit wasn't labeled.

"How do you know?" I asked.

"Ours look nothing like this," said Dustin.

I swung my rifle over my shoulder and took out my tablet, snapping a few photos.

"This must've belonged to some sort of cleanup crew. Covering up the crash," said Mav.

His words hung heavy in the air. We continued forward again in silence.

Another fifteen minutes passed before we saw signs of a second clearing up ahead. The trees were becoming sparse, providing less and less cover.

Dustin gave a signal with his hand that only his team understood. They took the lead as my friends and I fell back. Suddenly, everyone stopped just at the edge of the tree line.

Metal debris littered the icy ground before us. I was snapping a few more photos when Maverick tapped me hard on the shoulder. I looked up and saw, just before the trees began again, what appeared to be a dark wall blocking our way through a second clearing.

I squinted at it, trying to make sense of the anomaly. It only took me taking a few steps closer to realize it was hundreds of Morts, standing frozen in a compact drove. The sheer number of them was so dense that even if we let them sleep, there was no way to walk through them to get beyond.

My blood went cold. I must've turned as white as the snow beneath me. I took one last photo of the horrifying spectacle, then slid my tablet back into my cargo pants, adopting my two pistols. My hands were trembling, and I took a deep breath to refocus.

As the rest of us faltered, Six took action, removing a plethora of small cylindrical objects from his belt. He walked slowly out into the clearing. His body language was confident as he moved, but his face was filled with dread.

The Morts were in all sorts of shapes and sizes, their black eyes glazed over in some eerie trance. Some showed signs of being former military; some were Phase Twos, possibly even beyond that. Others wore torn hazmat suits. One in every ten bodies was so deformed, I almost wondered if it was an entirely different creature altogether.

Six weaved in and out of the unmoving Jumbees, meticulously placing explosives at strategic points among the horde. Before long, his decorated belt was nearly empty. Carefully, he made his way back to us.

He looked to Dustin, who gestured for us to brace ourselves. Three and Four then took the forefront, readying their flamethrowers.

Six removed a small clicker from his vest pocket. Dustin gave the okay, then counted down with his fingers. Three ... two ... one.

BOOM!

A heat wave blew past us, instantly melting the snow at our feet. I squinted at the flashes from the multitude of explosions throughout the clearing. Body parts flew in all directions and smoke rose in plumes towards the sky.

Less than a minute later, the screeching was so loud that I almost dropped my guns just to cover my ears. The legion had awakened and they were desperate to find the cause of their disturbed slumber.

A second heat wave kissed my skin, this time from the flamethrowers Three and Four let off. The shower of fire fell upon the crowd of rioting Morts, giving the rest of us just enough time to regroup and carry on.

Bullets zipped past me and havoc ensued. A storm of stampeding Morts swirled all around me, growling and flailing. Bodies dropped left and right. I fired half a clip into a group of them rushing me. My other pistol quickly matched it, blasting through the skulls of two more chasing after Archer.

Maverick took down another that pounced at me, giving me a fraction of a second to take a few more steps forward.

I lost track of half our group through the thick mosh pit of decaying monsters. I heard screams that weren't Morts, and could only pray it wasn't my friends. I pushed forward through the smoke and burning bodies, emptying the rest of my magazines. I holstered them and reached for the assault rifle strapped to my back. I took down four more before I saw it.

There in the distance, wedged between some fallen trees, a graveyard of metal surrounded the remnants of a massive plane. The ruins of what had started the hell we lived in now.

I felt a spray of blood hit my arm and turned to see a headless Mort standing over me. In the fraction of a beat that I'd stood there distracted, Five had saved me from a surprise attack. She'd found a vantage point on top of an abandoned emergency vehicle, her sniper scoping out the battlefield.

Dustin, Maverick, and Archer found me again. I was infinitely relieved to see them still standing. Maverick was expertly providing cover fire while Archer aimed and took out enough Morts to clear a path for me.

I held down the trigger, spraying bullets in a wave in front of me. We were halfway there. I saw the mighty stature of Nine, towering over the undead, taking out at least ten creatures before a rogue few managed to reach her and sink their teeth into her flesh.

Ten blasted a hole through a pod of them with his shotgun, just before a Phase Two clawed into his head, dragging him to the ground and pouring blood from its eyes into his.

I stumbled as I trudged on. Dustin was right beside me, firing round after round into the forehead of every Mort that came our way.

Archer was being forced further and further away as the mob rampaged on. I killed a few more in front of me, and tried to make my way over to him.

"Willa, no! Focus!" Dustin yelled, pushing a beast off himself.

I saw Archer run for shelter towards an abandoned Humvee in the distance and forced myself to accept that I could not help him. I had to keep moving forward.

Maverick was back-to-back with me, firing nonstop. I took a beat to switch from my assault rifle and reload my pistols.

BAM. BAM. BAM. Each bullet was precious, but I made every one count. I glanced back to see Two near Archer, helping him keep a throng at bay. I refocused. The plane wasn't much further.

Three was overwhelmed and mauled, despite Four continuing his firestorm along the perimeter of the battlefield. Nearby, Dustin pulled the pin out of a grenade and tossed it into the crowd. It exploded in a fiery burst, clearing the way forward.

"Willa!" Maverick urged, and followed closely as I darted ahead.

I was almost there. I jumped over metal debris in the snow. Pieces of the wings and engines lay all around. Dustin and Mav were still with me, holding off a group of Phase Twos as I raced for the jagged opening in the plane's hull.

I'd made it!

Inside was strangely quiet, the battle raging outside becoming muffled. I drew a deep breath, grateful to have my face covering. I quickly took in my surroundings. I'd never had time to imagine what the inside would look like, but I wasn't expecting what I found. There were oddly scattered seats around the hollowed cabin, but between them, rows and rows of fridge-sized tanks connected by a series of tubes and wiring filled the majority of the space. Almost everything was covered with soot from the wreckage fire.

Despite my confidence that Zenith and the plane theories were true, my shock was no less severe. To be validated by something so disturbing was no reward.

I snapped back to my mission. I could hear the fighting continuing outside. I quickly holstered my guns and ran towards the tail of the cabin. Panels from the hull were hanging off and warped from the crash. I combed through the broken pieces, scanning frantically for anything that stood out among the ash.

A few parts caught my eye, but none matched the neon orange color I was looking for. I heard a few bullets ricochet off the body of the plane, jump-starting me to move faster.

Finally, my scrabbling hands unearthed something cylindrical – and orange. I heaved it out of the debris, gently placing it in my pack.

Next, I rummaged through my stuff for the sample kits. I popped open the plastic box and removed one of the sample collectors. It looked like a small, black lipstick tube. I popped the cap off and found inside a cotton swab. I brushed it carefully along the singed walls of the cabin, recapping it and repeating the process with the other tubes. I also swabbed some of the tanks and seats.

After taking some photos and making a short video walkthrough, I stood before the cockpit door, an ominous feeling in the pit of my stomach. Who crashed this plane? What sort of evil, brainwashed person would sacrifice themself for such a dark cause? A hellish legacy to leave behind... or maybe it was never meant to crash. A historic mistake that would change the course of humanity for good. We'd know soon enough.

I put my hand on the divider's handle and slid it aside. At the first sound of the creaking door, a Mort burst out from inside the cockpit, slamming me backwards onto the ground. My tablet flew from my hands as the contorted creature grabbed at my arms and face.

Its flesh was burnt and bubbled, mixed with the rotting decay of its infected features. One of the most terrifying Morts I'd ever seen.

I struggled under its weight, desperately trying to reach for my pistol's holster. My automatic weapon dug painfully into my back.

BAM.

Suddenly, the pressure relented and I threw the body off of me.

Maverick stood at the opening with a smoking gun. He helped me to my feet.

"We need to go!" he said.

We wasted no time. I ran over to my tablet, finding the screen completely shattered. I knew the content had already been sent, but I hoped I didn't run into more evidence I wouldn't be able to relay. I had no time to pack the device away. I reloaded my rifle as a swarm of Jumbees started pushing their way into the plane.

With Dustin's help from outside, plus mine and Maverick's efforts within the cabin, we at least managed to make it back onto the battlefield.

There was still an uncountable number of the infected between us and the chopper, but our labors had significantly cut down their forces.

"Whatever it takes, get back to the chopper!" Dustin yelled into the com.

"I need help!" came Archer's distant voice in reply.

My eyes scanned the chaotic scene, finding him on top of the Humvee. We were too far away to help him, and even as I stepped in his direction I was intercepted by a Phase Two. I noticed Seven and Eight were still standing, running to assist him.

Dustin and I ducked behind a wing fragment protruding from the ground while Maverick was pushed to the side of the clearing, all the while emptying clip after clip.

I watched as Seven jumped into the passenger seat of the distant Humvee, fiddling with the wires in an attempt to bring it back to life. Archer was cornered against the turret gun above, firing one last round from his assault rifle before resorting to kicking away the Morts that climbed up after him.

"Help!" he cried as more of them tilted the Humvee with their weight.

Every cell of my body screamed at me to run to him, but there were too many. If I fell, I'd risk losing everything we'd gone there for.

I was relieved to see Eight fighting his way over to Archer, but the feeling was fleeting. He was taken down by a large and decrepit Mort only feet away from the vehicle.

The pack suddenly shifted their attention away from Archer for a moment as the sound of barking filled the air. Hound had darted headfirst into the chaos, sinking his canines into one of the undead climbing onto the vehicle. He growled voraciously and leapt up to plant himself next to Archer on the roof.

It gave Archer a beat to unlock the heavy weapon. Seven's attempt at hotwiring was unsuccessful. He abandoned his post just as Archer grabbed a hold of the turret gun and fired into the melee.

The boy's quick thinking cleared enough of an opening for us to advance back towards the woods. But, as if to avenge their fallen brethren, the horde fell even heavier against the Humvee.

I blasted multiple rounds into the backs of their heads, but it barely deterred them. The Humvee was covered in undead within moments, a pile-on that looked like a mountain of rotting flesh. Everything slowed around me as I watched Archer and Hound disappear under the weight of the swarm.

"*Archer!!!*" I screamed at the top of my lungs, making to run in his direction.

Dustin held me back as I violently thrashed. "Willa! It's too late! We need to go!"

Two and Maverick appeared to my left, covering me as I froze with terror.

"Willa!" Maverick urged, and only from pure panic was I able to run again.

We vigorously fought our way back into the woods. I was on complete autopilot as I sprinted in the direction of the chopper. The cold slowed the monsters from their usual abilities, but the small advantage only provided an unsure chance we'd make it. Maverick was at my back and Dustin led the way. Two, Five, and Seven joined our race.

At least thirty Morts had broken away from the masses to give chase. I was sure I was out of ammo, but I was still in too much shock to fire even if I wanted to. I was fully reliant on my comrades to cover me.

Two and Five tossed a few grenades behind us, taking out some of the fiends.

I could finally see the helicopter up ahead.

"Seven! Get us out of here!" yelled Dustin.

The man ran ahead, wiping his bloodied glasses quickly on his jacket, and jumped into the pilot seat. He toggled and switched a bunch of buttons in a flurry, the propellers kicking on a moment later.

A scream made the hairs on the back of my neck stand up. Five was being ripped apart.

Dustin jumped into the co-pilot seat and the rest of us hauled the cabin door closed. The chopper lurched as the remaining Morts slammed into the side, but their growling grew more distant when we finally took flight.

I threw my mask off and panted, letting out all the boiling turmoil that had built up in the last hour of chaos. Maverick did the same, then looked at me, his eyes glazed with anguish and relief all at once. We hugged tightly, as if this was the last time we'd see each other, and then, unexpectedly, we kissed. I didn't even know who initiated it, but our lips locked in a moment of desperate connection. We'd survived, but at what cost?

I broke away and cried into his shoulder.

"We made it 'cause of him," I said, my words muffled against his combat vest.

"I know... He did good. It's over now, Willa. We did it. It's over."

I rested my head on Maverick's shoulder as we flew towards the border. My body was drained to its last ounce of strength. My mind was clogged with an unsettling numbness. And my heart was broken beyond repair.

I couldn't gauge how long we'd been flying since takeoff, or if anyone was even speaking to me during. In total grief, I melted into the seat. Even Maverick's energy couldn't soothe me then, because he too was filled with a new darkness. I could feel his heart pounding even through his shoulder.

Dustin unstrapped himself and joined us on the bench. Two, having finished dressing her wounds, moved into his seat in the cockpit.

"We'll have to go through all the border protocols when we land," he said. "Mav and I will go through military process. You'll follow FORESIGHT's requirements. Willa, you should get hold of your contact and figure out what the next move is."

I'd heard Dustin's words, but I didn't move for another full minute until he handed me my radio. With a grueling effort, I walked to the opposite end of the cabin and dialed for Thirteen.

He answered in a blink. "*Willa?!*"

"Hey..." I said weakly.

"I'm so relieved to hear your voice. The evidence you've sent has had us all running around like a madhouse. Did you get the flight recorder?"

"I did. What now?"

He must've heard the defeat in my voice. *"Willa, I'm sorry, I didn't ask—are you okay?"*

I took a long beat before I could answer. "I lost more friends."

"... I promise you, their sacrifice, and yours, will not be in vain. Things are moving fast now. Once you arrive at the border, follow the protocols, but the FDR and samples should be left with your friend Dustin. His clearance will keep them safe until I can retrieve them. I'll contact him when it's clear."

"Got it."

"You'll never know how crucial a part you've played in what we're working on. Take care of yourself. I'll see you soon, Willa."

The call ended.

If Dustin hadn't walked over to me, I would've stood there staring blankly at the floor for who knows how long.

"I'll make sure they're safe," he said, handing me my pack. I removed the case of samples and the recorder and handed them over. "We'll be landing in twenty, then we'll have to go our separate ways."

The notion that both Maverick and Dustin would be separated from me at that deep of a low point was terrifying, even if it was only temporary. Not only were they sources of comfort, but Dustin's presence made me feel more connected to Tye. Those memories tethered me to my resilience. They reminded me there was still a reason to stay strong.

Just as we all strapped ourselves in, I spotted the behemoth border wall through the viewport. I was not looking forward to the assigned dormitory I'd be sanctioned to while they processed my return. The scratchy bedsheets and cold showers made the halfway camp feel more like a prison sentence than a refuge.

We passed over desert land and I couldn't help but scan the terrain for any sign of life. Tye would've at least passed through those parts if he'd escaped back into the contamination zone. I wondered how far he'd gotten.

The chopper finally landed in a designated zone adjacent to the towering wall. It was clearly a separate entrance for military personnel.

Like a well-oiled machine, a team of soldiers in hazmat suits surrounded the aircraft, some holding tablets and other testing devices. We were asked to step out and line up, and one by one we were tested and reregistered.

As predicted, both Dustin and Maverick were taken to proceed with their military protocols while I was escorted through the familiar entrance to begin mine.

"Look here, please," said a portly man in uniform behind the desk. I looked into the camera of his tablet. "Willa?" he asked.

"Yes."

"Welcome back. Thank you for your service."

"Mm-hmm."

"Your results are negative and it shows you've already been vaccinated, so you can proceed ahead," the man said flatly. "Please place all your belongings in the bins. Once we've logged them, we'll return what's registered to your name. You're assigned to zone eight, dormitory one. Go through security and show this ID card. Follow the street signs."

14.

Because of my expedited entry, I was sanitized and escorted directly into the encampment. I looked around at the familiar, dystopian neighborhood homes that had been converted into holding dormitories.

Following the repurposed street signs, I found my way to zone eight. All around me were young adults, meandering through the streets like it was some overcrowded college campus. There were ten times the number of refugees since the last time I was there. Even still, the environment was orderly.

I wished Archer was there. And I knew Hound would've loved running through the surrounding fields.

I approached a red brick house labeled with a large *1.* A soldier stood outside with a tablet in hand.

"ID—" he began automatically, but I was one step ahead of him. He took it from my hand and scanned it. "You'll be in room three."

And soon, I was. I immediately plopped onto the squeaky bed. It was the first time that day that I was able to catch my breath. It still hadn't hit me that I'd made it back there alive … but I'd always imagined the next time I'd be there would be with Malik.

Suddenly, I remembered the last page of his notes that was still in my pocket. My hand pulled it out slowly, debating if I had anything left in me to stomach what it might read. But I couldn't resist. Any ounce of connection to him I could get a hold of was welcome.

Willa, this is not how I ever pictured life would turn out for us. Even now, in my final moments, I'm not thinking of my accomplishments or unrealized ambitions—not my friends, or regrets. Just you, and how incredible of a sister you are. Your light is way too special to be dimmed by things that were never in your control. I hope if you find these notes, you remember me the same way and find the strength to stay bright, even with the burden of what I've shared.

I am comforted by the fact that I know you will still go on to do great things, even as the world crumbles around us. You're more powerful than anyone I know. Don't forget that, you hear me? I love you in this life and the next.

Malik

If I had any more tears left in me, the pillow under my head would've been drenched. I pressed the letter to my face, as if to pour his words into the void his absence had left in me.

This is what it feels like to have no one left...

My parents, Maverick, Dustin—none of them knew me in the way Malik did. No one understood me like him. I had Imani, and even Tye to remind me that that type of connection could happen more than once in a lifetime... but even they had been taken from me.

On the other hand, Tye was still out there. He probably felt just as alone. Why did he run? Whatever his logic, he had to have known he'd be cut off from all of us by doing that. His best quality was how loyal he was to his friends, so whatever had scared him off would've outweighed the knowledge that he'd be isolated.

Dustin said his blood may have special properties. I could only imagine the severe protocols and horrible testing he'd be subjected to if that were the case. I shuddered. Running didn't seem so implausible after all.

I jumped at the sound of the phone going off.

RING… RING… RING…

It sat on the small desk across the room. I folded Malik's letter again and put it back in my pocket before answering.

I was half-expecting it to be Thirteen on the line. "Hello."

"Is this Willa, zone eight, dorm one, room three?" came a monotonous voice.

"Yes."

"We require you at the Military Affairs building tomorrow at eleven AM for your FORESIGHT debrief. Please be there promptly with your newly issued ID."

"Okay."

The call was to the point, but vague. I sat on the edge of my bed, dreading the fact that the following day I'd most likely have to rehash everything I'd seen and lived through. I decided that, instead of sulking in my tiny chamber, I'd try my best to take care of myself, and food was a must.

After a quick, less-than-warm shower, I made my way to the cafeteria building a few blocks away in no real rush. As I recalled, the food was poorly reviewed.

Inside, rows and rows of packed tables surrounded scattered food bars. I felt transported back to my high school, except here, we were all dressed in the same jumpsuits.

Once I got my unappetizing tray of food, I sat at one of the long tables. A few people smiled at me, but I let them know by my expression that I preferred to be left alone.

I heard laughing from across the room and looked up to see a group of teens making the most of their dinner break. I noticed that each of them had a distinct yellow armband around the sleeve of their jumpsuit. A marker I recognized as the FORESIGHT training emblem.

Like me, they had enrolled and were amid their training window before they reentered. All of a sudden, their laughter seemed out of place. If only they knew what it was like out there. What it had become. I really hoped they'd enjoy those last laughs.

I ended up back in my room after a long walk around the perimeter fence. As tired as I was, I couldn't bear the thought of spending unnecessary time in the confines of that cramped room. The fact that some people spent months in the halfway camps before being released into the inner cities was unreal. They could've at least left some books to read in each room.

RING... RING... RING...

Despite the irritating ringtone, I was grateful to have a momentary distraction. Maybe this time it was Thirteen, ready to tell me our next moves. "Hello?"

"Did you find him?!"

I was thrown off by the female voice. "Who is this?"

"Sorry! It's Ava!"

"*Ava?!*" I spluttered.

"I marked you as family when I found out you reentered. They just updated me that you're back. Did you find him?"

"Tye, you mean?"

"Your brother."

I couldn't say the words out loud, but she interpreted my silence correctly. "Willa... I'm so sorry. Look, if you ever need anything at all—

somewhere to stay, *anything*—you can come here, and stay with Otto and me at my mom's."

"Thank you ... Have you heard anything about Tye?"

"Only rumors from unreliable sources. We've been worried sick. If Otto wasn't here, I don't know how I'd be getting through the days."

"I'll try to find out more while I'm here. It's been hard on me too."

"Really though, Willa, please let me know if you need us. We're still here for you."

I felt unexpected tears welling up, but I kept my tone even. "I believe that. Thanks, Ava. I'll stay in touch."

The next morning, I arrived at the Military Affairs building. Unsurprisingly, there was a line I had to wait in before checking in for my appointment.

I was escorted by two soldiers down a series of crowded hallways. I had no idea what to expect of the debrief, but I was anticipating a miserable and mundane hour ahead.

One of the soldiers opened a door to a conference room and as I stepped inside, it closed quietly behind me. Across the room, a suited man in round spectacles rose from his chair to greet me.

"Willa."

His voice stopped me in my tracks. I recognized it right away. "... Thirteen?"

He smiled warmly. "So good to finally meet you. Please, take a seat."

I couldn't hold back my own smile. There was the oddest sense of familiarity with Thirteen, like he was an old family member I hadn't seen in a while. He really had been through so much with me, however distantly. That voice on my radio had become a staple of my journey.

As I was scanning the room, he caught my eye. "We can speak freely here," he assured me. "I've already filed all your notes and observations for this debrief. Omitting your latest findings, of course. I knew this would be the last moment I'd be able to speak with you securely. My team and I are building a massive exposé on Zenith. We're just sifting through all the data and sources to support your evidence before going public. Of course, your contribution will remain anonymous."

I could feel the passion emanating from him as he spoke.

"And you?" I asked. "Aren't you scared something will happen to you when you speak out? Midas already silenced all those people who tried..."

His eyes widened in surprise when he realized I knew that name.

"I am, of course. More for my son. But it's for the greater good. We now have undeniable evidence about the plane theories, and once it's out there, once the press spreads it like wildfire, Midas won't be able to hide anymore. Especially in this current climate. The people are demanding answers from a government that, so far, has provided very few."

"I hope you're right, Thirteen. I really do."

"And if, God forbid, something does happen to me, the cause will continue on. And as we solidify, we hope to bring more and more experts into the group. The biochem samples you brought back could potentially lead to a cure—an actual *cure*, that gives hope that our world could maybe, one day, see a normal future again."

"Speaking of, do you know about my friend Tye?" I asked. "I hear his blood could help with a cure too. The government is looking for him... He was with me when I first got here, then escaped."

Thirteen looked a bit taken aback by the sudden change of topic. "I know of the search for him, but when we've looked into his files, it's clear they're keeping it tightly zipped. It does seem his blood tests showed very rare attributes."

"What's the latest you've heard?" I persisted.

Thirteen just stared at me, distress in his eyes.

"Come on, I helped you, now you help me. I want to find him before they do."

"Willa," he said carefully, "one of your greatest and most admirable qualities is your persistent loyalty to the ones you care about, but is there any part of you that wants to relent? You've been through so much. More than anyone your age should have to bear. Stop hunting now, and try to settle. Maybe go see your parents and try to live the best life you can under the circumstances."

His tone was caring and soft, and although all of that sounded great in theory, I already knew my parents were safe and that my friend was not. Even though I hadn't known Tye that long, I would never be able to rest knowing he was in potential danger. I had to find him. I knew he would do the same for me.

"*Please,* Thirteen."

That was all I said. And I know he could see it in my eyes, that this was very important to me.

He shifted in his seat. "I figured my attempt at subduing your fire was going to be futile, but it was worth a try." He handed me a Post-it note with some coordinates prewritten on it. "His last known location. Spotted by a search party two days ago. He's been good at evading capture, it seems."

I clutched the note like it was an irreplaceable heirloom. "You're a really good friend, Thirteen," I said. "Words aren't enough."

Despite my determination to find Tye, there was no denying that I needed to rest if I'd be reentering the contamination zone again. I took the next three days to sleep in, eat as much as I could, revitalize my hygiene, and process the losses I'd suffered. I could see it in the melanin of my skin that I was regaining my health. I was feeling much better than I had in a long time, physically at least.

I sat in the cafeteria one afternoon, sipping on some hot tea. It was one of the very few things there that tasted the way it was intended to. I nearly dropped the plastic mug when I spotted Dustin walking in.

I stood up so he'd see me. "Dust!"

He joined me at the table, hugging me tightly before we sat. "Finally," he said, smiling at me. "Had to go through a long protocol process."

"Have you seen Mav?"

"We're in different divisions, so no, not since we got here. How are you? Everything okay?"

"I've been resting... Feeling alright. I heard from Ava."

"Bless her. Me too."

"What happens now?" I asked tentatively. Part of me wondered if I'd even know how to go back to a normal life.

"You'll probably be contacted any day now to be decommissioned from FORESIGHT. I expect they'll give you a psych evaluation, then release you to your parents once all the paperwork's done. Have you called them?"

I'd thought about it, but I wasn't ready to break the news to them about Malik. Not only was I still fragile, but I saw no need to make them suffer longer than they had to with the news of his death.

"No." I lowered my voice. "Dustin, I want to find Tye. He needs us."

His gaze broke away from mine. "I know, Willa, but everyone's after him. What are we going to do, even if we find him?"

"He must be terrified out there. We all suffered for months, clawing our way to the border and we *finally* made it out, but he... he has to stay out there longer, and alone. We can't let him go through that. Something clearly scared him when they found out about his blood. We need to at least find him and let him know he still has us, and figure out why he ran."

Dustin looked at me again, evaluating. "Of course I want to find him. He's one of my best friends. But as Special Forces, I don't even know if I can reenter like that. I'm on reserve here. I'd have to look into what's possible. Are you staying in FORESIGHT, then?"

"I don't know," I said honestly. "I don't want anyone tracking us if I'm in a government program. Tye has to stay safe."

I sat alone in my dorm, thinking about Dustin's words. What were we going to do even if we did find Tye? He wouldn't be able to reenter freely.

There was a knock at my door.

"Who is it?"

Maverick appeared at the threshold. "Hey," he said somberly.

I jumped up to greet him. "Mav! I was starting to wonder what happened to you..." I took a step back and looked him up and down. Something looked different about his body language. And his tired face was troubled. "Are you okay?"

"Yeah, just haven't slept much. I think it's all just hitting me, now that I've had alone time. Archer... Malik."

I pulled him down with me to sit on the mattress. "I know, me too. It's okay."

Like we'd done on the boat, we embraced and followed each other's deep breaths until they were in sync. I cradled him in my arms from behind as we shared the stiff pillow.

Although I'd never had sexual desires for anyone, intimacy and romance were not the same. I still liked the connection and feeling of being close like this with someone. Emotional intimacy far outweighed any physical lust. And Maverick had become more than a friend to me. A byproduct of the complex circumstances we'd endured.

"What have you been up to?" he asked softly.

I reached across to the bedside table and unfolded the Post-it note in front of him.

"What's this?"

"Coordinates. Tye's last known location."

He bolted upright on the bed. "How did you get those?"

"Thirteen."

He took the paper from my hand and scanned it. "So... you're going back in?" I didn't say anything. "Well, I'm going with you, you know that, right?"

I smiled. "Dustin said he would too, but he's trying to figure out how he can leave his post."

"We'll be okay without—"

"Mav, he's Tye's friend too," I reminded him. "And mine."

He looked at me, schooling his expression back to something more neutral. "Well, word is, the military forces out there are dwindling. *Both* of us could volunteer to be deployed. But we'd have to reenter separately from you and find you once we're back in."

I smiled a little wider than before. We looked into each other's eyes, but just before it got too intense, Maverick broke away and stood up.

"Anyway, I told the soldier out front I was just checking on you quickly... I should probably go."

"Oh... Alright," I said. "Well, try to get some sleep. I'm going to register for reentry tomorrow. You let me know."

I woke with a vigor inside me that I hadn't felt since the day I'd heard Malik had gone looking for me. After scoffing down breakfast, I made a call to Dustin and Maverick from my room and synchronized our reentry plan. We would all be going back that afternoon. The two of them as newly deployed recruits, intending to join the forces on the frontlines, and me as a discontinued asset to the FORESIGHT program. The coordinates would be our meeting point.

I was notified that once I reentered, my program status would only protect me for the first forty-eight hours before I would be considered, and treated, like a civilian. This meant coming back to the camp would potentially be impossible. Additionally, none of my FORESIGHT gear would come with me, but the few personal belongings I did have registered to my name would still be useful: my flashlight, lockpicks, firestarter and ammo, all packed in my old backpack. And, of course, my two sentimental pistols in their respective holsters, now strapped over my cargo pants at the perfect level for a quick draw.

Part of my previous program benefits included a one-time courtesy transportation when requested. It was usually used to reunite with loved ones within the safe zone, but that afternoon, I was using mine to get as close to Tye as possible. Of course, I kept the real reason secret, remaining quiet throughout the journey as the four soldiers in the Humvee basket talked among themselves.

I must've been crazy. Reentering for a second time was the only thing closer to insanity than doing it once. But whatever was pulling me back in was deeper than my conscious choices. It was a powerful need to save the ones I cared about.

An hour's drive later, the escort crew unceremoniously dropped me in the middle of the desert after confirming the exact coordinates I'd been given. I was surprised at how barren the surroundings were. How Tye had evaded capture in such open land was baffling, but I knew him to be sharp-thinking.

The soldiers waved me off, leaving me in the wake of the Humvee's dust cloud. I coughed and rubbed my eyes, taking in the environment. I could see some canyons and scattered rock formations far in the distance. Cacti and dried bushes pockmarked the sandy clay terrain.

I walked in the direction of the canyons, scanning for any sign of life. Clearly, I wouldn't find Tye out in the open, but maybe he'd found refuge among the rocky forms.

I was grateful we were in the colder months of the year or else I would've melted under the high sun. I could feel the back of my neck burning, but the breeze was brisk enough to keep me from sweating.

I wasn't walking for long before a glint on the horizon caught my eye. Something was nestled against the canyon wall. I picked up the pace, and as I got closer, I saw it was an RV. It was in terrible shape, but it was an obvious shelter close to Tye's last known location.

I approached with caution, drawing my pistol. "Hello?" I called out.

Only the gusts of wind answered me. I pulled the rickety door open. Inside was a mess, and the closer I looked, the more disappointed I became.

It had clearly been searched through thoroughly, more than once. Most of what was strewn across the floor were loose panels from the interior and broken parts. The search for Tye had been aggressive.

Desert nights could get very cold, so for that day, it would have to be my final stop. I expected Mav and Dustin to find it easily. I began to clear the inside of all the debris, then did a more meticulous search through the cabinets and drawers.

I found some empty cans of food, some toilet paper, and a map. I took the map and spread it over the dusty countertop. I was hoping if Tye had been there, he might've made some informative marks on it…but it was untouched.

Nothing in the RV gave any clues that assured me Tye had been there at all. Only that it had been ransacked in the hope of finding him. Though I did manage to find an unopened can of corn that I put aside for later.

The sound of moving gravel made me look outside. A Phase Two Mort was wandering toward the vehicle.

"Are you kidding me…All the way out here?" I said under my breath. I pointed my pistol through the open window and fired. It fell with a grunt.

I got out to take a closer look. The decayed man wore a fisherman's hat, just as tattered as his skin. It could've possibly been the original owner of the RV. The fact that it was still walking about meant that another Mort would've fed on and revived it. As isolated as it felt out there, I'd have to stay on my guard.

It felt like forever waiting for night to come. I had nothing to do but organize the disheveled encampment, and with no real ETA on Mav or Dustin, I decided to get to bed the moment it turned dark enough. The ragged pullout couch would have to do.

I'm watching Malik and Imani run through grassy fields. At first, I think they're running from something. They're not. They're laughing and holding hands. At peace.

I notice Archer's there too, but Tye isn't. Someone taps me on the shoulder and I turn. He's behind me. His shaking hand reaches for mine. We touch.

I woke abruptly from my shallow sleep, hearing the distant sound of a buzzing engine. For a moment I thought I was still in the disorientating dream, but I quickly rolled over and realized it was the morning sun blurring my vision. I stayed low, peering out of the window.

I could see a cloud of dust growing closer and closer. I finally stepped down from the RV when I spotted Dustin at the wheel of a four-seater dune buggy. He pulled up and shut it off, eyeing the bloated body on the ground between us.

"Ah, so Maverick got here first?" he teased.

I couldn't help but laugh. "You little shit." I approached him and we hugged. "Any trouble with Special Forces?"

"A bit, but I used your plan to frame it like I wanted to support the frontlines and they let me out."

"That was Mav's idea, by the way," I pointed out.

He ignored that. "So, should we move this body?"

Holding our breath, we seized its arms and legs and dragged it as far as our strength would allow, finally dropping it into a ravine.

Dustin turned with his gun up at the rumble of an approaching motor. It was some sort of military-grade dirt bike. He lowered his weapon when the rider did a wheelie before putting it in park and removing his helmet.

Mav's sweaty white hair gleamed in the sunlight. "Are we staying in that RV back there?" he asked, as if wanting to jump right in.

"At least for tonight," I replied.

Dustin didn't say much, just nodded and started back towards our new camp.

Maverick parked his bike next to Dustin's dune buggy, and only then did I notice that both vehicles had solar panels built into their frames. A welcome convenience, considering it'd be a while before we found any cars to pilfer from.

As we stepped inside the RV, it was obvious right away that the space would be too cramped for the three of us to hide out comfortably.

Mav studied the open map on the counter. "We're pretty far from any town, but we should head towards the nearest one and see if we can find better shelter. Tye would've done the same."

"This one's not too far off," said Dustin, his finger landing on a small town called Palm Acres. "If he was trying to avoid the border camps, he would've gone that way. And assuming he's on foot, there's no chance he got much further."

"Well, if we're looking for him there, the search parties will be too," I said, pocketing the map. "We have to be careful."

15.

Strapped into the passenger seat of Dustin's buggy, I directed us towards the town. The small car was fast on this terrain, easily gliding over the rocky gravel. Mav had no issues keeping up on the bike.

We covered a few miles before a large structure caught our attention. We pulled up to find the cavernous building was an old airplane hangar. By the looks of it, it had been abandoned long before the epidemic.

We parked outside the battered warehouse doors and carefully slid them open. Luckily, there weren't too many places inside for Morts to hide. It was essentially one vast, open hangar. Old airplane parts, trash, and shrubbery littered the ground throughout, only illuminated by the dim glow of the sun through the dusty broken windows.

"So, whaddya think?" Dustin asked, kicking over some rusted engine part. "Seems cozy."

"I mean, it'll do. I think we need to have a basecamp so we're not spotted," I said. "We can do scouting trips from here to track Tye, but we'll be safe from the elements and any watching eyes."

"I like the idea of staying low-key," Mav agreed. "Dustin and I are breaking about a hundred laws."

With that, we began clearing the center of the hangar, dragging away old scraps and trash to form a clear space for us to anchor. The dirt bike and buggy were brought inside for safekeeping and to keep our presence from being discovered by any passersby.

"Willa, come look at this," Mav called from across the room. He was looking down at something within the litter: an array of bullet shells scattered along the ground. Even more concerning were the nearby bloodstains.

I knelt beside the marks, noticing some small footprints that looked like they'd been left by beach sandals. "If Tye was here, it looks like he had a run-in with a smaller Mort."

Dustin joined the crime scene. "There's definitely more out here. The fact there's no body means another one revived it. They're out there walking around."

"Should we figure out a night watch system?" I asked.

"I say we try to stay in pairs," he said. "A Mort sneaking up would be easy enough to take down, but if any military comes through, we should be ready."

I saw the two guys exchange a look, realizing they most likely would have to endure each other's company at some point while I slept.

"That's fine," said Maverick, unconvincingly.

The rest of the afternoon was spent organizing. Dustin started a fire in an old oil drum using my firestarter. There was plenty of dried brush and plywood to burn.

We shared some of the canned corn, set up the two sleeping bags Mav and Dustin had on hand, and situated ourselves by the warmth just as the evening breeze started funneling through the hangar bay.

We each had a sip of water from Mav's canteen and tried to settle in the new space. I was used to bouncing from place to place. I'd done so much of it in the last year. The places I'd stayed with Imani ranged from old factories to luxury homes, but none ever felt right. Home wasn't just Seabird. It was a safe feeling. And that never came.

"So let's say we find Tye," said Dustin. "What do we do then? We can't just bring him back to the safe zone."

We'd talked about this before, but the question was still unanswered. I was trying to focus on one thing at a time.

"I just want him to know he's not alone," I said. "Talk to him to find out if he's okay and why he ran. I don't know, maybe Thirteen can help get him a new identity and we can smuggle him in. He can live with me and my parents if he doesn't have anyone..." Both the boys looked at me like I was in way over my head. "Or maybe he'll come back with us and help them make a cure. We don't know."

They seemed slightly more open to that idea.

The night came in cold and I was eager to bury myself within the sleeping bag Dustin had loaned me. We'd have to make do with only the pair. Dustin and Maverick were taking the first shift. I'd have a few hours to recharge before switching back to high alert again.

A burst of white light. Tye and I sit across from each other inside a bright green house, laughing.

We laugh hard, until we're both crying. The crying turns to harrowing sadness.

Someone is draining Tye's blood. I yell, begging them to stop. And then, a piercing gunshot.

"Your turn with Dustin," said Mav, gently waking me.

I was dreaming about Tye a lot more lately, and I didn't think it was just because we'd been talking about him. I felt he was closer.

I watched Maverick scoot his sleeping bag away from mine to the other side of the oil barrel, which surprised me. He usually tended to stay as close to me as he could. Lately, his energy had shifted. Either because of Dustin being around, or worse, the kiss we'd shared.

Maybe he finally realized he'd never actually get all of me. The inevitable conclusion every guy I'd ever known would come to. I'd been called a tease more times than I could count. One would think I'd eventually get used to it, but even knowing men's nature, I was always disappointed when their intentions were revealed.

I avoided his eyes and sat near Dustin, closer to the entrance. I could still feel the fire, but it was many degrees colder away from our camp. Dustin shared his camo thermal blanket with me.

"Thank you."

"How long d'you think we'll be out here this time?"

I shrugged. "I hope Tye didn't go far and he's just hiding. I think he's close."

"How do you figure?"

"I can feel him."

Dustin busied himself with a small bottle cap by his boot. I think he was doing his best not to dismiss my feelings, even if he didn't fully understand them. I saw him look over his shoulder at Maverick, who was already fast asleep.

"... What now?" I asked reluctantly.

"I told you how all military personnel in the States were notified about the search for Tye... Somehow, Mav missed the memo. I asked him how."

"He was separated from his unit—"

"Right, he said the same thing to me. I just don't trust him."

"Clearly. But what are you saying, then?" I asked. "Why would he pretend to not know of Tye when he does?"

"I'm not sure. Just seems odd to me."

I caught myself looking at Maverick with suspicious eyes. Dame had already sullied my taste for friends who omitted important details. But Mav had been an amazing friend to me since the beginning. I had to believe it was just Dustin's protective paranoia.

"You met him at a tough time. He's going through a lot too," I assured him. "Just take it easy on him for now."

We talked about our other friends for a few hours before Dustin began dozing off in the silences in between. I eventually woke Mav for his final shift together with me.

I offered him part of the padded blanket, but again he made distance between us.

"You get any sleep?" I asked, trying not to overthink it.

He nodded. "That felt like the first rest I've had this week. I can't fully shut off when we're at the border camp."

I looked him in his weary eyes, trying to gauge his mood. "Are you okay, Maverick?"

"All things considered," he said with a shrug.

"Did I misread us? Did the kiss bother you?"

He shifted uncomfortably, seemingly not expecting such directness. "No, I'd been wanting to. I think I'm just new to these kinds of feelings..."

"What kind?"

"All my past relationships were drug-fueled and toxic. I don't know how to do this."

I nodded. "You and me both. I've been figuring us out too. I know I care for you as more than a friend, but I'm used to guys needing more than I can give them. I've felt safe with you... but you've been different lately."

"I think I just have a lot going through my head right now," he admitted. "With Malik gone, I'm feeling disconnected somehow. Like his existence was what was holding me together. I'm sorry, I shouldn't even be saying that to you. It's nothing like what you're probably—"

"Mav, we can both feel Malik's death in our own way. My loss doesn't devalue yours."

He finally looked me in the eyes. "I hurt a lot of people in my past, Willa. I'm scared to do that to you."

I took his inked hand in mine. "Then don't. You're not that person anymore."

He said nothing out loud, but I saw a lot happening behind his eyes.

We both heard it from outside. A wet, rattling snarl. Abruptly, we were up and armed. Maverick stepped towards the hangar door, aiming his gun into the black night. I jumped when Dustin came up on my left, his gun at the ready too.

Our trio walked just beyond the threshold. I had to strain my eyes to spot anything, but there they were: silhouetted in the moonlight, three Jumbees of different sizes running towards us.

"Our gunshots are gonna be heard for miles. Should I knife them?" asked Dustin, removing a large combat knife from his boot.

"That's way too risky," I said. "If it was one, maybe—"

The Morts screeched with rage. In a blink, Dustin leapt forward, driving the blade into the skull of the tallest one. Maverick maneuvered under the chomping jaws of another, tackling the creature to the ground, then removing the knife from its fallen brother's forehead and plunging it into the Mort at his feet.

My moment of hesitation cost me. The last of the monsters clawed at me, pushing me to the ground and wrapping its decayed fingers around my head. Dustin quickly kicked it away from me, retrieving his bloodied blade and slicing its throat. It gurgled violently, but did not relent. Maverick grabbed it by its mangey hair, pulling it off of me, and impulsively, I fired a single round directly between its black eyes.

The bullet echoed around the surrounding canyons. We froze in the silence that followed, half-expecting to see a platoon of soldiers marching towards our base. Luckily, no one came.

On the ground around us, ruby liquid glittered under the moon's glow.

"We'll have to burn these," said Mav, finally breaking the silence.

With adrenaline pulsing through us, none of us were able to get back to sleep. We used the energy to burn the bodies outside, extinguishing the fire as soon as the job was done so the light would not draw any attention. For the rest of the night, we made a few fortifications to the broken windows in hopes that the wind chill would be lessened.

Come sunrise, we regretted patching up the holes as the hangar trapped the stifling heat like it was baking us in an oven. The most comfortable option was sitting just outside the door in the shadow of our shelter.

"We should start scouting before the sun's too high," I said, leaning against an old storage crate.

Mav was scanning the horizon with his binoculars. "I say we split up to cover more ground. If one of us is caught, it won't compromise the others."

"I feel like we should stick together," countered Dustin. "Or at least one of us stays at camp and the others scout ahead. We don't know what's out there so it's safer as a pair, and we'll be lighter on our feet if we leave most of our supplies here."

Maverick's jaw muscles clenched. "Willa?" he asked, passing the baton.

"I think two of us should scout and one of us stays here," I conceded. "If Tye hasn't come through here yet, there's a chance he could very well come by looking for shelter. Since you two clearly won't see eye-to-eye, I'll go out with Mav today. Dustin, you stay here in case you're needed. We can switch off tomorrow."

Maverick stepped out into the sun. "Alright then. Lead the way."

We decided to carry out the mission on foot rather than use the dune buggy. Walking would not only allow us to get the same point of view as Tye, but we'd call less attention.

Mav and I started towards the canyons, the only other obvious hiding place outside the hangar. The soft breeze was still crisp enough to keep us cool, but I knew we'd be walking for miles. I squinted at everything, taking in as much as I could along our walk.

My hope was to find any sign of life or a trace Tye might have left behind. However, with the relentless desert winds constantly shifting dust and sand, it was hard to believe that any remnants remained uncovered.

When we reached the canyon, the vast shadows they cast were a welcome break from the sun's rays. We followed the clear path etched by the crevice, both of us with weapons at the ready.

Besides the remnants of a dead buzzard we passed, very little seemed out of the ordinary. We walked for an hour, trying our best not to lose the direction of our basecamp while looking for any sign at all that someone else had been through these parts.

Along the way, Mav would periodically use his binoculars to check all peripherals, but other than a few directional words, he was being very quiet. His steps were lagging and his overall energy was sluggish. I chose not to call attention to it. I felt like I'd been overanalyzing him lately, and I didn't want to make him feel worse.

"Do you remember the first time I ran into you? At the Supernatural Pancakes show?" I tried.

He grinned, but stayed fixated on his search. "I do. We were in the mosh pit and you accidentally decked me in the face."

"I was convinced Malik had asked you to spy on me. He was overprotective like that."

"Nah, he knew you could handle yourself, but I always kept an eye out for you anyway. In case you needed me."

"And you still do," I said with a smile.

He smiled back, but it was still strained.

More hours passed as we zigzagged through the crags, exploring every possible nook, every logical hiding place. We stopped a few times for short water breaks, but were nearing the point where we'd have to turn back before sundown.

Just when I felt the scout had been in vain, I spotted a stream of water trickling down the side of the cliff. Looking closer, I spotted some footprints in the damp sand underneath.

"Sneakers," I said, lining up the print with the side of my boot. "Definitely the right size."

"That pattern isn't any military boot," Mav said. "Could really be his."

“Tye!” I called out. My words reverberated off the rocky walls and I strained my ears for any answer. “Tye! It’s Willa!” I called again, desperately.

“We should keep it down—”

At first, I thought the sound I heard could’ve been a Mort, a distant, growling rumble, but within seconds, the unmistakable thrumming of helicopter blades became clear.

I ran for an underpass in the cliff’s wall, ducking for cover. When I looked back, Mav was still staring listlessly up at the chopper.

“Maverick!”

He snapped out of it and joined me just in time before the military helicopter passed overhead. We stayed pressed against the rocks, hiding in the shadows. We didn’t move a muscle. The aircraft circled several times before the engine whir grew distant again.

Finally, it moved on far enough for us to relax.

“What the hell was that, Mav?!” I demanded. “You’re sleeping at the wheel today. We were almost caught.”

“Sorry, I was distracted.”

I frowned skeptically at him. “Let’s get back to camp before they circle back.”

We got back to our base just as the sun fell. We shared a ration bar around the small fire and filled Dustin in. He was optimistic about the prints we’d found, but nervous at the news of search parties nearby. Who knew what our fates would be if any of us were caught? Both treason and being a mere civilian were grounds for punishment. Or worse, execution.

Maverick practically begged to get some sleep first, which he clearly needed more than either of us, so Dustin and I took the first night watch.

“Is it just me, or is he not looking so good?” asked Dustin, out of Mav’s earshot. “I’m not roasting him. He looks beat.”

“He’s definitely been off his game. I think it’s more mental than anything. Losing Archer and my brother has been hard on him.”

"If we didn't get the airborne vaccine, I would think he's infected. He's acting hella sketchy."

"Dustin, relax. He's a good guy if you give him a chance. He's done a lot for me. And my brother trusted him like family."

"The world's different now, Willa… People change when things get bad."

Dustin's words stuck with me until the morning. I was at least happy to see that he and Mav made it through their shift. Mav was fixing something on his bike, while Dustin loaded a few ammo reserves into the back of his dune buggy.

"You guys covered our area yesterday, so we should venture a little further out today," he said, jumping into the driver's seat. I strapped myself in and Maverick waved us off as we sped out into the open desert.

The buggy sailed over the bumpy terrain, its solar engine only emitting a low hum.

We traveled in the direction of Palm Acres, Dustin focusing on driving while I used the binoculars to survey the land ahead. We passed clusters of dried palms and cacti that I tried to memorize in case we needed landmarks to find our way back.

Before long, we were in another area entirely. The sun was high above us, but the day was actually quite chilly, almost making me shiver as the buggy sped through the desert.

We slowed down when we reached the outskirts of the town. I could see a wide main road lined with a small collection of rundown shops and stores.

Although it was technically on the map, this tiny town looked more like a village than anything else. It was hardly a good hiding spot for anyone on the run, considering it was so isolated out in the desert and would be an obvious first stop.

Regardless, we jumped down from the buggy and readied our weapons to scout ahead. Each shop showed signs of being searched and ransacked. Tire marks from military vehicles were obvious on the asphalt.

"Tye!" I called out. No answer.

It didn't take us long to realize Tye wasn't there. I prayed he hadn't been found already.

As we made our way back to the buggy, one store caught my eye. A bright green hut—some sort of souvenir shop. Why it grabbed my attention so suddenly was beyond me, until I took a step closer and remembered I'd seen it in my dreams.

"What's up?" Dustin asked as I slowly approached it, entranced.

Ignoring him, I looked around the disheveled store. Almost instantly, my eyes were drawn to a white plastic bracelet on the ground. A hospital band from the border facilities!

I almost choked with how fast I inhaled. I held it up to Dustin, both of us reading it at the same time. All of Tye's info was labeled there, cut down the middle by whatever blade he'd used to dispose of it.

"Holy shit," Dustin said, hugging me. "I'm glad we found it, but he shouldn't have left it lying around."

"Maybe he did it on purpose to throw them off his course. He could be in the total opposite direction."

We headed back to the car, looking around with more intent than ever. However, what we spotted in the distance was bad news. A batch of military four-wheelers were zipping towards us.

"Let's go!" Dustin said, strapping himself in.

I quickly dropped the bracelet on the ground and kicked sand over it.

Peeling away, Dustin swerved to avoid the approaching soldiers. A bullet zipped between our heads. I ducked, then turned in my seat to fire in their direction.

One of the machines dodged my bullets, returning fire tenfold. Our only protection was the dune buggy's metal cage over our heads. Dustin put his foot down, zigzagging to avoid the heavy fire.

Two of the four-wheelers made to cut us off. Dustin fired with his free hand, killing one of the drivers. The other continued to chase us, still firing.

We swerved dangerously as a bullet scuffed Dustin's arm. He flinched in pain. I had to take the wheel momentarily as we slowed to a stop.

"I'm hit!" he said. Blood was soaking through his sleeve.

I pulled him out of the driver's seat and we ducked behind the buggy, using it as a shield from the onslaught of bullets. I didn't want to have to kill them, but if it was us, or them, I had no choice.

I managed to fire two lucky rounds, killing another driver and popping the tire of the third. The two remaining soldiers mirrored us, using their four-wheelers as cover. We exchanged shots back and forth.

"You are in a restricted area!" one shouted at us.

Groaning, Dustin stood up and got a few shots off before ducking again. It seemed the rain of fire eased up, a sign that he must've taken out one of the remaining soldiers.

"There's one more. You take right, I take left," I said.

My partner crawled towards the hood of the buggy while I took the other end. I saw a female soldier with her gun resting on the seat of her quad. She fired at us three times before we both popped up together and fired from both angles. Caught off guard, she slumped over the clutch in a bloody mess.

Although it was a relief to be out of harm's way, the reality of Dustin's wound hit me hard. Red dripped onto the sand at his feet.

"We need to get you back! Maverick can help."

16.

By the time we got back to base, Dustin was in such agony that it was hard to even watch as Mav tended his wound.

"Luckily it only grazed him, but it cut deep," he said, gluing the sanitized wound together.

"That was too close a call," I said, holding Dustin's hand.

Mav finished tying a strip of gauze around his forearm. "How does that feel, man?"

Dustin shook his arm out to test it. "I should be good. Thanks, Mav."

"Of course."

I couldn't help but grin at the moment of comradery. It showed that at the end of the day, we still had each other's backs. It gave me hope in moving forward.

The following morning, we updated Maverick about Tye's hospital band. He agreed it didn't necessarily mean we'd find Tye in the area where we found it, but it did mean he had to have at least passed through.

Preparing for a long journey, we packed up our camp. Given the distance we'd be covering, we needed to remain flexible, ready to seek shelter wherever we ended up. It was all hands on deck as we'd be scouting as a trio that day.

With our provisions tightly packed, we took off without looking back at our shelter. Mav's dirt bike tailed us. I had my gun in one hand and the map in the other. On the horizon, there was one significant area we hadn't yet explored: a collection of rugged crags. These would likely be Tye's final option for cover within a reasonable radius.

With search parties still in the area, I was optimistic that Tye hadn't been captured yet. But whether he was still anywhere near his last known sighting was yet to be seen.

It took us quite a while to reach the towering formations; they'd looked deceptively closer than they were. Both vehicles maneuvered through thin pathways created by the bluffs as we slowed to inspect them more closely.

Halfway through, there were signs of bullet shells and tire marks, but nothing unique to Tye. Even the footprints we managed to spot were too vague to place, and most seemed to match the underside of Mav and Dustin's military boots. We were energized to continue looking, though, as that area had clearly seen a lot of activity.

An hour later, Dustin turned a Mort into roadkill, clearing our path of its threat. Something both he and Mav shared a laugh over. Half a mile later, our track marks were still red with its blood.

We searched for many more hours with few breaks until golden hour was upon us. Three times we had to reroute and strategically position ourselves between boulders to avoid the looming eyes of search helicopters. We'd just avoided one, now flying far into the distance, when—

"Stop!" I called out, spotting a small cave off the main path.

The buggy skidded to a halt. Mav quickly parked his bike beside us. I hopped down and approached slowly. A bundle of dried branches scattered at the opening of the cave caught my interest.

"Gathered firewood."

The boys followed me into the mouth. A few bats hung from the high ceiling. At the far side of the rounded chamber of the cave was a small collection of stones placed in a circle. It was filled with ash—a campfire.

Dustin knelt beside it, scrutinizing. "There's two pairs of footprints. Sneakers and military boots. A woman's, maybe?"

Some of the tracks were the same as the ones I'd seen near the waterfall, identical in size, but the smaller bootprints threw me off. "If it's Tye, he's with a soldier... His captor?"

Mav was studying the wider part of the cave. "It looks like he was walking around freely, though. I don't think he was being held."

I couldn't help but smile. "We're onto him. I just *know* he was here!"

"If they're his prints, it's a good sign, but he could be miles away by now," said Mav.

Dustin seemed to share my enthusiasm, but Mav was being very matter-of-fact.

I wanted to preserve my hopefulness, so I changed the subject. "We should shelter here for tonight. It'll be dark once the sun goes behind the canyons."

I gathered the remaining sticks from outside while Dustin and Mav collected more. It was an odd feeling to be mirroring what I thought to be Tye's exact movements, in the very same place he must've stood.

Our fire ended up being small, but at least provided enough warmth to get us through the night. To conceal the glow and avoid drawing attention, we draped the quilted thermal blanket like a curtain over the cave entrance, though it was a difficult sacrifice to make as the temperature continued to plummet.

Sitting around the firepit, we shared a ration bar. The taste of them was starting to become nauseating. Not only had they been my only source of nutrition for so long, but their mere association with survival made them hard to stomach.

"Where do you guys think you'd be right now, if none of this ever happened?" I asked.

They looked at me with squinted eyes, but I could tell they didn't mind the prompt.

At first, Dustin poked at the fire with a twig, looking thoughtful, until something he recalled brought a smile to his face.

"A month before the outbreak, I was planning a trip to Hawaii with this girl, Jade. I was so excited about getting to spend more time with her and we made all these plans for that year, half of which we couldn't even afford." He laughed. "I guess I like to think we'd have ended up there together. My parents really liked her..."

Dustin's heartfelt response took me by surprise, but it made me glad I'd asked the question. "Aw, Dust, I didn't know you were a romantic," I teased.

"How about you? Where would you be?"

I'd been thinking about it before I brought up the topic. "I would've been spending as much time with Malik as I could. Once he went to school, we were a little disconnected and I hated that. I would probably be visiting him every other week."

The mention of Malik's name made Maverick shift where he sat.

"How about you, Mav?" I asked softly.

He stared into the fire, and I watched the reflection of the flames dance in his eyes.

"I'd reconnect with my parents. Tell them how sorry I was for what I put them through... and just work on repairing stuff with them. They would've loved that."

The pain was obvious in his voice.

"Do you know where they—"

"HOLY *FUCK!*" Dustin shouted, jumping up quickly and grabbing his weapon.

I spun around immediately, both pistols drawn. The blanket was pulled aside and a familiar boy stood at the cave mouth, but I couldn't place his face right away. Then, I nearly buckled at the knees.

"*Tye?!*" I said in awe.

"Willa," he said, wide-eyed.

I lowered my guns with shaking hands. Mav still had his drawn, but it was pointing at a second figure standing in the entrance: Dame.

Surely I must've dozed off without realizing and this was one of my hyper-real dreams. I was torn between a smile and tears.

"Wait... What's going on? What?!" Tye exclaimed, seeing his old friend. Dustin ran at Tye with open arms. They embraced tightly, laughing like two little kids. "Dust! I didn't know you'd be here too! What the hell?!"

I was gobsmacked. "How... ?"

"This is your friend, right?" Tye asked me, gesturing to Dame.

She nodded hello, like she was a bit embarrassed to show up again. "I was on my way back to the border camp," she said, "but I realized I'm probably wanted for treason by now, so I can't reenter. I was stuck out here and Tye tried to take my shit in the night. After I stopped him, and we traded some words, we decided to stick together. I had no clue this was your friend until he started telling me his story and I pieced it all together. We've been tracking you guys."

"We've been tracking *you!*" I said, still in disbelief.

"Well, that's probably why we all ended up in the same spot," Tye laughed.

He looked so different from how I remembered him—clad in mismatched clothes he'd clearly pilfered off fallen bodies, and older somehow, though not much time had passed. He was weathered, with the shadow of some scruff around his jawline and more experience in his eyes.

Dustin hugged him again. "This is unreal. We have so much to catch up on!"

"Yeah, like your new haircut!" Tye teased, rubbing Dustin's buzzcut. He nodded to Maverick. "Who's this?"

Mav finally lowered his gun. The arrival of the duo seemed to have stunned him. "Maverick," he muttered.

"You look like shit," Dame joked, throwing down her bag and sitting next to the fire.

"I know this was your camp, but sit, please," I said to Tye, and we all took a seat together.

He held my hand. "When I heard you were out here again looking for your brother, you don't know how happy I was. I thought I'd never see any of you again … but Dustin? Why are *you* here? That's the best surprise."

"I'm in Special Forces now. When we found out you ran away from the facility, we had to come find you. Fill us in."

"Special Forces … ?"

"We're doing this under the radar," Dustin explained. "I'm here as your friend, not on duty."

"Mav was friends with my brother. He came to help me find him," I said to Tye.

"Where is he? Your brother?" Dame asked, still smiling. It quickly faded as she watched my face. "Oh, Willa … "

Tye's expression flickered between shock and sorrow. "I'm so sorry."

I nodded. "I know. I'm just glad you're okay. What happened? Tell us everything."

His body language sank, like he was cowering from an unseen force. "They found something in my blood. They were running so many tests, like taking blood over and over while keeping me like a prisoner. I don't know exactly what they found, but look." He pulled at the collar of his shirt to reveal a thin black scar on his shoulder. "This was an infected wound, from the Mort in 556. It healed completely."

I flashed back to that moment when I first met him, and the monster trying to devour him on the hotel floor. I gently touched his old wound. It was hardly visible.

"Even I didn't know all this," said Dame. "You said you were on the run, but damn, I didn't know you were some sort of miracle."

"You got a fat bounty on your head now, buddy," said Dustin. "Clearly your blood's been made a high priority. But why did you run? If your blood can make a cure, wouldn't you want that?"

Tye's cheeks flushed. "Maybe I'm being a selfish piece of shit … but I'm terrified. It's as simple as that. I don't know what they'd have done to me, or how my life would've been. I was only there for two days and I nearly lost my mind. They'll never let me go if I become a science experiment. Being a lab rat for life, and imprisoned for blood draining? I'd rather die."

Mav was listening intently, but remained silent.

When no one else had a rebuttal, Tye went on. "Anyhow, I think there's others like me. There were other kids being studied too. I'm not the only chance for a cure so I don't get why they're coming after me so hard."

"We went to the site of the plane crash," I told the new arrivals. "The one that started this all. Seems the virus was being intentionally spread. We've turned in the flight recorder and samples for proof. A lot of things are going to change now. They might even be able to find a cure with the new information."

Their expressions seemed to glitch, Tye's from the news and Dame's most likely from hearing we went to Ground Misery.

"So it *was* the planes? Like everyone suspected?" Tye asked, visibly dumbfounded.

"We don't know how deep the conspiracy goes, but the plane we saw was absolutely involved. It could be the start of unraveling the whole thing."

A collective chill ran through the group, clear in the way everyone tensed up.

"Where's Archer?" Dame asked suddenly.

None of us could make eye contact with her.

"...No. When? How?"

I met her teary gaze. "At the crash site. It was swarmed."

She put her face in her hands. "*No me digas.*"

On that heavy note, I scanned the group and took in everyone's exhaustion. "Look, this is the best outcome any of us could hope for. It's about time something went right. Let's get some rest and figure out a game plan in the morning."

"No chance I can get to sleep with how stoked I am to see you guys. I'll take night watch. You guys sleep," Tye offered.

"I'll try to," said Dustin. "But only because throwing a party for you isn't an option right now."

He and Tye hugged again.

"I'll join you," I said. "I won't be able to wind down either. I've been thinking about this moment for months."

His face flushed and he gave me a sweet smirk.

The others readied for sleep inside the cave while Tye and I sat on a large boulder just outside, huddled closely under the stars.

"It feels so out-of-body that you're here," I said. "Like I'm dreaming. That's been happening a lot since you left."

"Dreams about me?"

"If you can call them that. Some weren't so good."

"I dreamt about you too. Out of all my friends, I almost feel guilty how I thought about you the most."

"Really? What did you see?"

"I could never fully remember when I woke up, but I just felt connected."

I smiled, feeling validated by our bond.

"How are the others?" he asked, looking worried.

"I heard from Ava last week. She's with her mom and Otto. And Dustin told me Riley found her dad."

Tye's eyes instantly welled up. "That makes me happy."

I rubbed his back. "We're gonna figure out a way to get you back there, Tye. We'll think of something."

He nodded, looking up at the sky, deep in thought.

"How long ago did you run into Dame?" I asked.

"Been together for about a week. I thought she was part of the search party at first, but realized she was on the run too. And you know how it is out here, you meet someone and get close quick. We started sharing our stories and freaked out when we realized we both knew you."

"Fate never fails... And what do you think of her?"

"I like her. Definitely wouldn't be here without her help."

I didn't know how much Dame had shared with him about our parting of ways, but I decided not to bring up her past. Like he said, she was the reason he was there in front of me, and for that, any past drama had become irrelevant.

Tye turned to me and rested his forehead against mine. "Willa... I felt so alone these last few months. Thank you for looking for me."

I grinned. "In this life and the next."

We talked for another hour about anything and everything, from foods we missed to the ins and outs of our time apart. I broke down a lot of what I'd been going through, particularly about mine and Maverick's complex dynamic and the tension between him and Dustin.

As if we'd summoned him, Dustin joined us in the middle of the night. "Okay, I'm getting FOMO. I can't sleep. I need some Tye-time."

"What happened to your arm?" Tye asked, spotting the bloody bandages.

"Oh, just a gnarly scratch."

"You guys run into trouble out here?"

I stood up. "You two catch up. I'm gonna try my best to get some shut-eye before sunup," I said, leaving the two to banter.

Next to the fire, Maverick was staring up at the ceiling, still awake. Dame, on the other hand, was knocked out, probably grateful to have eyes on night watch again.

"Can't sleep?" I asked, crawling into Dustin's sleeping bag.

"Well, a lot happened tonight."

"Fair. I don't think it's even hit me yet... Which part shocked you the most? Tye finding us, or Dame being with him?"

"I think I'm more confused than shocked... She said she was tracking us, but how'd she even know we were in this area?"

"Maverick, let's not look for reasons for things to go wrong. We don't need to be best friends with her, but she did get Tye here. Let's just sort out a plan in the morning."

He was eyeing her over the flames, but let it go for the moment. I was caught off guard by his hand reaching for mine.

"Move closer," he said to me.

I held his gaze for a moment, trying to read him. Maybe our last talk had softened him. I moved my sleeping bag closer to his and rolled over. I could hear Tye and Dustin holding in their laughs outside and couldn't help but fall asleep with a grin.

Now that Tye was back, I was curious if I'd experience another dream, or if I'd wake up and realize all of the previous day was the dream. To my relief, my friend was still there when I woke, and for once, my sleep had been restful. With Malik gone and Tye's return, I had no one to save anymore. My driving force was fulfilled, and a new weightlessness had formed within me. I could literally feel my breathing ease and my head was euphoric with clarity.

The sun had just started to rise, warming our abode by a few degrees. Tye and Dustin were sitting by the smoldering fire, clearly having not slept at all, while Dame and Mav walked in from their shift outside. I wondered how that had gone over.

"Did you two get acquainted?" I asked her, pointing at Dustin.

"A bit. Looks like you all go way back," she said. "We were talking about getting some real food. We saw a few desert hares out there. I could cook one up if we can catch one."

"I'd do anything not to eat another ration bar," said Dustin.

"Okay, but first, something very important," said Tye. We all turned our attention to him. "The floor is lava, quick!"

He jumped onto the sleeping bag closest to him and we all shuffled to find the nearest landing point. I stood on the other sleeping bag, Dame and

Mav took the high ground on top of some big cave rocks, and Dustin balanced clumsily on his backpack. We all started laughing.

"Now what?" I called, shoving Tye's arm.

"I don't know, actually, just seemed fun."

And it was. We were thrown into a fit of laughter, realizing how we'd all instantly committed to the claim the floor had become deadly. All of us were standing in the most silly positions. I was grateful for the moment of levity.

" ... Do you hear that?" Tye asked, his face suddenly serious.

A few of us kept laughing, thinking it was another game, but his expression was too grave. We strained to listen, all of us moving quickly to grab our weapons. It sounded like a distant engine somewhere.

"Out! Now!" I urged.

Together, we hustled to pack and run for our vehicles. Dustin and Tye took the front seats of the dune buggy while I took the back with our supplies. Dame jumped on the back of Mav's bike.

TING! A bullet ricocheted off his handlebars, missing him by inches.

We shot off down the canyon's path, hearing the engine of whatever was chasing us grow louder. I readied my weapons, pointing them over the backseat. Two large Humvees turned the corner, firing in our direction with their turret guns. I dodged as part of the fabric of my seat exploded. I carefully fired off a few rounds, aiming specifically for their tires.

Mav's dirt bike zipped past us, Dame providing cover fire with her automatic. Large, flared cracks appeared on the front windshield of the foremost truck, but it didn't slow.

We came into a rounded space between the canyons. It almost reminded me of a colosseum ring. Fitting, as our two small vehicles faced the behemoth military trucks head-to-head.

Gravel exploded around us as we swerved left and right to avoid the shots. Dustin made a hard turn to circle left, firing from the driver's seat as we fell in parallel with one of the Humvees. He managed to hit one of the tires dead-on, piercing it with a loud pop and a hiss.

The truck tilted to one side and toppled over, screeching to a halt as it scraped along the rough ground. Five soldiers emerged from within, ducking behind it and resuming fire.

The other Humvee was still in pursuit of Maverick. "Hop off!" he called to Dame over his shoulder.

She quickly let go and rolled off the speeding bike. Mav then sharply pivoted the bike to face the oncoming Humvee head-on. They fired at the motorcycle, sparks blooming from its body, but just as Maverick was in range for a deadly collision he jumped from the bike, releasing it at full speed into the windshield of the oncoming truck. The dirt bike smashed into the glass, killing the driver instantly. The vehicle slowed until the other soldiers jumped out.

Our buggy zoomed around the two groups of soldiers firing at our party. Dame and Mav took cover behind some protruding rocks, managing to kill a couple of them.

Tye took another one down before having to duck again when our buggy took heavy fire. Dustin was forced to put distance between us and the soldiers.

"We can't leave Mav and Dame!" I shouted, looking back at the clearing. They were completely outnumbered.

"I know, I'm on it!"

He swerved again, making a wide turn back towards the battlefield, but just as we started picking up speed, he slammed on the brakes. A chopper rose from behind the canyon, kicking up dust all around us.

"Oh, fuck," said Tye, dread flooding his face.

The helicopter landed in the open area, a whole team of reinforcements pouring out of the cabin.

"Head for the rocks!" Dustin called.

We ditched the dune buggy, ducking for cover near the rock outcrop where Mav and Dame had taken refuge. Bullets rained on the boulders we now all hid behind.

A voice boomed from a loudspeaker. *"You are in possession of a fugitive. If you aid him, you will be treated as fugitives too!"*

Tye's face paled like flour. Mine must have looked the same. We were totally surrounded. Mav and Dame looked over to me, as if I was meant to come up with some sort of plan.

I was overwhelmed by the realization that I had put all our lives in danger by coming to find Tye. I'd never considered what would happen after we found him, and now we'd all be prisoners together instead of reunited and free.

"Put your weapons down and—"

A petrified scream echoed around the canyon, quickly joined by several more under the cracking of gunfire. We peeked over the rocks to see a horde of Morts flooding into the clearing. Some of them were clad in military uniform, fallen soldiers now infected.

Mav took full advantage of the distraction, running towards the Humvee he'd hit. He grabbed his dented dirt bike and heaved it upright, kicking it on just before the Morts could reach him.

I grabbed Tye by the arm and made a break for it, Dame and Dustin following my lead. Tye and I ran for the dune buggy while Dame and Dustin closed in on the vacant Humvee, shooting a few Morts along the way.

Before I knew it, Mav's bike and the military truck carrying Dustin and Dame were behind us, and our procession fled the bloody scene.

17.

We drove for miles, leaving the echoing cries of the soldiers behind. Finally, we parked our vehicles beneath a sprawling underpass in a rugged canyon, hidden from prying eyes. Tye's regretful gaze met mine, burdened by the weight of our predicament.

His voice trembled with remorse. "I'm so sorry..."

"Tye, stop," I said firmly. "We knew what we were signing up for."

Dame's lips parted to speak, but she stopped herself.

A cough from behind us made us jump and spin around. Our guns all pointed at a bloodied soldier, struggling out of the backseat of the stolen Humvee with a bullet hole through his shoulder.

"Jesus Christ," Dustin muttered. "Where were *you* hiding?"

The man had clearly wanted to escape the melee just as much as we had, but now our location was compromised.

The man reached for his radio but Mav pointed his gun directly at his face.

"Don't move," Mav ordered.

"I don't have a weapon," the man pleaded, holding his hands up. "Please, help me."

Blood seeped from his wound, staining the dirt beneath him. Dustin instructed him to sit, propping him against the canyon wall.

"I'll ask the questions, and your answers will determine your fate," Dustin said, his tone unwavering. "What are your orders? What are they planning to do with Tye?"

Tye swallowed hard a couple of times. His anticipation was palpable. The soldier merely winced.

"Answer us," I urged, raising my pistols slightly.

"I don't know what they're doing with him," he sputtered. "We were ordered to find him and take him to the camps at Ylem."

There was an ugly silence. Tye's jaw clenched.

"Ylem? Where is that?" Dame prodded.

As she was fellow military personnel, the fact that she hadn't heard of it worried me. Mav's face was unreadable.

"Where? What is that?" I repeated, more sternly.

"Where the virus hasn't reached... the untouched land. They're rounding up people like him, the ones with unique blood," explained the soldier, almost going cross-eyed. "He's the most wanted kid on the list right now."

His words hung in the air. That was quite the revelation.

"I told you what I know... Please, I need a med kit!" he pleaded.

Mav kicked the man's radio out of reach. "I'll patch him up and we can leave him here. We'll be long gone before he reaches help."

"We can't take the chance. He knows our faces now and you know we're breaking every law in the book," said Dustin. "We'll put him out of his misery."

"Why do you always say the opposite of everything I say?" Mav demanded, his tone suddenly becoming hostile. "He's a fellow soldier, unarmed, just doing his job."

"And his *job* is to hunt and take Tye! We can't take the chance," Dustin repeated. "There can't be any witnesses."

"Are you protecting Tye, or do you just want to fight me on everything?!" Mav yelled, getting in Dustin's face.

I stepped between them. "Both of you, stop—"

A gunshot shattered the air and the soldier's body crumpled. A bullet had penetrated his skull. Tye stood across from him, the end of his weapon still smoking. No one spoke as we all stared at him. The others looked to be in as much disbelief as I was.

Tye took charge, his voice cutting through the shocked silence.

"Let's make camp and stay low today."

Hours passed, yet Tye's cold execution of the soldier lingered over me, a stark testament to his evolution since I'd first met him. Survival had reshaped him, toughened his resolve.

We shared a ration bar around a new campfire. Between the five of us, we were dangerously low on supplies. Even the canteens were starting to feel light.

"We really need to figure out what to do next," said Dustin. "It's clear they won't stop searching for him."

I suddenly had no appetite. "We know there's others like Tye, so I don't get why they're so set on getting him."

"Well, with the amount of resources they're using on the search, it's clear there's something about him that's made him a high priority," Dame mused.

"I did kill two men when I escaped," said Tye. "Maybe they want me for that."

"The body count means nothing to them," Mav chimed in. "This bounty's about something else."

"They never told you anything when you were at the facility?" I asked Tye. "Had you heard of Ylem?"

"No. Just that my blood was healing my infection somehow."

"He said Ylem was *untouched*. Somewhere the virus hasn't spread yet," Dustin said pensively. "Probably one of the contained states."

"Or another country entirely," I said. I'd never even considered that there was a place that didn't have some sort of outbreak by that point. While some states were able to be zoned off quickly, more news of distant outbreaks seemed to sprout weekly.

The silence settled, heavy with the weight of our uncertainty.

"What was your plan after escaping? Did you think about what you'd do once you were out?" I asked eventually. I was hoping his ideas were more thought out than mine had been.

"All I wanted was to get out of there. Once I did, I was wandering, just trying to survive out here. I guess at some point, I did think maybe I could make my way to another country. To start a new life."

"Hmm," Dame murmured under her breath.

"What?" I asked.

"So many things could go wrong... but I'd been thinking about doing the same. Before I was drafted into EMBER, I was in aviation. We were working on flying cargo planes with supplies to some of the infected cities in Canada. I have a friend there. A guy named Rex."

I gaped at her. "Are you saying we smuggle Tye out of the country?"

She shrugged, as if disregarding the suggestion.

Dustin spoke up. "The air base isn't far from here, right? A few from my training program were stationed there."

"About two hundred miles," Dame replied. "Before I ran into Tye, that was my next move."

I could see Tye's mind racing, searching for a path in an uncertain future. "What about your mom? Your sisters?" he asked. "You're gonna leave them?"

The shame was written all over her face. "What choice do I have? It'd take a miracle for me to get back in without severe punishment for treason."

Mav and Dustin traded a look. We were all in the same boat. The only difference was that our treason wasn't on record yet. I hoped to keep it that way.

"What are you thinking?" I asked Tye. "I don't want to leave you, but your freedom isn't our decision."

His eyes darted about as he thought it over. "I don't think they'll ever stop hunting me. And even if I stay with you guys, or make it back to the others, I'm putting everyone in danger."

"So, is this the plan?" Dustin asked, his voice cracking with emotion. "We get you out of here?"

The truth hit me hard—protecting Tye meant losing him. As our eyes locked, my tears welled up.

"Willa ... you said it yourself," he reminded me. "I'll see you again, even if it's in the next life."

I laughed, despite myself. "I don't want to wait that long."

He hugged me tightly.

Dame picked up the fallen soldier's radio. "Give me some time with this and I can comb through 'til I find the base's channel. Rex owes me one."

We lay low until sundown. I cherished the time I still had with Tye. The specter of separation loomed, and an imaginary hourglass hung over me. Amid the anxiety, I fought to stay present, to savor every fleeting second. What was I going to do with my life once Tye was gone, and hopefully, safe? My first stop would be my Aunt Solana's house, to reunite with my parents. But then what? Everything as I knew it was so warped now that readjusting seemed impossible.

While Dame fiddled with the radio in the corner, fragmented words reached our ears. Each sound was a breadcrumb leading us to our next move, a desperate gamble for Tye's safety. She had to be careful not to alert any search parties to our location, but she claimed to know exactly what type of jargon to listen for that would indicate she'd found the air traffic channel.

I tried my best to sleep before my night watch shift, but all I did was toss and turn. As I lay there, I would've traded the horrors that showed up in my head for any nightmare about Tye. I kept hearing Archer screaming, Midas laughing, all intermingled with flashes of Malik bleeding out on our parents' bed.

I thought I'd feel fulfilled once I got Tye back, but it was becoming apparent that my old habits had resurfaced. I'd mastered the art of burying my traumas under an avalanche of distractions. Searching for Tye had been just another driving force to keep my purpose intact, but now that he was with me, the stuff I'd been avoiding was creeping back in again.

I sat up, wiping beads of sweat from my temples with the back of my hand. As if he sensed it, Tye awoke next to me.

"You okay?"

My heart was pounding. "No," I said weakly. "I feel like I'm having a panic attack."

He jumped to his feet and grabbed the canteen, drizzling a little water over my head and into my mouth. "Deep breaths," he encouraged.

Each shallow breath felt insufficient, as if the very air around me had thinned to a suffocating mist.

Mav and Dustin were sitting at the mouth of the underpass, keeping watch. They came over to see what the commotion was.

"What's going on?" asked Dustin.

My chest was heaving up and down with panic. A distant part of my mind tried to reason with the chaos, reminding myself that I was safe, that there was no imminent danger, but my thoughts continued to churn, spiraling into an abyss of overwhelming anxiety. I started crying into my hands.

"Sorry, I'm just not feeling good," I said, my voice coming out muffled through my fingers. "I think it's all hitting me now."

Dame woke up next. She didn't need to ask what was happening. My demeanor must have given away the burdens that were haunting me.

Mav sat beside me, rubbing my back. Normally his presence would've calmed me, but his recent cryptic behavior had put me even more on edge lately. Tye was the only one who had that ability now.

"You're okay. You're allowed to feel all these things. None of this is easy stuff," Tye said, his voice like a soothing balm on my wounds.

And then, just as swiftly as it had engulfed me, the storm began to ebb. My racing pulse gradually slowed, the constriction in my chest loosened its grip, and the world began to regain its focus.

I took a shaky breath. My body still trembled, but the worst of it was over.

"I can take your shift," Dame offered, getting to her feet. "Sun's almost up anyhow."

"Thank you," I said, still rattled.

"Want to take a walk?" Tye asked, offering me his hand. "We'll stay in the tunnel."

I took his hand, the only thing that could make me feel better right then, and we walked away from the others as they tried to get back to their tasks.

We spoke softly. "Did you have a bad dream?" he asked.

"Somewhere between sleep and awake, yeah. I just think there hasn't been any time to process all that's happened. It's getting to me."

"I can't imagine. I had nothing but alone time for so long, I think it helped me work through some things, but you've been nonstop. I can't believe you reentered *again*."

"I had to."

"I know. I'm sorry about Malik. I can't imagine how you feel ... but I'm happy we found each other."

"Me too."

We planted ourselves on a smooth rock at the far end of the underpass.

"I was having a hard time sleeping too," he said. "What he said about Ylem—rounding up other kids? There's still so much going on out there that we're totally unaware of. How much worse is this world gonna get?"

That very question had crossed my mind many times whenever I thought of Zenith and what may have been going on behind closed doors.

"Before my brother died, he left me a note that revealed so much more than we knew before," I said to Tye. "That pharmaceutical tech company,

Zenith, was using planes to distribute treatments into the atmosphere, but the guy who bought the company somehow tampered with it all and caused the virus. One of the planes crashed. That's why the US took the biggest hit. The crash site's only a few states away."

His brow furrowed as he digested what I'd said. "Why would they want the world to turn into this? What's the gain?"

"Hard to say just yet, but there could be other powers at play here."

His expression became earnest. "If I do make it out of here, promise me you'll keep yourself safe? I know you're a lot stronger than me, but we can't take on all of this conspiracy shit like we're superheroes. We're just kids."

He possessed an uncanny ability to read my thoughts and emotions. It was undeniable that I had taken on the role of uncovering the truth myself and ensuring that those who'd shattered our lives faced the consequences. My determination to avenge Malik, to seek justice for my friends and myself, burned fiercely within me.

"We *were* just kids," I said, "but we can't be anymore. Not with everything this world's become."

The sun started to crest over the edge of the cliffs, casting shadowy streaks across the ground. It was time to rejoin the others.

Everyone around the camp was still awake, probably still spooked from my episode.

Dustin was the first to greet me. "If you're feeling up for a distraction, I was gonna go hunt down one of those hares. We're past the point of ration bars doing the trick, and we're low."

The thought of escaping for a minute was instantly appealing. "I'm up for it."

While Dame continued her radio monitoring, Maverick and Tye chatted among themselves. I almost wished I could eavesdrop, but I set off with Dustin.

Under the intense morning sun, the rugged canyons sprawled before Dustin and me, a vast wilderness of possibility and risk. We desperately needed some food, but eluding the ever-present search parties was equally as important.

Every footstep was a careful negotiation with the terrain, a balance of avoiding alerting not only our prey, but also any scouts in the area. The gravel's crunch threatened to reveal us, so we moved like shadows, blending into the landscape.

We scanned our surroundings, seeking any hint of movement, ears attuned to every sound. Dustin and I exchanged wordless cues. I was grateful to have a friend with me and something to keep busy with. I couldn't risk another panic attack out there.

Dustin's good arm shot out, halting me in my tracks. His gaze locked onto a distant movement, a flash of fur against the harsh backdrop. We crouched low, our eyes locked on the unsuspecting hare.

A gunshot in the ravine would echo for miles, so Dustin took out his knife. He moved with stealth, closing the gap between him and the animal. In an instant, he pounced, his quick hands securing the hare. Relief washed over me and I beamed with admiration.

The rabbit flailed in his grip, squealing.

"Okay, you little fucker, it's time to become lunch," he said gravely, pressing the blade to the back of its neck.

His aggression surprised me. "Dustin, don't."

"What? We have to kill it to eat it."

"I know, but don't talk to it like that. It's giving its life for our survival. We should be grateful."

He looked a bit taken aback, but I could tell my point had landed. "You're right. I'm sorry." I could see in his face that he regretted his moment of savagery and was almost embarrassed. It wasn't like him. "Maybe you're not the only one bottling things up."

He gave the animal a soft kiss on the forehead, then ended it quickly. With our prize in tow, we retraced our steps.

On our walk back, I could sense that something was still bothering Dustin. "I didn't mean to get on your case. I was just trying to share my thoughts," I said gently.

"You don't have to explain. I think I just realized that I've had to change myself to live like this... Everything we've gone through has kind of made it hard to even recognize myself anymore. I feel like I've had to separate the two sides of myself, or else all of it, never finding my parents, losing friends—it would all be too much."

I nodded. "I get it, Dust. We're all doing what we need to do." A deep understanding passed between us.

The short trip wasn't just about the hunt; it was about outwitting the military who hunted *us*. Our return felt like a victory, and our friends smiled when they saw the hare.

"No way!" Tye said, hopping up from the dirt floor. His eyes moved from the catch to me. "Are you feeling a bit better?"

I managed a smile. "A little, yeah. Better when we get some food in us."

"Well, there's more good news," said Dame, holding up the radio. "I spoke with Rex."

All our attention turned to her, the prospect of a meal taking a backseat.

"He'll do it. He'll bring Tye aboard his next supply run. I have the coordinates of where he'll land to pick Tye up in three days. We'll have to be ready. If he's grounded for any longer than ten minutes, he'll be flagged by air traffic control and our plan will be blown."

The gravity of the situation was sinking in, making it undeniably real. On one hand, a glimmer of relief washed over me knowing that Tye had a chance to escape and forge a potential future. On the other hand, the uncertainty of what awaited us all loomed large.

"And when I land, then what?" Tye asked, a hint of fear on his face.

"Then you're on your own," Dame said simply.

A tense stillness settled over him.

"Where's the coordinates?" Mav cut in. He'd been so quiet lately that his voice sounded almost unfamiliar.

“Here,” she said, showing him a mark she’d made on our map. “About one hundred miles north. There’s a massive stretch of open terrain he can land in.”

“Little more than a two-hour drive, I’d say,” said Mav. “When should we leave?”

“We should eat and pack up tonight. We can leave at first light,” I suggested, and tried to focus on the impending meal. In reality, it was to distract me from the fast-approaching moment when I would have to part ways with Tye.

That evening, Dame retrieved an old pan from her meager supplies and placed it over the crackling flames, its worn surface a testament to the countless improvised meals it had prepared.

The rest of us gathered around the fire, anticipation and hunger making our stomachs growl as the scent of cooking meat wafted through the air. It had been weeks since I’d enjoyed a proper meal, and the prospect of a warm, satisfying dinner brought a glimmer of happiness to my weary soul.

Dustin’s wound had reopened during the hunt, so Maverick tended to it while Tye’s imminent departure hung unspoken in the air. There was some added unease knowing the Morts we’d encountered just days earlier could still be around. I kept looking out into the darkness beyond the fire’s glow, half-expecting to see their twisted silhouettes.

Dame took the pan off the fire and set it between us. “Careful, it’s hot.”

Dustin was already reaching for one of the crisped legs, blowing on it to cool it down. None of us could wait, so we ignored the burning and dug in.

“Wow, Dame. This is so good,” Tye said through a mouthful.

She took a seat in our circle. “Best I could do without seasoning.”

The hare, though small, was a welcome respite from the monotony of our usual rations. Despite the stress of our circumstances, I savored each bite, finding peace in the momentary comfort.

I had my first shift that night with Dame. I insisted I could do it on my own since she'd taken over for me the night before, but she was adamant about joining me.

We sat under the tunnel's stone awning, not talking much at first as our past tensions hung in the air.

"How you holding up?" she finally asked, sounding genuine.

"I'm not sure I am," I said with a feeble laugh. "I just miss being strong. Before Malik died, I felt like I could handle anything."

"It takes time to rebuild yourself," she said. "When my *abuelo* died, I was so busy making sure my mom and sisters were okay, I forgot to grieve myself. It all crashed down on me a year later. It took me forever to even hear his name or see a picture of him without spiraling."

I didn't know what to say. I just gave her an empathetic smile so she'd know I appreciated her sharing with me, and we sat and listened to the small chirps of bats in the dusky sky.

"I never got to thank you for saving my life," she said after a while. "You could've left me for dead at that mall, but you didn't. I regret lying to you guys. I regret what I did."

"We've all done some heavy things to get by," I pointed out. "Let's leave it in the past. I'm grateful you brought Tye to us. And I'll be forever indebted if this plan works out. It wouldn't be possible without you... and I'm sorry I left you on your own."

I could tell that meant a lot to her. Her eyes got teary and I could see the reflection of the moon in them. "I wish Archer was here," she said hoarsely.

I nodded. "I know. He fought so hard. We wouldn't have made it out of there if it wasn't for him."

She laughed painfully through her tears. "That little badass. And Hound? They went together?"

"Yes."

"We should make a little shrine for him. Since he didn't get a proper send-off," she said, getting up and helping me to my feet.

Under desert stars, Dame and I crouched on the sandy ground, gathering rocks and pebbles and arranging them in big letters that spelled out Archer's name. Each stone was placed with care, a dedication to the memory of our fallen friend.

As we worked, we quietly shared memories and stories of Archer—his laughter, his courage, sweet moments between him and Hound.

Dame went and fetched a small hare bone from the campfire and carefully placed it beside the arrangement of stones, a symbolic gift for Archer's loyal companion.

We stepped back and admired the small memorial. A feeling of closure settled upon me. We exchanged a knowing smile, but there was something different in Dame's expression. Like she wanted to tell me something but was holding back.

"What?" I dared to ask. I didn't know if I could handle any more surprises.

"I don't want to cause any rifts in the group, but I have to tell you," she said, lowering her voice. My stomach dropped, and I braced myself. "It could be nothing, but last night I was half-awake and I saw Maverick walking off down the tunnel. He was talking with someone on the radio. I couldn't hear what about, but he never mentioned it after that."

First Dustin, then Dame? Was piling on Maverick going to be a recurring theme? Everyone taking turns sowing seeds of doubt about where loyalties lie? It felt like Dame and I had finally reached a stable point in our relationship, but even though Mav and I were somewhat distant right then, I couldn't bring myself to suspect him of having any malintent.

"He's been off lately," I said, unable to hide the hint of frustration leaking through my tone. "I'm sure he was just helping find the air control channel."

"Maybe you're right. I just thought it was odd and worth mentioning."

I nodded. "Thanks."

18.

The following morning arrived with a palpable sense of anticipation. A buzz ran through our group as we hurriedly gathered our last belongings and loaded up the dune buggy and Humvee with whatever supplies remained.

I caught Maverick having a private moment in front of the memorial. His face was sullen and pale with a mixture of everything he must have been internalizing as the survival journey finally caught up with him.

Dame's earlier warning echoed faintly in my thoughts, but it was still hard to look at him with suspicion when so many of my feelings for him were that of half-realized love, making it a complex tangle of affection and uncertainty. Something was eating him alive from within, but I wasn't in the best state to console him.

All I could do was gently place my hand on his back. He hugged me, but turned his face away so I couldn't see him cry.

"You guys ready?" Tye called from the passenger seat of the buggy.

"Coming," I called back, breaking the embrace. "Mav, do you want to go back to the border? I know you want to be here for me, but if it's all too much you should take care of yourself."

His hesitation in answering indicated to me that he was considering it. "... I'm okay, Willa. Really."

Nothing about the way he said it made me believe him, but I nodded.

We took our places in the vehicles. Dame drove the battered Humvee, Mav straddled his dirt bike, and Dustin piloted the buggy while I sat in the back, ready to fire at anything that might tail us.

The drive that day would be our most daring stretch so far as we'd be out in the open for most of it. With a series of nods to each other, we were off, steering through the twists and turns of the canyons. The coordinates Rex had given us acted as our North Star, guiding us through the rocky landscape.

Conversation was sparse; everyone was focused on the journey. The minutes ticked by as we pushed ahead, the sun climbing higher in the sky. We encountered a handful of wandering Morts along the way, but the gentle morning light kept the gorge trail chilled, preventing them from catching up to us at full speed.

"It's about twenty more miles 'til the meeting point!" Tye called out over the noise of the grinding gravel.

Relief swelled within me as we neared the finish line, but the thought of Tye's departure was still haunting me. Our unique connection had always been clear, but my time apart from him and the prospect of losing him forever forced me to confront my emotions. Maybe my romantic feelings for him were deeper than I'd ever admitted to myself.

Our journey took an unexpected turn when an ominous hum cut through the calm sky. A military chopper flew overhead, casting a shadow over our convoy. We jumped into defensive maneuvers, swerving left and right to avoid the inevitable gunfire.

Loud cracks reverberated through the valley as the chopper fired from its turret gun into the roof of the Humvee, causing Dame to fall behind. Tye and I stood up in our seats, firing at the helicopter. It sparked and rose higher, but our bullets were no match for its thick hull.

"Get us closer to Dame's truck!" I yelled to Dustin over the noise of the blades.

I had my eye on the Humvee's mounted turret gun. Its heavy-duty rounds were the only thing capable of piercing the chopper.

The buggy fell back, Maverick's bike taking the lead as he fired to cover us. We dodged more gunfire from above and maneuvered so we were parallel to the Humvee, when a massive round hit the front of our buggy, taking the bumper clean off.

"Sheesh!" cried Dustin, zigzagging to avoid another fatal hit while I tried to gauge a jump from our car to Dame's.

"Closer, Dustin!" I pleaded, holding onto the buggy's cage as I readied myself to make the jump. One wrong move and I'd be crushed underneath the wheels.

Tye provided cover fire just long enough for Dustin to line up with Dame's Humvee. I gambled with my life and jumped, landing hard on the side of the truck and quickly grabbing hold of its protruding armor.

Dustin veered off, joining the shootout while I climbed up to the turret gun. With a loud click, I released its locks and angled it skyward.

BAM BAM BAM BAM!

With a deafening shriek of metal, one of the chopper blades exploded and fell clean off, sending the helicopter into a spinning death fall, its mayday alarms whining. We continued forward as an explosion behind us confirmed that our pursuers had been thwarted.

We caught up with Maverick just as the location of the coordinates came into view. We couldn't be sure if we were still being followed, so finding cover was important. Now that we were in an open valley, the only logical place for cover was a cluster of stone pillars. It would barely protect us, but it was better than being out in the open. We parked in its shadows.

"You absolute boss!" Tye cheered, hugging me from behind. "That was insane."

I appreciated the acknowledgment, but I had more pressing things on my mind as I took in the land that would be the setting for our last day as a group.

"How do they keep finding us?!" Dustin exclaimed in frustration, his shoulder bandage bloodied yet again. "It's like they have a tracker on us."

"Yeah, Mav, how do they keep finding us?" asked Dame.

Her question hung in the air, momentarily stalling the conversation. Her sudden change in expression told me the words had come out more pointedly than she'd intended.

"What's that supposed to mean?" he asked after a beat, narrowing his eyes at her.

She shifted uncomfortably, scuffing a pebble with her shoe. "Who've you been talking to on the radio at night?"

In unison, the group seemed to hold our breath, as we all awaited Mav's response.

He turned to me, frustration etched on his face. "If any of us are helping them, it's her! She just found out why they want Tye, and she has the most to gain—"

"Are you *kidding* me?! Why would I lead them to us when I'm hiding from them too?" she shot back.

The increasing intensity of the situation was unsettling. Dustin intervened, keeping his voice measured. "Then who were you talking to on the radio?"

Mav's expression was murderous. "I was helping to find the channel we needed."

That had been my initial instinct, but somehow I wasn't buying it, and he seemed to know it. His gaze turned to me, imploring me to trust him. He gripped my shoulder and his eyes locked onto mine. "You really think I'd jeopardize you? Dame's the one who betrayed her entire unit. She *killed* her fellow teammates. Of course she's gonna deflect the blame!"

It was clear Tye hadn't known about that part of Dame's past. His eyes were darting between each person in the group, like he was trying to process the sudden dynamics.

"I don't know, man," Dustin said. "You've been acting hella weird since we reentered. You're off."

I could see an immense attempt to restrain himself in Maverick's almost unrecognizable face, but just when I thought he'd explode, he turned and walked off, taking his bag with him and disappearing between some rock formations.

There was a moment where we all let the dust settle.

"Let's make camp and cool off," Tye suggested. "Maybe we shouldn't make fire tonight so we don't draw attention to ourselves."

As the night drew in, we huddled together, preparing for a cold one without the solace of a warming fire. The temperature dropped, and the only sounds were crickets and an occasional coyote howl from far off. Tye and I shared a blanket, while Dustin and Dame nestled close, using his sleeping bag as a makeshift cover.

Sleep seemed to elude all of us as we lay there, all too aware of our exposure to potential danger. Though the cold could slow down Morts, the earlier tension kept me on edge.

Maverick remained absent for the rest of the evening, probably having set up his own camp somewhere to get some space. It was clear that something weighed heavily on him. I felt a pang of guilt that I couldn't offer him the support he clearly needed. Malik had always known how to reach him. It was a connection that had once saved Maverick's life.

"I'm gonna check on him," I said, ignoring the disapproving glances of the others.

Slipping away, I walked around some of the towering pillars until I reached his campsite. I expected to find him sitting with his arms crossed, still fuming, but instead I found him convulsing on the dirt floor!

Instinctively, I reached for my weapons, fearing the worst—was he infected?—but guilt swept through me when I got closer and realized he was having a seizure. Panicked, I turned him on his side, attempting to support him.

"Maverick! You're okay. I'm here. *GUYS!*"

My calls for help brought the others running, their worried faces illuminated by the pale moonlight.

"What's wrong with him?" Tye implored, taken aback by Mav's frantic movements.

"I don't know! Dustin?!"

Dustin slipped Mav's bag under his head to keep him supported. "Has this happened to him before?"

"No!" I said anxiously.

Finally, Maverick's tremors settled. He was drooling from the corner of his mouth and his glazed eyes stared up at the stars. I wiped his mouth with my shirt and signaled for Dame to hand me his canteen.

"You're okay, Mav," I reassured him, pouring a precious splash into his mouth.

He managed to take a few sips, his eyes gradually regaining clarity. We stayed gathered around him until he seemed to refocus.

"Maverick, what happened?" I asked gently.

Without warning, he sat up and puked onto the ground next to him.

"Were you bit?" Dustin demanded, jumping back.

Maverick shook his head, dismissing the accusation. Finally, he spoke. "I'm sorry. I'm sorry..."

Those words became a broken record, playing on a loop for the subsequent hour as we struggled to fathom his meaning. He seemed disoriented, lost in a daze. Our only choice was to stay by his side through the night, hoping that whatever had him in its grip would eventually let him go.

When morning came, Maverick seemed more coherent, but he sat alone against a large boulder with his head between his legs, his temples slick with sweat.

"Willa..." said Dustin, pulling me aside. He handed me a small bag of white pills. "These were at his camp."

An instant wave of dread surged through me, plummeting to the depths of my stomach. Suddenly, everything made sense, and I felt like an idiot for not putting it together sooner. Maverick had fallen back into his old ways, right under my nose.

I felt completely unequipped to handle it. If only Malik was there. I tried to call upon his way of handling things. He always came at things like that with love and understanding.

I walked over and dropped the bag at Maverick's feet. Although I was bubbling with anger and disappointment, I tried to keep my tone even. "Maverick, what are these?"

He kept his head down. "They're to help me sleep."

"Is that what you're using them for?" I asked, working to keep from sounding accusatory. When he didn't answer, I went on. "I know losing Malik must've brought up some stuff, but you can't go down this path. I'm not him, but I care about you just as much. You can't do this again." I picked up the bag and crushed the contents between my palms, throwing the powder to the wind. "You told him you'd take care of me. Part of that is taking care of yourself! I can't do this without—"

"Yes, you can!" he shouted, catching me off guard. "I'm sorry, Willa, I'm sorry—"

"Stop saying that! For what?!"

"I BETRAYED YOU!" he shouted, his voice cracking.

A grave silence enveloped us, tension crackling in the air like electricity. Dustin's grip on his gun tightened, his wariness palpable.

"Running into you at the mall wasn't fate." Tears dripped down Mav's tattooed face. "The government sent me. They linked me to Malik and they knew you were friends with Tye. I was meant to shadow you to get intel on Tye's location. When we got back to the border, I told them the truth—that you didn't know where he was—but when they found out you were reentering to find him, they told me to go with you and bring Tye back. They have a lot of shit on me, Willa..."

My world spun, the ground beneath me feeling unsteady. "Maverick..."

"Everything we went through, all my feelings for you—all of that's real, I—"

"Stop," I pleaded.

Dustin's gun was now fully aimed at Maverick.

"I regret it all, Willa," Mav insisted. "It started as a mission, but I never planned on it going this far—"

"Dame was right," I cut in. "You've been feeding the government info on how to find us."

"I'm not right in the head, Willa. I don't wanna help them anymore. I'm so sorry—"

"If you say that *one* more time, I'm gonna lose it," I warned.

He fell silent, his face turning as pale as his hair. When he reached for my trembling hand, I instinctively drew my pistol.

Right then, I could see that Maverick knew he'd cemented the irreparable chasm between us. Fury raged inside me. Malik would be sick to his stomach if he knew.

"After everything my brother did for you? How you promised him you'd look after me?" I demanded. "I think you should go, Mav. Go far away and don't come back."

My words carried enough venom to end any hope of a friendship between us. Something inside him appeared to break. He ran for his bike, kicked on the engine, and sped off towards the canyons.

Although I'd insisted on it, watching him leave wreaked havoc within me. The memories we shared, those instances where I'd felt safe and secure in his company, now bore the stain of betrayal. Mav had been manipulating me all along, exploiting our connection to get to Tye.

My emotions churned like a turbulent storm, a chaotic mix of anger, confusion, and disappointment. I had always prided myself on my intuition, believing it to be as reliable as a compass. Yet there I stood, facing the sobering fact that I had misjudged our connection completely.

I'd lost so many people already. And although it wasn't a death, the devastation was no less. It felt like a seismic shift in my reality, as if the solid ground I stood on had suddenly given way.

I turned back to my friends. Their stunned expressions mirrored my own feelings. I had the strangest sense that I didn't really know any of them as well as I thought. Perhaps the weight of Mav's betrayal was warping how I saw everything and everyone around me.

A crackle came from the radio.

"Red Ruby."

Dame raised it to her mouth. "Oxtail."

There was a pause on the other end before the voice continued. *"Hey. Everything's on schedule for tomorrow. Landing at the coordinates at eleven hundred hours. All set on your end?"*

"Stand by, Rex." She looked at us doubtfully. "So, what now? If Mav gave away our location, they could be here any minute."

My head was still spinning. I was grateful when Dustin spoke for me.

"We can't bail on the plan now. Can we meet Rex at a different landing spot?"

"Not possible. Anything off-course will raise the alarm."

"We can take long night watch shifts to get through the night," said Tye. "In the morning, we can wait on high ground to spot any search parties before they see us."

Again, they looked to me for input. I just nodded in agreement.

"We'll see you at eleven hundred," said Dame.

"Copy that."

The radio fell silent.

Hours later, when the stars began to show in the sky and we huddled between the rocks to shelter from the windchill, my mind was still reeling.

Amid the turmoil, a part of me wondered if I had made the right choice in sending Maverick away. He was suffering, and battling addictions that had a strong hold on him.

But then, my thoughts turned to Tye. He was the last person in my life, the one connection that still mattered. He shouldn't have to carry the weight of something that wasn't his fault. He deserved to be free.

Words were scarce that night, the sound of the wind filling the long gaps in conversation. I figured all of us were processing the latest turn of events in our own way.

"I'm sorry I didn't listen to you guys," I eventually said to Dustin and Dame. "I let my feelings get in the way."

"He's not your problem anymore," said Dustin. "We're still here."

Dame could only offer a feeble smile.

"Willa and I will take the first half of the night. You two get some rest," Tye said, standing and offering me his hand.

We walked to the perimeter of the spires. The cold wind was a lot sharper there, but the stars illuminated the night sky brilliantly—a cosmic display untouched by city lights.

"Tomorrow's a turning point for us, isn't it?" Tye asked thoughtfully, looking up to the heavens. "What do you think happens from here?"

Thinking about reality without him was painful.

"You'll have a new life," I said. "I'm sure it'll be hard at first, but nothing you haven't gone through already. You'll make a new name for yourself... find new friends ... "

"Come with me."

His words hit me with a force that resonated deeply.

"Tye—"

"We can *both* start over and wait this out!" he insisted, his eyes bright with hope. "With everything you've uncovered, and the other kids with immunity in their blood—maybe all of this will resolve in a few years and we can come back to everyone."

His words made my heart sing. For a moment, I allowed myself to indulge in the enchanting sweven, and all I felt was pure happiness. The thought of being with Tye and leaving everything behind was intoxicating, but the weight of reality anchored me again.

"My parents," I said, bursting the daydream. "They still don't know about my brother. They haven't heard from me in ages."

He nodded. “Right.” He put his arm around me, providing the warmth and sense of safety that had been evading me for so long.

“You were close with your parents, right?” I asked, hoping to learn as much about him as I could within the little time we had left. There was still so much we’d never had a chance to unpack. “What were they like?”

He smiled, but there was pain in his eyes. “Yeah, we were close. They were opposites, which made growing up interesting. He was very serious and she was an eccentric hippie, but they always supported everything I did.”

“I hope things with my parents get better.”

“Maybe this will all be a wakeup call for them, and they’ll cherish you more. You deserve that.”

I smiled. “Thank you, Tye.”

“Will you tell the others where I went?” he asked suddenly. “Tell them I’m gonna come back and find them one day, and everything’s gonna be right again. And look out for them, okay, Willa?”

His last words quivered with emotion.

I nodded. “Like family.”

His grip tightened as our eyes locked. “I... I love you, Willa.”

The words carried weight, but they didn’t startle me. We’d conveyed the sentiment before, even if it wasn’t out loud.

“I love you too, Tye.”

19.

I dreamt of Tye again, but now, they were visions of happiness. We floated in a glass boat on a celestial river, finally at peace in this lifetime.

Despite Maverick's gut-wrenching betrayal, and the fact that I could smell him on his sleeping bag I now slept under, Tye's words cocooned me in a newfound calmness. I stretched as I awoke, squinting into the bright sun.

It took a moment to register that it couldn't be sunrise; the sun was too high. Dustin was still asleep nearby, while Dame and Tye were noticeably absent. Only the radio and Tye's gun were left behind.

I shook him awake and he sat up, instantly alert.

"Dustin, what time is it?"

He pulled his sleeve up and looked at his watch. "What the hell?! It's ten!"

My response was swift, almost instinctual. I shot up so fast, spots danced in my vision. I hurried to where we'd parked the vehicles. The Humvee was gone.

"Dustin!"

He appeared beside me, rubbing his eyes as if it would reappear. "Where do you think they—"

"She took Tye."

My conviction was firm, a certainty born from the core of my being.

Dustin's voice rang with disbelief. "*What?!*"

"She took Tye!" I yelled. "She's turning him in!"

"No ... No, maybe it was Mav—"

"Dustin, she left us asleep! There's one hour 'til that plane lands! She turned on us!"

Dustin pointed to a trail etched in the dirt, the marks ending exactly where the Humvee should have been.

"Drag marks. She must've knocked him out." With grim determination, he threw our stuff into the back of the buggy, then leapt into the driver seat. "Let's go! We're going after them!"

While Maverick's betrayal had left me stunned, this one lit a hellfire under me. The pure evil it must take to do something like that in the final hour, after all the kindness I'd shown her since the day we came across her in the woods—it was unfathomable.

My grip on my pistols tightened, my knuckles almost blue. Whenever I laid eyes on Dame, I vowed to empty the entire clip into her skull, and there wouldn't be a shred of remorse.

We tracked the tire marks back through the winding canyons until the terrain changed from dirt to gravel. Dustin's foot stayed firmly pressed on the pedal, propelling us forward as we aimed to close the distance on Dame.

He swerved onto a slope, ascending to higher ground along the canyon's ridge. From the elevated viewpoint we gained a broader perspective, but the Humvee remained out of sight.

Not only were we racing to catch her before she turned over Tye, but we had less than an hour to get him back to the landing zone ... unless she'd taken her scheming a step further and called off the plan altogether. I prayed our excursion wouldn't take us too far or alert any search parties. Time was of the essence.

A gunshot in the distance made Dustin slam on the brakes.

"I heard it too. That way!" I shouted, pointing west.

The buggy fired up again, its wheels kicking up dirt in its wake. We heard a few more rounds, enough to guide us towards the source of the noise.

We sped around the canyon's bend and found the Humvee cornered against the cliff. My blood boiled when I spotted Dame, ducking behind the truck with her weapon aimed at Tye, who took cover behind a collection of boulders. His attempt to escape had clearly fallen flat.

"Tye!" I yelled.

A bullet ricocheted off the dune buggy's rim. Dustin and I crouched, drawing our own arms. Tye stayed still, looking relieved to see we'd found him.

"Put the gun down, Dame!" Dustin shouted. "You tried and failed. This isn't gonna end well for you."

She responded with more gunfire, forcing us to stay down. Her brazenness ignited me further. I ducked and rolled out from behind the buggy, firing both pistols at her. She ran, but not for cover—she darted towards Tye, grabbing him and pressing her gun under his chin.

I had to cease fire. Tye had no weapon. He was helpless, and now, so were we.

"Why are you doing this?!" I yelled at her.

"I have no choice!" she yelled back. "I thought long and hard about this, Willa! It's not personal, but I'm not ready to never see my family again! Turning him in's the only thing that'll clear my name! I'll be a hero instead of a traitor!"

I stepped towards her threateningly, but she pressed the gun barrel harder against Tye's skin.

"If you need him, then you won't shoot him," I challenged, my voice unwavering.

"Then I'll shoot you. Wanna test me?"

Tye was trembling in her grasp. The madness flickered on her face as she slowly nudged him towards the Humvee.

Dustin fired at one of the tires, popping it with a loud hiss. "You're not gonna get far, Dame. Give it up!"

"HE IS THE *CURE!*" she yelled. "I NEED HIM, AND SO DOES THE WORLD! SO DOES MY FAMILY!"

She opened the car door, shoving at Tye with the barrel to his temple.

"Dame! Don't do this!" I pleaded once more, my heart fracturing as I took another defiant step toward her.

"Don't come any closer!" she screamed. "Get back in your car and—"

BAM!

I buckled at the knees on seeing blood explode across Tye's chest, his eyes wide with terror...but he didn't fall. Instead, Dame toppled to the ground, a bullet hole in the side of her head.

I looked up to see Maverick standing at the canyon's crest, silhouetted against the sun and his weapon trained on the fallen figure. I held my breath, thinking for a moment that he was there to intercept Tye. But when my eyes fixed on his, they were filled with sorrow.

Tye ran toward me, our embrace carrying the weight of reunion after what had felt like an eternity.

"Willa, we have to go, now!"

Dustin's urgent shout snapped me to attention. He held up his watch for emphasis.

Without a second to process what Mav had done, I grabbed Tye and the three of us took off in the buggy.

"Red Ruby, Red Ruby," chimed Rex over the radio.

"Oxtail!" I yelled into the com.

"Landing in ten."

I felt the buggy jolt into high gear. Tye was holding my hand tightly, both of us huddled in the backseat, our time together about to be over. The final act of our journey had begun. He had only just come back into my life and was soon to be gone again.

Dustin sped back to the landing zone as if competing in a Grand Prix. The buggy caught air several times as we zipped over boulders and dips.

Just as the open valley came into view, we spotted the cargo plane in the sky, its wheels deploying for landing as it descended.

My heart sank. I looked into Tye's eyes, somehow just as vivid as I'd seen them in my dreams. They glistened with emotion as he held my gaze.

He cradled the back of my head and pulled me in gently, yet kissed me with great passion.

I felt all of our connection and history through his lips. I'd never known comfort like that in any kiss that came before.

We broke apart when Dustin brought the buggy to a halt.

He hugged Tye tightly. His tears wetted the back of Tye's shirt. "Just make sure you live long enough so we can see each other again."

"I plan on it."

The plane had a large red X spray-painted on its charcoal plating. The engine roared as it touched down, kicking up sand around it like a storm cloud.

Suddenly, the sound of another motor cut through. Maverick's dirt bike pulled up behind us. I raised my weapon when he dismounted.

"Don't come near him!" I shouted in warning.

Somehow, he still looked shocked that I was not the same Willa he knew before. "Willa, I'm on your side!" he pleaded. "I never wanted to hurt you, you know that!"

"*Do* I?!"

Dustin drew his weapon on him too.

"Board immediately," said Rex over the radio.

I didn't even know if I could trust the pilot at that point; any friend of Dame's was an enemy of mine. But it was Tye's only chance at salvation. I'd have to hope the universe was on our side.

The plane's turbines grew quiet as the ramp lowered. But a new, yet familiar sound rang out: groaning, choked and guttural.

Twenty or so Morts funneled out from between the canyons and out into the open, drawn by the whir of the plane. Half of them were once soldiers, probably from the very search parties we'd taken down.

Dustin fired first as they ran towards us.

"Tye, go!" I yelled, firing both pistols into the horde.

I could see his obvious reluctance to leave us, but he took off towards the aircraft.

The Morts swarmed around us. Maverick joined in the shootout, taking down a few running after Tye. I killed a couple more before reloading while Dustin covered.

I saw Tye make it onto the platform, but three Morts were right behind him. He kicked one forcefully away, while I finished loading just in time to get rid of the other two.

A Mort tackled Dustin to the ground, his weak arm making it hard for him to shake it off. Maverick quickly jumped to his aid, kicking it off of him and firing into its neck. Dustin was able to instantly return the favor as another grabbed Maverick from behind.

I ran towards the plane as its engines kicked on again. Morts were hanging onto the ramp as it started to close. I could just make out Tye ducking behind the storage crates inside the cabin. I fired from both pistols, killing the remaining creatures as our eyes met for one final moment before the ramp fully shut.

The plane took off with a deafening roar, eventually leaving behind an eerie silence. Bodies lay all around the three of us as we watched the cargo plane shrink until it was no longer visible among the clouds.

I was the last to look away. Tye was really gone. Instantly I regretted not going with him, although I knew it just wasn't possible. Not without choosing him over my family.

I also felt an unexpected guilt. Had I just let a major part of the solution to this outbreak slip away? I hoped the evidence I'd brought to light, and the other kids like Tye, would reveal more avenues to a cure.

Dustin pulled me close to him, offering comfort, but also putting himself between Maverick and me. His weapon was still drawn.

"Now what?" he asked me, his eyes on Maverick.

I finally turned to Mav. It was hard to look at him now. Every time I did, I was conflicted between anger and overwhelming sympathy. I remember Malik explaining to me how complex addiction was. How someone could completely lose themself and it wasn't entirely their fault. How the disease controlled them.

"Please, Willa," he said, dropping to his knees. "I need help. Don't abandon me now."

Letting Tye go had broken my heart, but Maverick had destroyed it.

"What happens now, when you go back to them without Tye? How do I know you won't tell them where he went?"

"I'll say we never found him. We left no witnesses so they'll never know. Give me one more chance to show you I can get clean and get back on track."

In the end, he had played a pivotal part in Tye's escape, but my inner alarm was still going off.

"I don't know what to do with you," I said honestly. "I don't know what to believe."

His eyes glossed. "I'm not on their side. They used me like a pawn. Everything I've helped you with is genuine. "

Dustin leaned into me.

"My dad used to lock up junkies," he said in my ear. "They *always* ask for forgiveness, and they *always* go back to their old ways."

I closed my eyes, trying my best to muster up the patience and understanding that Malik was so good at finding. I knew he'd never abandoned Maverick like that. And Mav had proven countless times on our journey that he cared about me deep down.

I turned to Dustin. "Where are you going from here?"

He shrugged. "I guess I have to report to the frontlines if I don't want any trouble. They'll be expecting me to finish my campaign there."

I nodded, then turned back to Mav.

He was still looking at me with desperation. "The border camps are full," he said. "I'll get you back in. Just give me one last chance to prove to you that you can trust me again. I won't tell them anything."

I took a deep breath, the clearest breath I'd taken in days. "I'll go back with you, but I need time to think. And you have to swear you're gonna get clean. Once and for all."

"I promise you."

Dustin huffed.

"I'm doing it for my brother, not him," I told Dustin. "Please be careful out there. I can't lose you too."

He hugged me for longer than usual. "Tell the others I'll see you guys soon." He turned to Maverick. "One misstep, and I'm coming for you."

For the first time, Maverick looked genuinely shaken by him. All he did was nod.

Dustin climbed back into his buggy, threw me a humorous salute, and took off across the desert.

Maverick and I stood facing each other, listening to the vehicle's hum dwindle. It was jarring to see how quickly our group had shrunk.

"Come on," I said sternly, climbing on the back of his bike.

He mounted eagerly and kicked us off towards the border. I held onto him to secure my grip, but the closeness was unsettling.

A few strenuous hours later, we began to see military presence ordering crowds of new arrivals away from the border, shouting to them about capacity and telling them to turn back.

Maverick flashed his ID at one of the guard checkpoints and we were admitted through towards the titanic border wall. Just before the reentry point, he parked his bike. His eyes widened when I immediately jumped off and put some distance between us.

"You have every right to be upset with me," he said feebly.

"You said they have something on you. What could be so bad that you'd turn on us?"

His face turned ashen, dread visibly washing over him. "Please don't make me say. It's in the past."

I tried to keep my voice down, but my temper was rising.

"You lied about not knowing Tye."

"I don't know why they're after him so intensely. They didn't let me in on everything. Trust me, I wish I knew what they were up to. Maybe if I had something on them, I could break out of this."

"What *do* you know then? Do you know about these Ylem camps?"

He swallowed hard. "Not a lot. I know every powerful person—anyone with enough money to make it happen—they're all there. Ylem's a heavily fortified city where the virus hasn't reached yet. The camps there harvesting immunized blood. That's why Tye was to be brought there ... Clearly something's different about his though."

My stomach was in knots. So, Tye's fears were spot-on. They were going to make him a lab rat. And Maverick would have subjected him to that.

"I hope you get help, Maverick. If not for me or Malik, for yourself."

A guard approached us before he could respond. "Major," he said, saluting Maverick. "May I assist?"

Mav looked at me one last time; he knew we probably wouldn't see each other for a while, if ever again. "Yes. This civilian needs reentry. She's registered under family."

I did a double-take at him, but this time he did not make eye contact with me. The soldier took my ID and escorted me towards the entry point.

I didn't turn to watch Maverick leave, but I heard his dirt bike heading for the military entrance.

Once again, I was subjected to heavy protocols of sanitation and testing, and administered a second dose of the vaccine. There was a time when I'd be grinding my teeth at the thought of an unknown substance being injected into my body, but now the world was so off-kilter, nothing really fazed me anymore.

Once I'd received my dorm assignment and registered my belongings and weapons, I made it into the holding atrium. An overwhelming wave hit me. The last time I was there I was with my friends, and Malik was still alive.

I approached the vast LED screen that listed thousands of names and their last known statuses. I scanned for Tye's name, finding it with a *Wanted* symbol beside it. I then found Malik's and almost instantly started to tear up, seeing him still labeled *Alive*. How I wished that was still true.

A man with a tablet approached me. "Young lady? Do you have any updates on the status of friends or family members you'd like to report?"

I couldn't handle seeing Malik's status change, so I shook my head. "I don't, no."

"Very well. When you're ready, please proceed."

I nodded, and he left me to continue studying the names. Archer's name wasn't even on the board. It was a reminder of just how many people I'd lost in a year, in more ways than one.

I peeled my eyes away from the screen and took the familiar path towards my new dormitory. This time I was in dormitory eighteen, room three.

The guard out front scanned my ID, then unexpectedly leaned in and whispered, "Thirteen's happy to see you're back."

I looked at him in surprise, but wondered if it was a test to catch me in some sort of investigation. I turned away and continued inside the house, hiding a small smile. If Thirteen was still watching over me, I was grateful.

A typical micro-room with its single mattress, small desk, lamp, and phone greeted me behind door number three. Rooms like these had become chapter closers for long survival journeys. Despite the claustrophobic dimensions, there was something peaceful about them now.

On the desk, a stack of paperwork, a pen, and the standard camp jumpsuit awaited me. I filled out the mundane personal information and the updated questionnaire about my circumstances.

Within the stack was an instructional pamphlet, explaining the next steps toward being released into the safe zone. I would be required to go through a psychological evaluation and a routine medical checkup before my parents or guardians were contacted to retrieve me.

The thought of seeing my parents again was panic-inducing. Not only to be in close quarters with them again, but to deliver the heartbreaking news of Malik's passing. I couldn't even bring myself to walk through that scenario in my head.

And then there was the staggering realization that I was going to be living a 'normal' life again. Whatever that looked like was yet to be determined, but I knew it'd be worlds away from the day-to-day I'd become accustomed to.

20.

Over the following days, I attended a series of medical appointments. At first, they felt like a nuisance, but at least the daily schedule gave me enough of a structure to decompress as I went. My hair felt clean, the blood and dirt under my fingernails had finally cleared, and the aches in my body had eased.

One morning, I found a new stack of papers left on my bed, confirming that my parents had been contacted to retrieve me later that very evening. I felt a jolt in my stomach. The time had finally come.

Under the pickup information, a series of names, addresses, and numbers were listed. I realized quickly that it was everyone I'd registered as friends or family. Their latest available contact info and places of residence were noted. According to the ledger, most of them were currently in refugee housing within the inner cities. Ava, Otto, Riley, and Aunt Solana were all listed there. I was looking forward to seeing my aunt again. I wondered how long we'd be allowed to stay with her.

I found high ground in the grassy field where some other refugees were passing a ball around. From the hill, I stared into the cityscape beyond the perimeter fence, watching helicopters patrolling the skies.

Reacclimating to the rhythm of life at the border had proven challenging. As each day passed, the stillness became increasingly unbearable. I felt oddly untethered, wandering without my usual burden of pack and weapons. Despite the absence of immediate threats like Morts, the unsettling feeling of a greater threat loomed.

I may have made it back alive, but the enigmatic forces behind Zenith were still at large, and wherever Ylem was, it had to be looked into. If it was a secret city where the powerful were hiding, I could only imagine which traitors had fled there while the world crumbled.

Midas Rothfield, the man who lit the match that set it all ablaze was not only the world's greatest enemy, but also mine. To think that someone could invade a pharmaceutical giant, that we're meant to trust, and orchestrate a biblical-level catastrophe was chilling. Evil incarnate.

I prayed that Thirteen would be successful in exposing it all. I'd thought about finding him one last time, but it was too risky to interact here. His operation was delicate and I was lucky not to have any known ties to it.

I couldn't deny that I had the urge to jump back into the fray and unravel Zenith's secrets. I feared that once I returned to what was now normal life, I'd be unplugged from the fight, unable to contribute the way I had been. Part of me wanted to let all of that go, but the other wanted to keep my sense of purpose.

I'd always wanted to leave Seabird in hopes of making more of myself. Everything I'd done with Thirteen and learned from my brother made me feel important, like I was doing something that mattered for once.

With the adrenaline of survival fading, it was finally hitting me that Tye was really gone, and that I may never see him again. My brother, Imani, Archer, and even Maverick, in a way, all gone... Tye was the last thing connecting me to my sanity.

On the walk back to my dorm, I became aware of that tiny familiar feeling, deep in my core, telling me that he wasn't gone forever.

The dreams I had left me feeling uneasy, hinting at the possibility of danger ahead. I held onto the hope that he'd stay safe. That he could start a new life in Canada and find some form of happiness, and like he wished, maybe one day when everything passed, we could all be together again.

After an entire day of anxious waiting, I was notified that my parents had finally arrived. With what few belongings I'd managed to keep, I was escorted on a golf cart to the pickup point. My heart thudded as we drove closer, finally stopping at what looked like an airport terminal.

I scanned the open hall, noticing a few other reunions happening simultaneously. I spotted my mom first, pacing back and forth. Some of her tied-up locs had fallen loose and dangled down her back. Beside her, my father tapped his foot anxiously, his arms crossed.

When they saw me, their eyes widened with emotion. But it wasn't joy, it was shock. As if they hardly recognized me.

My dad hugged me wordlessly; my mom was the first to speak.

"Is Malik with you?" she asked, fear-stricken.

As predicted, Malik was their priority. I buried my face in my dad's chest, delaying the answer. The smell of his morning coffee reminded me of home.

When I didn't answer quickly, my dad stepped back. "Where's your brother?" he repeated.

My eyes filled with tears. I winced as my mom let out a soul-wrenching cry. Two guards came over to check on what was happening.

My dad was silent but his face paled. I was relieved not to have to say the words out loud. They knew Malik was not coming back.

The car ride home was excruciating. I sat in the backseat listening to my mom sobbing as my dad drove in silence. I'd have to endure it for a two-hour drive into the inner city.

Neither had asked about me yet. I should've adjusted my expectations before my homecoming.

Through the window, I couldn't help but notice the stark contrast between the safe zone and the parts of the state that crumbled under contamination. Things seemed relatively like the old world if I ignored the prominent military presence. Every few miles, signs of past chaos would reveal themselves, but this part of the country felt utopian compared to beyond the wall.

"Wh-why did he go in to get you?" my mom gasped through a shuddering breath. "He should've let the proper authorities handle it!"

It was ambitious to think my relationship with my parents would be any different upon my return. This was always how our arguments started. Everything seemed to be my fault and nothing I did was right.

"He was trying to help me, but he didn't know I'd already made it to the border," I tried. She sobbed harder, my dad placing a comforting hand on her lap. "I went back to find him, but it's really bad out there ... "

My words offered no relief. Both of them seemed to be on the verge of exploding.

We eventually reached some sort of checkpoint outside of a suburban gated community. Similar to the border camps, these homes had been converted to refugee housing after their original owners had either fled or perished.

We pulled up to a middle-class, two-story home. My aunt stood outside, already in tears. Her voluminous hair was pulled back in a snug knot, something she only did when she cooked. She opened my door first and hugged me so tight that I felt myself melt into her arms, finally getting the welcome home I needed. I could smell the home-cooked meal on the linen of her shirt.

"Willa! I'm so happy you're safe!" she said, looking me directly in the eyes with love. "Are you okay?"

My parents both went straight inside without a word.

"Malik—"

"I know," my aunt said quietly. "Your dad texted me. Let's focus on your return right now."

We managed a smile.

Inside, she took my bag and left it at the foot of the stairs, doing a double-take at the two pistols holstered in the side pockets. She looked uncomfortable, but didn't comment.

A newscaster's voice carried into the foyer from the TV in the other room.

"—unrest at the capitol today as protesters flood the streets. There are reports that the president has already been evacuated as early as Monday as tensions continue to climb—"

The anchor was cut short when my aunt walked through and shut the TV off. "I made a room for you upstairs. It's small, but I made it nice," she said warmly when she returned.

The house was modest, but more than sufficient considering it had been repurposed. The décor and furniture left behind by the previous occupants were clearly not anywhere near my aunt's bohemian taste.

A timer chimed from the kitchen area. I already knew what it was just by the smell of spices. "You made brown stew chicken?" I asked with a laugh.

"Your favorite. Although, I had to improvise a little. A lot of the ingredients have been hard to find with the foreign supply chains down. But I think I made it work."

I followed her as she made her way to the stove. There were pots and pans all over the place. She turned the heat off and stirred the contents of the largest pot, never looking away from me.

"Sorry, I'm just so happy you made it back safe. I meditated every day for your safe return."

I smiled gently. I was back, but my mind was still reeling from the odyssey beyond the wall, and my mother's wails continued to reach us from upstairs.

"Things are going to take a while to fall back into place," my aunt said quietly while serving me a plate. "We'll have to be patient with them."

I took a bite of food. I couldn't even remember what the original had tasted like. This was heavenly compared to the ration bars I'd been forcing down.

"How are you doing? What happened after everything crashed?" I asked through a mouthful.

She shook her head like she didn't know where to start. "I was trying to piece everything together as it was happening, but things fell apart so quickly. I was packing a bag to run when a military party came through and evacuated us to a safe zone. A lot of us were living in tent cities for months until we were offered housing. I got this place in a lottery system I registered for. I checked to find you guys every day, and finally I heard from your parents. It was so tough waiting to hear about you and Malik. When that wall went up and things stabilized, it was tough to get any update from the other side." She swallowed hard. "Willa... how did you make it through? What's it like out there?"

There were no words I could use to describe what I'd seen. Part of me didn't want her to know, so she could continue living as normal of a life as possible. One with hope.

"It's... really bad."

I guessed she could see the horror behind my eyes and refrained from prying.

"Well, you're safe now," she said, busying herself with a sponge and pan in the sink.

"And what happens next? How long can we stay here?"

"To be honest, there's no clear timeline. It's been hard to feel settled knowing things can change again quickly. It was only a matter of time before Mother Earth fought back against us. But I'm doing alright, Willa. I'm grateful I'm still here with the ones I love."

I walked around the kitchen island and hugged her again.

My dad came in then, walking past us and making a small plate of food. "I'm going to try and get some food in her so she can rest. Today has been a lot." He looked at me before leaving. "Try to give your mom some space these next few days."

When he left, I exchanged a look with my aunt, disheartened. How much more space could she need? I'd been gone for over a year. I was still too raw to be exposed to prolonged toxic dynamics with my parents.

"I'm going to shower and try to get some sleep," I told Aunt Solana. "Thank you for making this. I'll have more tomorrow."

I went upstairs and tried to orient myself. There were doors to three bedrooms leading from the small landing. I could hear my parents' voices coming from behind the first door and I tried my best to pay it no mind, but my mom's words stopped me in my tracks.

"She's reckless! Always! She should've come with us to visit Malik! She should've evacuated when everyone else did! Malik would've never been in danger if she would just do things the easy way for once!"

A rage ignited within me. I wanted to kick the door down and defend myself, but nothing I could say would change the way they thought of me. Was this what I'd stayed behind and left Tye for?

I took a deep breath and made my way to the other room, slamming the door behind me. I wanted them to know I'd heard them.

Unsurprisingly, sleep did not come easy. The culture shock of being back inside a house with my family, no one having to be on night watch, having a private shower and a bed—it all felt so odd.

Thoughts of Maverick, Dustin, Imani, Archer, and Malik fluttered around in my head. All the usual suspects. And a feeling that Tye was somehow still in danger kept pricking at me.

The next morning, I went downstairs to find my parents sitting at the dining table by the bay window. My dad was reading the newspaper, the headline reading "The Fall of Healthcare." My mom was mindlessly stirring the coffee cup in front of her, dark circles prominent under her saddened eyes.

"Morning," she said to me, staring down at her cup.

"Good morning," I said, opening the small pantry to see what was available.

The shelves were pretty barren, but I was thrilled to find a single box of Cheerios on the top shelf. A bottle of milk was in the fridge, some strange brand of coconut milk I'd never seen before. I made myself a modest-sized bowl, most excited about having a refrigerated liquid.

"Why didn't you evacuate Seabird with everyone else?" my mom asked suddenly, looking like she was holding back a fresh wave of tears.

I froze, mid-pour. Some of the milk sloshed over the edge of the bowl. I knew where this was going.

"....I thought you guys were coming back."

My mom started crying again. "You should've come with us to visit—"

"Okay, I'm not doing this!" I yelled, loud enough that my dad's eyes broke away from the paper. "You're not going to blame me for his death! I tried *everything* to save him! You have no clue about the things I've been through out there!"

My parents looked at me, stunned. I threw the bowl into the sink with a crash and stormed past my aunt on the way up to my room, slamming the door behind me.

If that was any indication of how the next few months of living there would be, I would rather be back in the war zone.

There was a gentle knock on my door.

"Yes?" I said, evening out my tone, knowing it would be my aunt.

She came in and sat next to me on the bed, putting an arm around me. "Willa—"

"I'm not staying here if this is how it's going to be," I told her. "If they need time to mourn, in whatever way they need to, I don't want to be around that."

She nodded reassuringly. "I understand. But it's our only option right now."

"Not for me. I have friends," I said, the idea coming to me on the spot. "They're here in the inner city too."

"Willa, you only just got here."

"I know, and I'll still come around to see you, but I can't be near them if they're like this. It was bad before, but I can tell this is going to be a long transition. I need to heal too..."

My aunt looked defeated, but she couldn't deny my point. "I want you to do what you feel is best for your heart and mind right now." She kissed me on the top of my head. "I'll go talk with them."

When she shut the door behind her, I went through my bag, shuffling through the stack of papers folded inside. I was looking for the contact sheet, but seeing Malik's letter made me pause. One particular part caught my eye.

You're more powerful than anyone I know. Don't forget that, you hear me? I love you in this life and the next.

Malik

Even in death, he always had the right words.

Things could change again quickly once Zenith was exposed. As for now, I could choose to let my parents' words get to me, I could allow everything I'd gone through to crush me ... or I could take back control and reshape what the next phase of my life would be. And if I'd learned anything, it was that chosen family could become real family.

My eyes landed on Ava's number on the contact sheet.

I picked up the house phone on the bedside table and dialed. As it rang, I listened to my parents going back and forth with my aunt downstairs.

"Hello?" came Ava's voice.

I was so overwhelmed with emotion that I forgot to speak.

"Hello?" she repeated.

"Sorry, hi ... It's me. Willa."

"Willa! Oh my god, are you okay? Are you back?"

"Yeah, I am. I'm in the safe zone at my aunt's house."

"Oh, Willa! I just saw Riley yesterday! We were all just talking about you!"

"How is she?"
"Good! She looks so good."
"Good... Hey, can I ask you a favor?"
"Of course. Anything, you know that."
I took a deep breath.

"Do you think I could come stay with you guys for a while?"

EPILOGUE.

I tried to memorize every feature on Willa's face before the plane doors shut. Especially those hazel eyes that always made me feel transparent. I'd said I'd see her again, but deep down, I wasn't sure I would.

I just wanted this nightmare to be over. I'd had hope that all of us would make it to the other side and find normalcy again ... but then I was infected. At one point, I even accepted my end. At least my friends could go on together. That day we drove to the border, while my dark secret ate away at me, I had no idea that it wouldn't be my infection that caused my demise, but my immunity to it.

I felt powerless. It wasn't something I could change and frankly, I barely understood it. Even with all the others seemingly with blood like mine, the way the government was coming after me felt like there was something different about me. Their relentless hunt was chipping away at my will.

The last few months on my own had hardened me. I'd conceded that I might never see my friends again, that I was alone. There was something strangely empowering about seeing your deepest fear finally realized, and surviving it.

Once again, Willa found me when I needed her most. Not only had she reminded me that I still had friends in my corner, but also of what it felt like to love someone again. I'd become numb after so much loss. So much suffering.

It wasn't my time together with Willa that made me realize I loved her; it was our time apart. Even though we'd only spent a few weeks together before separating, I considered Willa as much like family as the rest of my group, if not more. It was that unspoken connection that made us feel like we'd known each other much longer than was even possible. Like she would say, in other lifetimes.

Were we destined to come in and out of each other's lives for only short bursts? It always felt so abrupt. That day I kissed her, I knew there may never be another chance. A hug just wasn't enough.

I was almost at my breaking point before I ran into Dame and heard of Willa's return. Seeing her and Dustin again made me so happy, and knowing they were together brought me peace. Dustin was a good friend, and I knew he'd protect her. They would need each other when things started to come to light. If what she'd said about Zenith was true—if the world was about to find out the root of everything—a different kind of war was sure to spark.

Memories of her and my friends were the last remnants of any driving force I had left. When this plane landed, I would have to endure an entirely new set of challenges, but at least I could stop running. The sleepless nights, the constant fear of capture, always being on the move—it was no way to live.

I wondered what the state of things was in Canada. Last I'd heard, our country was able to contain the outbreak enough to stabilize some states and areas, but I hadn't heard much about cross-border areas.

Based on the living hell I'd endured in the past few months, it was clear that the situation had taken a significant turn for the worse. I just craved a normal life again. A place to rest my head, where I wasn't watching my back all the time.

Anywhere would be better than the camps at Ylem. Whatever they were, I knew I'd be a prisoner there.

I was huddled behind a large storage crate that smelled like gunpowder when my ears popped. We must've reached a higher altitude.

Even with no Morts inside the plane, I felt incredibly vulnerable without my gun. There was no telling what would await me when we landed.

I braced myself against the wall with my feet pressed against the crate. The turbulence was intense, and the engine sound was almost deafening in this part of the plane. It didn't help the pounding headache that still lingered from when Dame had knocked me out.

I was on borrowed time once she found out about the value of my blood. I'd never reveal that to anyone in my new life. Immunity could be considered a blessing, but for me, I was marked.

I shifted uncomfortably, my back aching from the cabin's vibrations. I had no clue how long the flight would be, but I was suddenly aware of how hungry I was. My lips were almost cracking from dehydration.

"You can come up front now," came a distorted voice over the intercom. *"You'll have to hide back there again when we land."*

There was no doubt the cockpit would be more comfortable, but it dawned on me that I didn't even know the pilot. Whoever this Rex was, my life was now in his hands.

I clumsily made my way around the plane's storage compartment until I reached the cockpit door. Pushing it ajar, I peeked cautiously through the gap.

"You're fine. I'll give you a heads-up when we get close. Still a few hours left," said the guy.

I sat beside him in the copilot seat and took him in. He had wild hair, held back by a pair of vintage aviation goggles, maybe a family heirloom or novelty trinket. By the way he had his feet up and seat back, it was obvious the plane was doing most of the steering itself.

"I don't wanna know anything about you, but you and Dame must be close for her to call in her big favor on you," Rex said. "Obviously you're someone important."

Part of me wondered if he was trying to convince me that Dame hadn't spilled why I was wanted. "Something like that."

"Well, enjoy the breathing room while you can. You'll probably be spending a long time in one of those crates until I can unload you and get you somewhere you can run off to."

"What's it like there?"

"Canada?" He shrugged. "Was getting better, but things have plummeted in the last few months. The death toll's out of control. Lucky for you, these supplies are going to the part of the country that was able to stabilize. But don't expect paradise."

"Noted."

I stared out the window at the ocean of clouds ahead. Condensation trickled down the glass in glittering droplets.

"You have any water?" I asked.

He handed me a flask from the bag strapped to his chair. "Just don't put your mouth on it."

His warning confirmed he had no idea about my blood. I hoped to keep it that way.

A concerning *ping* sounded from the dashboard screens. I sat up. "What's that mean?"

He didn't answer right away. His whole body language changed as he grabbed the steering and swiped through the touch screen. "Seems like there's two aircraft tailing us, but we're not even in Canadian airspace yet."

"What? What's that mean?!"

"Calm down. I think—"

CRASH! The plane shook violently and alarms started to blare.

Rex yanked on the steering as the nose tilted downwards dramatically. "They're shooting at us!" he yelled over the warning sounds.

I grabbed the sides of my seat, bracing myself as the turbulence significantly picked up. I frantically strapped myself in. The plane continued to lose altitude.

"Are we crashing?!"

Rex was desperately hitting switches and maneuvering the steering controls back and forth. Before he could answer me, two oxygen masks dropped down from the ceiling.

The alarms continued to sound as we tried to fit the masks to our faces. In my panic, I was struggling. If only I'd paid attention on commercial flights to the flight attendants' demonstrations.

A fighter jet zipped past us with a sonic boom. We'd fallen through the clouds by then, and smoke was filling the cockpit. Patches of green fields blanketed the earth beneath us. It was getting closer and closer.

Rex finally managed to stabilize the plane from a nosedive, but our approaching speed was much too fast for a smooth landing. "Brace!" he yelled.

SMASH!

My neck nearly snapped from the collision. A deafening screech of metal on terrain exploded in my ears. My chest nearly caved in from how deep the straps of my seatbelt dug into me.

After several minutes of vigorous shuddering, the plane skidded to a halt. The alarms continued to sound, gradually pulling me out of my daze. Rex's head was bleeding, but he was already unstrapping himself.

"Are you okay?" I asked.

"Go hide in one of the crates!"

Without a second's hesitation, I ran for the storage cabin and opened the first crate I found that was big enough. It was filled with latex gloves. I climbed in, sealing it over my head. The overwhelming smell of latex almost burned my nose.

I could hear Rex opening the back ramp.

"Hands! Now!" came a new voice.

"I'm the pilot! What's this about?"

BAM!

I heard a body fall to the ground. My hands were shaking so much, I was almost sure I was making the whole crate vibrate.

For what felt like an hour, I listened to whoever these people were ripping open crate after crate, and decided this was as happy of an ending as it could get, all things considered.

I'd got to see some of my friends one last time, and leave some messages for the others. I even liked the thought of Willa thinking I'd made it to safety and feeling good about how she'd helped me.

I wished I had a weapon. If I did, I would go out fighting.

I heard frenzied sniffing from outside my box, then the unmistakable bark of a dog.

"Here," I heard a woman say.

My entire body clenched as the top was pried open. Several hands grabbed me and threw me to the ground at the boots of a statuesque figure. A team of military personnel surrounded me, the lasers of their guns aimed at my head, all of them clad in golden uniforms.

The menacing woman looked down at me, scanning my face with ice-cold eyes. Despite her foreboding presence, her features were beautiful. Well-kept, but fierce with authority.

I felt a painful prick in my shoulder. One of her guards had stuck me with a needle attached to some mechanism.

It beeped and flashed yellow. He handed it to the woman before pricking me with a second needle.

"God's Blood. It's him."

They were the last words I heard before everything went black.

www.ingramcontent.com/pod-product-compliance
Lightning Source LLC
Chambersburg PA
CBHW060806310726
48980CB00002B/258

* 9 7 9 8 9 9 3 3 3 1 5 4 6 *